A BRIDE'S TALE

JODY BRADY

BRADYREALMS

1

Cover pictures taken from the public domain at www.unsplash.com

Printed in the United States of America

First printing January 2023
Bradyrealms
The Justice Project

Millers Creek, NC

ISBN 9798374144550

WAS IT NOT YOU WHO CUT RAHAB TO PIECES, WHO PIERCED THAT MONSTER THROUGH?
ISAIAH 51:9 NIV

The castle battlements rise high above the town square below, the king's banners flapping vigorously in the growing wind from the higher towers. Shiny, black cannons point outward from the walls toward the ocean, protecting the sheltered port from roving pirate ships that can come suddenly out of the fog. They have come several times, but the cannons have kept them from taking the port.

Currently, three ships are anchored in the bay, and the cargo is being unloaded as men and animals labor through the day to pile the trade goods on the wharf. Other men scramble among the cargo, separating it and taking it to the king's warehouses. All the work is done under the careful eyes of the port guards, who ensure that the trade goods are delivered properly.

Between the wharves, warehouses, and the castle are stone and wooden homes, craft shops, bakeries, carpenters, textile shops, furniture makers, and others, all crammed together among winding, narrow streets. Off to the one side along the forested hills, next to the castle, lie the larger homes of the upper class. Small stone huts, army barracks, and stables are closer to the battlements. A gray haze covers the village from the smoke of many chimneys; however, as the wind increases, the haze clears out, revealing the streets filled with people going about their everyday lives. From the battlements, the people appear as ants to anyone standing in the higher guard towers.

A lone figure stands at the highest tower, facing toward the distant mountain range. He wears dark leather pants and a green shirt. A sword is at his side, with only the hilt visible because of a heavy, woolen cape tied around his neck with a golden brooch. The cape flutters back away from him in the strengthening breeze.

3

He is motionless, his gaze staring off into the distance. He is a young man, however wise beyond his age. He has to be because he rules the land as far as he can see from the tower. He is the King. And tomorrow, he is to be married.

He watches the building wall of clouds that gather against the rocky crags along the mountains far above the timberline. Great flashes of raw energy explode against the granite rock, followed by violent crashes of thunder. He glances at the cannons on the battlements below and thinks that the sound of the thunder reminds him of the cannons when they fire. He watches a guard walk along the wall and then turns back to the incoming storm.

Many times, he has stood and watched the storms gather along the mountain range before coming down upon his city, but there is something different about this storm, something sinister, something dangerous.

The King looks away from the approaching storm and back to the city below, where his subjects continue in their daily pursuits. From his vantage point high on the battlements, he can see the approaching danger, but the villagers far below cannot. To them, the thunder and lightning far off against the mountain range just meant they had to complete their tasks quicker before the rain came.

The king leans over the wall, "Guard!" he shouts.

The guard below turns quickly and looks up toward the king, "My Lord?"

The king shouts over the increasing wind, "Sound the alarm. We are under attack!"

The guard looks quickly across the mountains and sees nothing but immediately runs toward the closest bell tower. A moment later the bells sound the alarm. Below, in the city, people look upward toward the battlements at the sound and then immediately begin running to prepare for an attack.

Soldiers rush to man the defense walls. Multicolor battle flags are raised, and archers climb the ramparts as other soldiers load the cannons. It takes only a few minutes for the defenders of the castle walls to reach their preassigned posts. However, below in the streets of the city, panic-stricken citizens clamor among the tightly packed streets in search of safety as more disciplined soldiers march toward the coastal defenses along the shoreline.

The wind intensifies, and great walls of black clouds climb higher against the cliff walls, swirling unnaturally. Darker shapes circle in the cloud banks. Reptilian wings dive in steep circles of flashing fire, and the king shields his eyes.

Several armored soldiers emerge from one of the nearby doors and out onto the battlements. They stand with their great swords drawn, staring upward at the approaching storm, but only the king can see what monster flies within the clouds.

"My Lord," one screams over the howling wind as sheets of rain and hail assault them, "There is no attack! Only the storm! My Lord!"

The king draws his own sword, staring at the vision in the clouds that he can see even more vividly now. He steps back against the cold granite wall. Other guards emerge from the doorway, fully expecting to fight to protect their king. But they see the storm and sheets of gray, stinging rain, and white hail stones that pelt them with biting blows and bounce off the rocks to accumulate over the battlements. In only a few moments, the walkway and parapets are white with ice crystals.

"My Lord!" another screams, "you must get to shelter. No army attacks the citadel. Only the storm!"

But the king remains steadfast, holding his broadsword before him and staring up toward the cloud.

And the great dragon within.

CHAPTER ONE

Dark storm clouds gather against the cliff walls, and the cooling air smells wet as the storm approaches. The trees across the higher slopes bend back and forth. Leaves ride the winds off the slopes and blow down across the meadows below. Flashes of lightning illuminate the gray clouds, followed by the booms of thunder as if the King's artillery fires in the distance.

Then, the ground shakes below me, and I grab hold of the nearest tree to keep me from falling. Low rumblings that rise from the earth grow in intensity just as the lightning flashes above. For just a few seconds, the ground shakes, and far off against the mountain cliffs, I see crumbling rocks and a great cloud of dust and smoke. Then, the earthquake is over, and the world around me returns to normal. I step out from the tree and look across the meadow below me. I had experienced earthquakes before, but never one so strong. I need to get home.

I carefully climb down between two giant boulders and exit the dark forest into a lush, high mountain glade full of grass and late summer wildflowers. Birds flutter out from the thick grass at my presence. There is no breeze here. Beams of sunlight slant across the meadow. I check the basket that I carry and make sure that the mushrooms I have been harvesting are safe, and glance back over my shoulder at the approaching storm. I look back down across the meadow and judge by the distance that I should make it home before the storm overtakes me, but I must hurry.

Several hundred yards across the meadow, nestled in a small grove of oak trees by a small stream, stands my home, a modest stone cabin with a thatched roof. Next to the cabin lies a small vegetable garden protected by a wooden fence, and next to the garden a chicken coup. White smoke climbs skyward from the stone chimney.

I stand for a moment and stare at the scene below me. The small homestead is my entire life. It is all I know, and the valley is surrounded by the mountain crags that I have.

known since childhood. I live in a home with only my mother. I never knew my father. Mother never talks of him. I do not even know his name.

A small path leads away from the cabin, crosses the stream, and winds its way through a gap in the low mountains below my home. I know it to be the road leading to the nearest town, which takes several days of walking to reach. Because of the distance and the fact that we do not own a horse, we rarely leave our mountain valley, and few people ever find their way to our home. Which is fine by me, I think. When people do visit, Mother hides me from their view. The few times that I have ever gone to town, I hide my face from view as well.

The wind suddenly blows stronger, and the smoke shears away and low over the thatched roof. Several large raindrops fall around me, a few spattering over the mushrooms. I pull the hood over my head, grab at my homespun dress with my free hand, and run barefoot through the grass to my home. I glance back and see the approaching wall of rain falling from the black cloud slant across the mountainside. I grimace as I realize that I most likely will not find shelter in my home before being overtaken by the rain, but maybe I will.

The hood falls back from my head, and my waist-length, black hair, now free and empowered by the strong wind, blows across my face. I stop and pull the thick hair back away so I can see again and look back at the approaching wall of rain. I realize that the wind shifts suddenly, and the rain's direction of advance shifts as well. Only a few large drops spatter around me. I continue quickly down the hill to my home.

I slow my pace as I near the chicken coup and stop to investigate the shelter itself, where I notice the hens gathering from the storm. I see only one egg grab it and place it carefully among the mushrooms. Besides the occasional rabbit that I can snare, the eggs are our only source of protein.

The garden is mostly barren as well, but we have food stored against the coming winter. But now I did have food for at least today, I think as I enter my home through the front door, which is but a hanging deer hide. Mother once said that my father had killed the deer when I was but a baby.

My house is but two rooms and a loft. To the right of the main room is where the stone fireplace is situated, as well as a wooden table and two chairs. Shelves line the wall and, for most of my life, have been mostly empty. To my left is the door to the second room where Mother sleeps in a bed made of wood poles and a straw mattress, covered with several homespun quilts. The loft above is where I sleep unless the cold is too great, and then I sleep with Mother.

I lay the basket of mushrooms and the one egg on the table next to a few potatoes that I had managed to dig up from the depleted garden. The rest of the crop had rotted in the ground from some black disease that caused everything it touched to die. I glance over to the bedroom and see that Mother is sleeping.

I look longingly at the one egg but decide to keep it for the next day and instead, begin cleaning and cutting the mushrooms. I add an onion to the mushrooms and place them together in a pot with water. Stoking the fire a bit, I place the pot on the metal hanger and situate the pot over the growing fire. It only takes a few minutes for the soup to cook, and I dish out a portion in two wooden bowls and pull the pot back away from the fire. Outside, the rain begins falling. The storm that had been chasing me down from the mountain had finally made its way to my home. Soon, the old thatch roof will once more reveal its weaknesses, and raindrops will enter the home at several locations. I try to fix the thatch but can never seem to find all of the leaks.

Mother stirs in the other room. "Hannah?" she questions.

"Yes, Mother," I answer, "I've made mushroom soup."

Mother sits up in her bed. She carefully swings her legs to the side and stands up. She wears the same night dress that she has worn for the past several days of her increased sickness.

"Mother, don't get up. I will bring it to you," I say.

"No, no child. I am feeling better," she answers and slowly walks from the bedroom.

I hate to see her so sick, but it seems some of her color has returned to her face. Maybe the worst is behind her, I think. I set her bowl of soup on the table, pull out a chair for her and then take my own seat. The rain falls harder outside, and the wind blows, shaking the deer hide door. Rain begins to fall at several locations through the roof, but there is nothing that either of us can do to prevent it.

Our floors are dirt-covered in straw. After the rain stops, I will remove the wet straw and try again to fix the holes in the thatched roof.

For a few moments, we eat in silence, and then Mother speaks, "The soup is very good, my dear. Thank you."

I finish my bowl of soup and investigate the pot. There is enough for maybe two more bowls, but I think we can eat that tomorrow. I had set a few of my snares in the forest, so hopefully, I would catch a rabbit or two and gather more mushrooms as well as wild greens and roots.

Mother finishes her soup and stands up slowly, "Thank you, dear. That was very good," she says, smiles, and walks slowly back to her bed, where she lies back down.

I stare into the fire and fight back tears. I do not want Mother to see me cry, and I wish that I could run across the meadow and into the forest and climb across the mountains to the King's castle. I wish to be a princess, to wear fine dresses, to dance with the gentlemen, and to watch the other girls see me hold the hand of the king. But that would never happen, I reason. I feel the scars again and know that I am only wishing for a dream that will never happen to me. I lay my head on the table and cry. The only place where my dreams come true is when I sleep.

CHAPTER TWO

The brightly colored tent stood back against the hard granite walls of the mountain cliffs among a grove of large pines. Several smaller tents dotted the approaching slope between the cliff and the meadow below. A wooden palisade that stood ten feet tall and had only one entrance surrounded the encampment close to an acre in size. The camp overlooked a large valley.

Two soldiers guarded the entrance to the encampment. Two equally large soldiers stood immediately outside the largest tent while several others sat by the main cooking fire, eating wild boar that had been shot the previous day and roasted over the fire. Two teenage boys dressed only in loin clothes were serving them. All the soldiers wore full body armor that glistened in the morning light and stood almost nine feet tall. They were beastly-looking men with heavy locks of untamed hair hanging below their shoulders, thick beards, and black eyes. If one could stand their stench enough to come close, one would realize with surprise that each man had six fingers per hand instead of five. The soldiers were of the Nephilium Giants race and swore allegiance to the queen herself as personal bodyguards.

A lone warrior rode up the trail through the trees to the gate. He bore the markings of a captain, and even the Nephilium saluted the man, but only because their queen had ordered them to respect the man's rank. The Nephilium only respected greater strength, which was why they obeyed the queen and her alone.

The horse shied away from the two guards out of fear. The captain dismounted and tied his mount to one of the pines away from the gate. He saluted the guards in return and walked briskly through the gate and past the soldiers lounging by the fire.

The captain did not fear the Nephilium but knew full well that they were protected from them only because the queen willed it to be so. Only captains who displeased the queen needed to fear her bodyguards, and this captain had just located a major treasure for the queen. The two guards saluted him as he stood before the outer entrance to the tent. The flap was open, which meant that he could enter at any time. If the flap had been shut, no one could enter the tent, no matter the urgency, before the guards first entered. The captain acknowledged their salute and stepped into the small outer court and into darkness as the flap fell shut behind him.

He stood for a moment to allow his eyes to become adjusted to the darkness. An entrance to the main room remained closed before him as he waited, knowing that he did not have to introduce himself to his queen. She knew when anyone entered the outer door and would summon him when she was ready to receive him. From behind the closed door, he heard a hiss and then scraping noises like that of a warrior's chain mail being draped across a table or similar object. Suddenly, the flap opened, and a young girl no more than ten years of age bowed before him as she opened the flap wide enough for him to enter. The captain entered the door, and the girl secured the flap but remained outside the inner door in the dark space between the two doors.

The inner room was dark as well, with only one side lit by a single candle, which sat on a small table immediately to his left. The back of the room was totally black; however, the flickering candle did reveal the shadowed form of a large canopy bed in the middle of the room. The captain heard the metallic scraping again and a soft hiss like that of water being dropped on a hot fire.

A second candle suddenly flared up to his right, revealing a large dresser with a full-length mirror. He saw his own ghostly figure in the flickering light, revealing a tall man with black hair that was well-groomed and tied in a single braid and a thick mustache.

"Captain, you have good news for me?" a soft and very feminine voice spoke from the darkness behind the bed. The captain turned away from the mirror just as a third candle lit up the back of the room.

He immediately bowed in respect to the queen, awed as always by her incredible beauty and grace. She stood by her bed dressed in a gown that flowed down her long legs to just above her sandaled feet. Her black hair hung in thick, curling locks down to her knees. Sometimes, her servants would spend hours braiding elaborate, decorative braids intertwined with golden bands, but today, her hair was free and a bit disheveled, with only a single purple band tied around her head as a crown. Her deep green eyes sparkled in the candle's light.

"Yes, my lady, I do. Madam. I hope that I have not bothered you too early this day, but I wish to receive your orders. I have men watching the mountain gaps. I believe we have located the girl, but I am not for sure."

She walked to the dresser and sat in the chair in front of the mirror, and immediately, two girls emerged from the darkness that still lingered in the back of the room and began to comb her hair, each one taking a side.

The captain stood silently, watching as the two girls worked weaving the queen's thick hair into a series of braids. She looked up at him through the mirror, her back still to him. He had news to tell her but was still trying to gauge her temperament. At times, she displayed a violent temper but usually was restrained. At this time, however, she appeared to be in good spirits.

"You are not sure, Captain. Why do you think you have found her?" she asked.

"We searched all the villages from the river to the sea and did not find a girl who matched your description until a few weeks ago. One of the men saw an older woman and girl walking from one village toward the mountains. The girl covered her head with a hood. He rode past them quickly and noticed the scars. He followed them to the cliffs but lost their trail. They walked directly toward the cliffs, but there was no break in the mountain. At least not then. But just a few days ago, there was a great shaking of the ground, and there is now a broken cleft in the cliff walls. There is a small cabin just on the other side. A place that has been totally hidden until now."

The captain stopped and fidgeted a bit. He had something else to tell, something that may make the queen very upset.

She seemed to notice and asked, "You have something else to share, Captain?"

"Yes, my lady. On the same day that the ground shook and the cliff wall broke, another scout encountered a Bene Elohim warrior very near the trail to the cabin that we had found. I think that they have located the girl as well."

She thought for a moment about that news. She had not seen a Bene Elohim warrior for quite some time in this realm, which could only mean one thing. She turned in her chair to face the captain. The girls moved around her and continued their work.

12

The captain looked directly at her face, his desire to look down at her figure that glowed in the candlelight underneath the silky garment strong. The queen returned his gaze, questioning the statement that he had just made. She noticed that he glanced downward quickly before immediately looking back to her face. She enjoyed the effect that she had on men and used it to her advantage. To her, men were weak, driven by their lust, and unable to control themselves. But the captain had never yielded to her temptations and flirtations. Even though she would never allow any man to touch her, she still relished the stares that some gave her as she walked by.

"That could be a problem, Captain, if a Bene Elohim found the girl first. You need to find out if she is in that cabin. If so, kill the woman, but bring the girl to me alive."

"Yes, my lady. Will there be anything else?" the captain asked.

She thought for a second before taking a mirror to examine the servant girl's handiwork, nodded her approval, and motioned for the girls to leave the room. She knew exactly why the Bene Elohim were in the realm. They were searching for the girl as well. They had to be.

The queen smiled at the captain as she stood before him. He immediately stepped backward and bowed slightly as she extended her hand to him.

"Thank you for this information, Captain. Take your men and find the girl. Remember, she must be brought back alive. If she must die, I want it to be me that kills her. Do you understand?"

"Yes, my lady," the captain answered. She took her extended hand in his and gently kissed it as he bowed, her sweetness intoxicating to him.

"Will you be accompanying us?" he asked as he backed to the door.

"I will catch up to you later."

"Will you need an escort?"

"No, captain. I will be fine. My Nephilium will stay with me."

"Yes, madam."

The captain left the tent, leaving the queen with her thoughts.

13

CHAPTER THREE

I wake up suddenly from a most pleasant dream where I danced in a beautiful white dress. I try to catch the memory of the dream, but it fades away back into the world of sleep.

What had awoken me? A loud boom, possibly? I had been dancing in a grand ballroom, and then everyone had suddenly looked away toward the distant mountain range, and a great explosion rocked the castle walls.

Hard sheets of rain blow sideways in the strong wind. Water pours into my home from a torn place on the thatched roof, and I quickly stand up and look frantically around me. I hear Mother stirring in the other room, and then she quickly emerges, runs past me, and opens the front door to our cabin. Her long black hair blows back away from her, and she is no longer dressed in her nightgown.

I stand in total shock at the sight of her. She stands tall and strong before the door, dressed in a long, woolen dress dyed purple with a leather belt buckled around her slender waist. She holds something in her right hand, but in the darkness, I cannot tell what the object is. I have never seen her this way.

A few days before, she had been sick with a fever and had been bedridden for several days. But now she appears stronger than I have ever seen. There is a brilliant flash of lightning, and I step back at the sight of the object she holds in her hand. Mother turns slightly in the doorway, revealing a broadsword that flashes again as a second flash of light explodes over the mountain slopes.

"Mother?" I stammer.

She backs away from the door and turns to me as the lightning flashes again. Her hair is tangled around her head and face and wet from the rain, as is her dress.

The morning sun suddenly explodes over the horizon and pierces through a break in the thunderclouds. Shafts of misty light shine through the windows and illuminate Mother's eyes, partially hidden behind the mass of tangled hair.

I step back in fear at her fierce eyes, and then she pulls back her hair, and her eyes soften at the sight of my fear. She places the great sword on the table and reaches out to caress my cheek.

I remember only a short time ago when my mother had been so tall. Now we were the same height. She sighs and pulls me into a strong hug, and I am puzzled by all that has just happened. Am I still dreaming?

She looks into my eyes, "Hannah, I am sorry. I thought I had plenty of time, but I did not. You have been found," she says, and I look at her strangely.

"What?" I ask, and then horses approach.

Mother pulls me into the other room and pulls back the heavy shelves. To my surprise, a tunnel appears leading down into the darkness below the cabin.

She places a small leather pouch in my hand, "Hannah, you must run from this place. Follow the tunnel to the forest and follow the trail to the river. Take the ferry across. Find the carpenter in the village. He will help."

"What do you mean, Mother? Who has found me?"

"There is no time, sweetheart. You must leave this place, or they will kill you!"

She pushes me down into the tunnel, but I pull back away from her, "No! Mother. I won't leave you!"

She hugs me once more, places a heavy wool mantle over me, and pushes a leather bag into my hands.

She takes the small pouch from me and retrieves an object that hangs from a small chain that she places over my head and then hides under my dress. It hangs down between my breasts. I look at the object in awe, having never seen something so beautiful in my life.

"Hannah, never take the chain from you and never allow anyone to see it until the time comes for you to do so. You will know who to trust when the time comes. Find the carpenter. That is all I know."

I could not believe what was happening. I have so many questions.

"But Mother, what is it? What is happening?"

She wipes the tears from my eyes and smiles, "Oh, dear one. I thought I had more time to show you who you are, but I know now that you must find out for yourself."

15

Mother places her hands over my head and bows her head, "Please, God, protect your daughter. Show her who she really is. Show her the way."

I look at her, puzzled.

"I am Hannah. I am your daughter."

"Yes, my dear. But you are to be the wife of a king. Now go! You must hide and never come back to this place."

We hear men shouting outside the door and horses neighing, and Mother looks quickly behind her. She then pushes me down into the tunnel, and before I can pull myself back out, she pulls the heavy shelf back over the opening, and I am suddenly in the dark.

I tremble in the dark and try to push the door open, but it is too heavy. But I can shift the door a small bit and can now see into the other room.

Mother stands in the middle of the room, her back to me, and she holds the sword out in front of her. How can she handle such a weapon, I think? What is happening?

"Where is the girl?" A man's voice booms from just outside my sight, and then an armored warrior steps in front of Mother.

Mother flashes her left arm to the side quickly, and I see a swirl of gray smoke, and then I see myself running across the field through the opening in the window. How can that be?

"She is running to the forest!" I hear another man shout and see several warriors run across the window opening.

Mother holds the sword before her with both her hands now as the first warrior laughs and strikes forward with his own weapon. Mother parries the strike, sidesteps, and flashes the gray smoke again before striking with her own blade. Steel cracks against steel, and the warrior backs away.

Mother swirls, her hair flying out away from her, and her blade cuts below the warrior's outstretched arms, tearing into his chain mail. Blood spills out over the floor, and the man gasps and falls back against the table, dropping his sword. Two other warriors push Mother back into the bedroom, but she stumbles back against the shelf.

She flashes her arm again, and gray smoke swirls over the first man. He grabs his face and screams, and she slashes the sword at his exposed neck.

"Run! Hannah! You must run!" she screams.

16

I back away suddenly from the door. I only see Mother's purple dress in the opening as she struggles with a third warrior, and then blood sprays over the garment, and I hear her scream in both pain and rage as the third warrior falls with a heavy thud, dead from her dying thrust. The purple dress slides down to the floor, and the last I see before running down into the tunnel is Mother's raven-black hair covered in blood.

I run in the darkness, my hands stretched out before me to feel the walls of the tunnel. The ground is cold, and in some places, it is wet. The

The darkness is total. My soul screams with anguish and pain. All that I ever knew lay dead behind me.

But what had happened? Who was my mother? How had she transformed into the woman who had bravely fought and killed three warriors? What magic had I witnessed?

I stumble against the cold tunnel wall and fall backward into a pool of cold water. The leather bag falls away from me.

Who were those men, and why would they kill me? What did Mother mean when she said I was to be the wife of a king?

I cry in the dark. My mother lay dead. What was I to do?

I reach out and retrieve the leather bag and pull myself carefully back up. I know that I must get free of this darkness. Mother had said to follow the trail to the river. So that is what I must do. I wipe the tears from my eyes and more carefully make my way through the tunnel.

After a few moments, I see a small sliver of light far off in the distance, which gives me hope that I will soon reach the end of the blackness. In the tunnel, at least, I think. My soul, however, lies in the blackness of grief and fear.

I continue through the tunnel until I reach the light, which reveals a small opening that is only large enough for my hand to reach. How was I to get out?

I push at the dirt, and to my relief, the clay falls easily away. I lay the leather bag down and pull the loose dirt away until I can crawl through the opening. I roll out into a bed of soft grass under the limbs of an ancient hemlock tree. I am in a great, old forest growing next to a mighty river that flows across the valley and to the ocean, or so Mother had always told me.

I remember the bag and reach back into the opening pull it free as well, and take a moment to look inside. To my surprise, I find baked bread, potatoes, and apples in the bag, as well as a small canteen full of water.

I pull the mantle tight around me and place the bag over my shoulder by its leather strap. I press my hand over my breast and feel the jewelry Mother had placed around my neck.

I find peace at the thought of the object being there, even though I do not understand what it is or what Mother meant when she said that I would know when and to whom to show the object. But I know that I must listen to her last words. And so, I continue down to the river and see where I am to go next.

A trail leads through the tall grass beneath the dark shadows of the great forest. The sun's light is just now reaching the forest, and golden slivers of light shine down through the breaks in the forest canopy. Forest animals scurry in the brush, and birds sing and flutter among the branches.

I scan the forest off into the distance, looking for any sign of my pursuers, whoever they may be, but see no one. I continue down the path toward a river and a future that I know nothing about.

CHAPTER FOUR

The captain pierced the deer hide with his broad sword, tore the skin from the door frame, and stepped cautiously into the room of the small cabin. He had heard fighting just a moment before, but now all was quiet inside the cabin. Outside, mounted warriors rode across the meadow, chasing a girl who ran upward into the crags.

Three of his men had forced their way into the cabin, and then the girl suddenly sprinted from the door across the meadow. How had she gotten by them? He thought to himself as he took another step. Something was terribly wrong.

Dark blood stained the table and dripped down onto the floor. A sword lay on the floor. He held his own sword before him and stepped around the table to investigate the second room, ready for a sudden attack. One man lay on his back, blood covering his throat, his dead eyes staring into nothingness. He saw the feet of a second man and stepped fully into the room. He also lay dead, a sword embedded in his mid-section, blood oozing from the wound and slowly spreading across the floor.

Who could have done this?

A low moan and sudden movement, and the captain turned quickly to see a third warrior trying to pull himself up, but there was too much blood. His throat had been cut. The captain leaned down to the wounded warrior and pressed him back against the wall. The wounded one tried to speak but could not. His eyes were wild with pain, and the captain suddenly realized that he was in terror.

"Who did this?" the captain asked.

The wounded man pointed toward the floor next to the cabinet, but there was no one there. There was only a sprinkling of blood across the cabinet and a bit of purple fabric.

The captain turned to ask again, but the wounded man slumped over as the last blood drained from his body. The captain stood up and sheathed his blade. Whatever had killed his men was no longer in the cabin. He walked back out into the yard.

Other horsemen approach from the broken mountain cliffs through the same entrance he had used to enter with his troop just a few moments before. He swore to himself. She would not be happy unless his men on horseback found the girl.

The captain stood by his horse by the door of the cabin and waited as the warriors rode up. There were six armored warriors riding black steeds in a line, with another riding a gray horse just behind them. The six fanned out across the front of the cabin and to each side as the one behind rode up to the cabin and dismounted.

The captain bowed and then stood at attention as the seventh warrior dismounted and handed the reins to the horse to one of the others. The warrior pulled the hood back from her head, revealing long black hair that fell across her face and shoulders. She pulled the hair back and tamed it with a single leather band. She stood as tall as most of the other warriors and had strong silver-green eyes with a prominent jaw and a long, slender neck.

She wore form-fitting black leather pants and a shirt that buttoned in the front with jeweled buttons. Her cape flowed down to her black riding boots, and when she pulled it slightly back, it revealed a short sword in a brown scabbard at her waist.

The queen took one long glance at the captain and then peered into the doorway, then looked back at the captain again.

"It's all clear, my lady. Someone protected the girl. Whoever it was killed three of my men. The girl escaped toward the mountain cliffs," the captain remarked as the woman gave one more disapproving glare and then entered the cabin.

The captain entered the door behind her. She walked around the table, took off her gloves, and held them in one hand. She knelt by the first dead body and, taking her free hand, softly caressed the dead man's cheek and then placed her hand over his dead eyes. She remained there for a moment and then walked to the second man and did the same thing as the captain stood by. He had seen his queen do this several times before.

She shook her head, "A woman?" she asked, "A dark-haired woman with a sword."

The dead man was impaled by a broadsword through his midsection. She pulled at the sword, but at first, it did not break free. She stood up and placed one foot on the man's chest and pulled again, and the sword broke free with a grisly cracking noise, and blood and water burst forward. She backed up quickly from the gore and examined the sword carefully.

"But not this sword?" she questioned.

The sword clattered loudly against the overturned chair as she dropped it and knelt again to touch the dead man's eyes.

"A trained warrior, this one. Your soldiers took her for granted, Captain, because she was a woman. But no ordinary woman, this one."

The captain took a step forward. His queen had second sight, he knew, and could somehow see a person's last sight just before they died. He watched as the woman walked to the third dead body, the one with his throat slit, who leaned against the wall. The one that had pointed to nothing on the floor in fear.

She knelt again and caressed the man's cheek and then covered his eyes with her hand.

"Magic!" she exclaimed, "How can this be?"

"My lady?" the captain questioned.

The queen glared at her captain and then glanced around the room until she saw the purple fabric lying on the floor. She reached down and picked it up and held it out before her. "It was a Watcher that killed your men, Captain. She is the reason the girl has been hidden from us all this time." The queen threw the fabric down across the face of the dead man and walked back out the door.

"But where did she go? No one came out of the cabin but the girl, " the captain asked.

The queen gathered the reins and mounted her gray horse, looking down at the captain. She carefully replaced her riding gloves and noticed a bit of blood on one of them. She leaned down and wiped the blood on the captain's tunic.

"If she is indeed a Watcher, Captain, she is doing just that," the woman remarked, "Keep searching for the girl, Captain. We have to find her before it is too late."

The woman whirled her horse around and rode back toward the mountain pass from where she had come, and her bodyguard circled around her.

The captain stared off into the mountains. He had heard of Watchers, ancient magic from the before time. But why had one kept the girl hidden? And where was this watcher now? Was she hiding somewhere nearby, tracking him and his men as they were searching for the girl?

Far off at the far end of the valley, he saw dark figures on horseback who were fanning out in a broader search, and then suddenly, one of them called, and the horseman turned toward the river. He mounted his own horse and rode to catch them. He would face the Watcher when the time came. Next time, they would not take anyone for granted, he thought.

CHAPTER FIVE

The river glistens in the early morning shafts of light that pierce through the giant oaks. Misty shadows float among the forest. Gray fog lingers over the water. The trail leads through a thicket of ferns, the ground covered in a thick mat of moss as well. Off in the distance, I see a small shack partially hidden by the trees. In the middle of the river, a figure of a man pulls at ropes that cross the river, pulling a ferry across the current back toward the shack. A horse neighs, and I see the black shape of a mounted horse standing between the trees by the shack. The horse steps to the side, and I see the glint of steel from a sword. The rider dismounts as the ferryman nears the shore.

I quickly duck behind a tree at the sight of the swordsman. Could he be one of my pursuers? How am I to know?

The ferryman slumps lower over the ropes to pull harder. With every pull, the wooden ferry draws closer to the shore. The man appears to be ancient with a long gray beard and balding head, but he is strong beyond his age, as proven by the pull of the massive ropes.

The man steps away from the black horse, holding the reins in one hand, and the horse steps behind him as he walks to the shore. He stands with his side to me, so I cannot see his face. He has long, black hair that hangs over his shoulders, a purple band tying the great locks of hair out of his face. He is large and muscled, and when he raises his left arm in greeting, I see a brilliant, multicolored tattoo covering his entire arm, but from this distance, I cannot make out what the tattoo is. The man pulls at the horse, and his great, black cloak falls back over the arm. I have never seen such a magnificent figure of a man in my life and take a step closer to get a better view, taken in by his beauty and pure masculinity. The ferryman pulls the ferry up to the shore and, with surprising agility for a man of such advanced age, jumps from the boat to the muddy shoreline. They speak to each other, but I cannot hear what is said. The ferryman bows to the man and takes the reins of the horse to lead the animal onto the boat. The man suddenly turns toward me as if he hears something, and I duck behind the tree.

Did he see me?

I wait for a moment until I hear the splash as the ferry boat breaks free of the sticky mud and peer around the tree to take another look. The ferry boat is floating empty beside the bank and there is no one to be seen. I duck back around the tree, and my heart stops in fear. He did see me! I had to get away from here, but where?

I take a deep breath to calm myself. Mother told me to go to the river and cross the ferry. But the dark horseman scares me. Here I am now, being chased by men that I do not know, and I do not know what to do or where to go. I calm my beating heart and crawl to the other side of the tree. I cannot stay where I am. The man must have seen me, but where is he now? I see only the horse standing next to the shack among the trees, and then I hear someone move among the brush nearby. They are near!

I suddenly jump up and run toward the ferry boat. Among the brambles, I see the ferryman turn in astonishment as I run by him and the flash of a black cape among the giant pines. And then, high on the ridge, warriors ride, their armor glistening in the morning sun.

The ferryman shouts, and I run faster. My only hope is to get to the ferry and cross the river before the men catch me.

"Stop, girl! We mean you no harm!" the caped man shouts.

But I continue to run. The ferryman falls among the brambles, cursing as I pass him. The other man turns and stands for a moment, the sun glaring behind him, casting him in a brilliant shine, and I swear I see dark wings flashing behind him. And then the horsemen begin to descend, and the caped man turns suddenly and is lost in the brilliant light.

I am now on the ferry, but I do not have the strength to untie the ropes that hold the boat to the dock. I frantically look around for anything to assist and see the glimmer from a sword sheathed in a leather cover tied to the black horse. I desperately pull at the sword until the leather cover releases and run back to the ropes. I swing at the first rope, and the sword cuts the great cord, to my surprise, with only one stroke.

I look up and smile as I jump on the shifting deck of the boat. The ferryman is running toward me. The horsemen are desperately trying to descend the cliffs down to the water's edge, stirring up great amounts of dust. One horse panics and throws its rider, who tumbles down among the boulders.

I swing at the second rope, a glancing stroke that only half cuts the cord, and look up again as the ferryman stops at the shore, breathing hard. The boat is now too far out in the river for him to board.

"Don't be a fool, child....... The current is too swift....... You will be pulled down to the falls!" he shouts between heavy breaths.

I see the horsemen finally reach the bottom of the canyon, and suddenly, the second man is standing next to the ferryman as I swing a second time and cut the final rope. The boat suddenly swings far out into the middle of the river. I hold tight and look at the caped man as he stands staring at me. I see his face now. He is the most beautiful man I have ever seen.

I realize my hood has fallen from my head, and I instinctively pull it up to hide my scars. I am mesmerized by his strong, piercing blue eyes. He bows to me as the current pulls me downriver.

I fall back as the current pulls the boat in a wide circle with the current, but the ropes tied to the opposite shore lead the boat across the current as well. A few moments later, the boat slams into the rocky shore, and I fall, but I quickly gain my footing and jump from the boat to the safety of dry land. I grab the sword and stand facing the far shore. The horsemen rein in their horses next to the river, watching me off to one side of the ferryman and the caped man and then turn and gallop down the river. Strange, I think, that they never seem to have acknowledged the ferryman and the caped man who still stands by the shack watching me. I take a step closer to the shoreline to get a better view of them. The ferryman turns to say something, and the caped man answers him. He then salutes me again, and they are suddenly lost in the morning mist.

"Did you see her scars, my lord? Poor girl to be scarred in such a way. No one will ever have her," the ferryman stated.

"She is the most beautiful young woman I have ever seen, ferryman," the caped man answered him, "Truly the bride of a king."

The ferryman looked up to his companion, puzzled at the statement, as the other man turned toward his horse. He would have to find another way to cross the river now. The girl was on the other side, which was where he needed to be.

I stand by the river, trying to see through the mist that thickens along the far bank. I am rather proud of myself, and then I remember that I still do not know where I am going. But I know that I must not be caught by the horsemen. They had killed my mother and, for some reason, were chasing me.

I think of the caped man with the tattoo, hoping to see him somewhere in the mist. Who is he? And why did he chase after me when he saw me in the forest? His eyes were so kind. Maybe I should not have run from him, I think. But it is too late now.

I look down at the sword in my hand. I had stolen it from the horse, but I had no choice. It was the only thing that could cut the ropes.

The sword is short and well-balanced, with a cutting edge on both sides of the blade. I touch the edge carefully and feel how sharp the blade is. The handle is made of dark wood, and there is a red coat of arms emblazoned on the handle of a set of bird wings. How strange, I think.

I carefully replace the sword back into its leather sheath and tie the weapon at my side. I pull my mantle tighter around me and am satisfied when I see that the sword is hidden from sight. I re-position my leather pouch and make sure the chain necklace is safe where Mother had placed it. I look upward, away from the river, and see a trail leading off into the forest. For now, I must trust the trail, I think to myself. I have no other choice.

Mother had told me to find the carpenter in the village. Hopefully, the trail through the forest led in the right direction. I had only been to the village a few times in my life. I knew it to lie at the far edge of the forest among low hills filled with grass and sheep.

CHAPTER SIX

I quietly crawl across the face of a granite rock on a summit overlooking a wide meadow to get a better view below me. The glistening silver of water shines in the afternoon sun, a long sliver that meanders through high grass. Six dome tents lay in a circle next to the stream, each at least ten feet wide. The grass is trampled down between the tents, a fire crackling in the center of them. To one side of the tents, I count at least twenty horses standing in a row, tied to a wooden fence. Three large wagons sit between the tents and the horses.

One man walks among the horses, a bow in one hand, a sling of arrows over his shoulder. He carries what appears to be two large rabbits spotted with blood in his other hand. Several women stand next to the fire, which has a metal tripod to one side and a large pot hanging over a smaller bed of coals. A small wooden table sits next to the tripod covered in dishes and vegetables. The breeze shifts, and I smell the food cooking. My stomach growls loudly.

I hear laughter and turn to see several small children playing in the tall grass as another man walks by them carrying a load of sticks and branches. I am hungry and need to eat, but can I trust these people? Will they help me? They seem to be a small clan of several nomadic families. Surely, they would help me, I think. But how can I be sure?

I step around the boulder and hide among a thicket of brambles and shrubs. The smell of roasting meat floats on the breeze, and I breathe in the intoxicating aroma. I am so hungry but am afraid to show myself to the people below me. Then I feel that someone or something is watching me, and I turn slowly to look into the dark eyes of a small child who stands next to the boulder I am hiding behind.

The boy is dirty and has disheveled hair that covers much of his face. He stands not three feet high, his eyes wide with amazement. I smile at him, and he smiles back nervously. He glances at the camp and then back to me and takes a step back in fear. I hold my hands out to him in submission and then place a finger to my mouth. Please don't scream, I plead in silence.

27

I hold his stare for just a moment and then realize that her will scream, and he does and turns quickly to run away. He darts past the rock as I reach for him and screams again as the man with the firewood drops it and grabs the boy as he runs by. I panic and run back into the forest as quickly as I can as several men approach the rock.

I am overcome with fear at the thought that they will chase me and continue through the forest away from the meadow for several minutes until I realize that no one gives chase. I stop, breathing heavily, and look around me. I am now deep in a darkened forest of thick, pole-sized pine trees that shield the sunlight from reaching the forest floor. Even though the sun still shines over the meadow, I stand in a darkened, silent world.

Now, what am I to do? I ask myself. This forest hides a darkness that I can feel around me like a living, breathing organism that hides in the shadows of trees in a world of half-light.

I have lived my entire life in the forest and meadows around our small cabin. I had always felt totally secure in the forest of my youth, but I knew that there were places in the forest that I should avoid. There were spirits of the forest that held a different power, an ancient evil from the before time.

And now, because I had panicked at being seen by the boy, I had run into a place where I should never be. My heart beats fast, and my breathing increases in fear. I look all around me and see nothing but the constant row upon row of pine trees that stretch far off into the distance of gathering darkness. Soon, the place will be consumed by the blackness of night, and I will be trapped.

I close my eyes and gather my thoughts. I slow my beating heart and breath as well and open my eyes. The darkness grows around me with each passing minute. There is no sound, no breeze, no life. Only the poles of dying pines and the growing ancient evil.

I take a step back toward the meadow from where I had run and then another. I think of running, but I think maybe the evil presence that gathers will know I am trying to escape, so I take one slow, quiet step at a time toward the meadow. I can see a small bit of light in the direction of the meadow, but
even that light is growing dim. I step a bit quicker but still try to be as quiet as I can for fear that whatever lay in the shadows might hear me.

28

There is a sudden flutter of wings above me, and I jump back from the sound and look upward. A black raven lands on a branch of the nearest tree and flicks its head to one side. The raven's eyes shine black and stare directly at me, and I think I see intelligence in the raven's eyes. For a moment, I stare back at the raven, and then, with a sudden realization, I understand that the raven is intelligent.

I draw my sword and hold the weapon upward toward the bird, but the raven is unmoving at my threat. The bird continues to stare at me with black eyes that suddenly turn green, and I hear laughter all around me. I panic and turn toward the meadow, and run as fast as I can through the thick pines. The raven flutters above me, and I hear laughter all through the forest behind me. I fall out into the meadow, and the last rays of the sun sink beyond the horizon.

I turn back to the forest on my knees and see glowing green eyes just inside the blackness of the trees. They move slowly closer to me as I gain my footing and back away. The eyes move to the very last tree, and I see a woman's shape materialize in the last light of the dying sun.

What evil is this? What have I awakened in the forest? Who is chasing me?

A voice calls from the forest like an echo, "What king would ever have you, girl? You are nothing but a slave. I see you now, the daughter of this world. You may run, but I will soon find you."

And the woman's shape fades away before me. I turn and run as fast as I can toward the light of the nomad's fires. Anything is better than what I had just experienced, I think.

I run across the rocky meadow, still holding my sword. Suddenly, a shape stands before me, and I try to sidestep but trip over the rocks. Hands reach out for me as I fall, and I slash with my sword.

"Bi curamach!" someone shouts in a language I cannot understand.

"Dia dhaobh, a chailin! Nil aon dochar againn duit!" someone shouts as I fall and hit my head hard against the rocks.

"We mean you no harm, girl!" someone else shouts, and I understand what he says this time.

I turn frantically to try and get back up, but my head explodes in pain, and there is sudden blackness all around me.

I smell flowers. What a strange thing to smell flowers, I think. I hear movement somewhere close by and whispered voices of women off to one side. I open my eyes, and the sudden light shoots pain through my head, and I quickly close them again. My head hurts terribly. I reach up and feel a bandage over the side of my head. I open my eyes slowly this time, and the pain subsides, and my vision clears. I am lying in a tent in a bed of firs. A girl who seems to be my own age stands by the bed, holding a wash basin. There are flowers lying all around me.

When she sees that I am awake, she smiles and calls, "Mother, she is awake."

The girl kneels next to me, takes a cloth, and dips it in the basin. She removes the bandage and I immediately feel the warm, healing power of some strong herbal fragrance when she places the cloth on my wounds. She replaces the bandages.

"Thank you," I say and smile.

The girl smiles back, "You took a nasty fall out there in the dark. When they brought you in, you were out cold."

I sit up still a bit confused about what had happened. I look around me and see my leather pouch and sword lying across the tent, propped up against the tent wall. I immediately place my hand on my chest and feel the amulet under my shirt. I notice the girl looking at the scars that cover the right side of my face and turn my head slightly as she glances away.

"Where am I?" I ask.

"Our home," she stands up. "We are Faireadoiri. My name is Raham."

I have heard of Faireadoiri. Once a long time ago a band of Faireadoiri came by the cabin. They travel the realm, selling a multitude of household items and tools, building and repairing work for hire, and then travel on.

"My name is Hannah," I introduce myself just as an older woman enters the tent.

"Good child. I am glad you have woken up. We were worried for you," the woman says as she leans closer to me and inspects the bandages.

"Well done, Raham," she says and then looks at me, "Child, what are you doing out here all along? Do you have family nearby we can take you to?"

30

How am I to answer her? The only family I have ever known lies dead in my home.

"No. I have no family."

The woman sees my scars but says nothing. She leans back down and looks at me directly. Her eyes are green, and I immediately trust her, which is strange to me. But something about the way she looks at me causes me to do so.

"No worries, child. You are safe with us. Is there somewhere you are trying to get to?"

"Yes. I need to get to the village at the end of the trail. I don't know the name."

She turns her head, questioning my answer, "That would be Glenmorrow. We are heading that way ourselves."

She smiles and pats my shoulder, "You rest a bit more, child. Raham will get you when our dinner is ready. Glenmorrow is but a few days' travel."

The woman leaves the tent, and I lie back down and then realize that I had been out most of the day because the last thing I remember was running from the forest during the night.

CHAPTER SEVEN

I run through a thicket of trees toward a distant light that fades further away as I run toward it. Something flutters in the treetops above me. Giant wings crash in the darkness. I fall over a downed tree onto a muddy forest floor and struggle against the wall of saplings and briers to get back up.

Flashes of red flame shoot through the trees above me, and great, leathery wings crash against the trees, breaking them like matches. For a moment, I stare upward in fear as a great, winged dragon struggles toward me through the tangle of trees. Yellow eyes glow in the darkness, illuminating the ground around me as I back away from the glowing light.

Limbs and leaves fall all around me as I get up and run again. The dragon screams and flies higher above the treetops, chasing me in the air, its yellow eyes searching the forest with glowing light. I push through another thicket, the briers tearing at my dress and skin, and then suddenly, I fall through the thicket and land on an open trail that leads toward the distant light.

I quickly stand back up and run along the trail as the dragon crashes into the undergrowth behind me. The creature has found the trail as well and now walks on the ground. I glance back and see a massive dark form on the trail, twin yellow eyes glaring in the blackness.

And then I am suddenly free of the forest and stand under a star-filled sky and full moon. The dragon now circles high above me at one point, covering the moon. The monster turns to the side and glides off over the mountains. The smell of fire and sulfur floats in the gentle night breeze.

And then I see a woman standing among the grass, her eyes bright and glowing in the dark. She walks closer as I tremble in fear and back away from her to the very edge of the forest.

"I mean you no harm, child," she says, but I do not believe her. Somehow, I remember her from a time before.

There is a flash of steel, and the woman suddenly turns and disappears in a swirl of smoke and leathery wings.

I see long black hair swirl and purple in the smoke, and I awaken suddenly from the dream, lying in the bed in the tent. There is a split second just as I wake up that I swear I see the shape of a woman disappear behind the canvas door.

"Mother?" I question.

Raham enters the tent.

"Good, you are awake. Mom sent me to get you. Dinner is ready."

I sit up in the bed and place my feet on the grass floor. I realize that I have no shoes. The dream flurries around in my mind like ghosts; parts of it are so vivid that it seems like it had happened in this very tent, and other parts disappear in the half-world between sleep.

"Had someone else been in here just before you came, Raham?" I ask.

Raham looks around, "No, just me," she answers as she checks my bandage and helps me retrieve my leather shoes.

I have lived my entire life in the cabin by the forest with only my mother. Very rarely have I ever been anywhere with other people. We rarely traveled to the village and never stayed for more than a day or two. We received very few visitors.

The forest and meadows around my home were the only real world that I have ever truly experienced except through the nightly stories Mother had shared with me. She would spin tales of wondrous cities, gallant knights, and grand balls where the women dressed in beautiful silt gowns and wore elaborately crafted jewelry.

I have often dreamed of such balls where I, too, wore a beautiful dress and danced with kindly and handsome gentlemen, much like the man I saw at the ferry only a few days ago. In my dreams, my scars are gone, but in real life, one side of my face is covered by the scars of a fire when I was but a small child. I had also dreamed of sitting at a dinner table with a family to see other children my own age and to see loved ones share a meal together. And now, I find myself sitting on one of many tree stumps positioned in a circle around a makeshift wooden table beside my new friend, Raham. The early evening breeze has a bit of a chill about it. The sun sits just above the forested slopes to the west in a sky void of any clouds.

33

The Faireadoiri are loud and boisterous at the table, speaking a language among themselves that I cannot understand. Every now and again, I hear a word or two that is familiar, however. They are a happy family. Raham shares with me that they are an extended family of three brothers, their wives, and children. Raham is the eldest, an only child of the older brother. Among the table sits eleven cousins. The youngest is but a babe that now suckles from her mother's breast as the woman eats with her free hand. At the far end of the table sits an ancient, dark-haired woman who is quiet with green eyes and a soft face. She wears elaborately carved earrings and a jeweled necklace.

She notices that I stare at her, and she smiles, and I quickly look away. All the women wear brightly covered dresses and jewelry, as is the Faireadoiri fashion. The men wear basic woolen pants and tunics with wide, black belts and leather boots. Their arms are tattooed with great colored animals of all sorts. I remember the man by the ferry at the sight of these men.

I think that it is strange that they seem to have totally incorporated me into their family. Just before I sat to eat, Raham's mother introduced me and told the family that I would travel with them to Glenmorrow. The older brother greeted me and pointed to the food. And that was that.

We eat rabbit and potatoes, carrots, and homemade bread, and I drink water, but I smell the distinctive smell of mead around me. Raham's father stands and points to the fire and says something in the Faireadoiri language, which makes the children jump up suddenly and scatter toward the fire that burns at the side of the table in the center of the circled tents.

He then looks at me, "Hannah, child. You are welcome to come. Tonight, we tell stories."

Raham smiles and grabs my hand, "Come Hannah, my Da is a wonderful storyteller. But he will speak in our language. I will try to translate it for you."

The younger woman with the baby gathers the children to a place by the fire where firs have been placed. She lays the baby on a fir and then lounges next to him as the other children fight among themselves for the best seats closer to the blaze.

I follow Raham to a place behind the children and next to a rocking chair where the grandmother sits with assistance from one of the older children. The child places a blanket over the woman, and she smiles and pats the child on the head.

I sit down beside Raham, watching in awe at the scene before me. I had never witnessed a loving family in such a way.

A few more logs are placed on the fire, and the orange flames respond with a sudden shower of sparkling embers, which blow up and then disappear in the night sky. Smoke stirs in the soft breeze and blows over the children before lifting them back up into the night.

Outside the range of the fire's glow, the world is lost in the mantle of darkness that only reveals shadows of the closer trees. Several lanterns offer bits of light at each of the tents arranged in a broader circle around the central fire.

Raham's father, or Da, as she called him earlier, stands by the fire with a small stick in his hand. To one side of him, a drum made of some type of animal hide stretched over a wooden barrel sits on the ground. The drum is beautifully decorated with multicolored tassels, feathers, and beads.

He bangs the drum once with the stick, and all is suddenly quiet except for the crackling of the fire. For a few moments, the man stands motionless and holds the stick over the drum as if he will strike it again. I fully expect him to strike the drum, but after a moment longer, he grins widely and places the stick on the drum itself.

Raham scoots close to me. I glance at her face and then back to her father, but he no longer stands by the drum. Where did he go? I think. And then I see his shape swirling in the glow of the fire and smoke before he emerges on the other side of the fire and closer to the children. I think of what I know of Faireadoiri, of how they often entertain in villages by performing plays in street markets and fairs.

He speaks in his own language.

"Bhi ri ann uair amhair a chuardagha bhrideog."

I have no clue what he says, but Raham speaks softly in my ear.

"There was once a king who searched for his bride."

"Bhi si cruthaithe ag Dia direachdo."

"She was created by God just for him."

The father blows in his hand as he speaks these words and throws something on the fire and dark blue smoke; the Faireadoiri's color of purity falls over the children as they stare, wide-eyed with excitement and awe. No doubt they have seen this many times before, but the magic never grows old to them. I am immediately pulled deep within the story and the magic of what I see before me. I notice a shadow gathering strength in the half-light just outside the fire's reach.

"Ach chuir mallacht an chire daonna ar feadh na milte blain bac uirthi fias a bheith aire cerbh i go firineach."

"But the curse upon mankind for thousands of years prevented her from knowing who she truly was."

The father disappears behind the fire again with this statement as the children boo and shake their heads.

"Just wait until you see what Uncle James does next," a child speaks next to me, and I look over and see the small boy who first saw me as I hid by the rocks.

"Shh," Raham scolds him softly and scoots closer to me.

The boy sits almost on my lap, "My name is Johnny," he whispers shyly.

"My name is Hannah," I answer, and he smiles.

"Someone is very attracted to you," Raham whispers.

Then James beats loudly on the drum, startling me. I jump at the sudden noise, and Johnny laughs, and the children scream in delight. The shadow behind the fire is one of the other women who gracefully swirls out from the shadows and begins to play the violin with quick rhythms that grow stronger as the drum beats faster until, with a final strike, both drum and violin fall silent.

"Ansin go tobann bhi crith talum mor ag bas ahus athbhreath ri."

"Then there was a great earthquake at the death and rebirth of a king."

And James once again disappears behind the fire as the violin plays softly. The children lean forward in anticipation as I do.

James speaks now from behind the fire, "Agus chonaic an dragan mor an bhrideag a bheith agus chuir se a arm chun i a mhara. A ch bhi an cath buaite ag an ri da bhrista cheana feirs."

"And the great dragon saw the bride to be and sent her armies to kill her. But the king has already won the battle for his bride."

36

James jumps suddenly from the fire in a swirl of red smoke, wearing a great dragon's head as the violin gains intensity. The children scream, and I jump back at the spectacle of the fire-breathing dragon before me. The dragon jumps toward the children as they scramble backward, falling over themselves as they scream and laugh all at once.

And then the violin player swirls in front of the dragon, and I notice her more now. Long black hair cascades over her face, and she wears a long purple dress adorned with multicolored ribbons. I am suddenly shocked at the sight of her dancing before the dragon, playing the violin like a weapon toward the heaving dragon. I think of my own mother in the purple dress, fighting to her death to save me. I fight back tears at the thought of her.

Suddenly, the dragon disappears in a heavy puff of red smoke that covers all the space between the fire and the audience. The music slows to a soft, slow rhythm and then is silent. I wait, breathless at what is to come next. My heart races with anticipation. My emotions are undone at the drama and majesty of the performance and of the vision of my mother swirling in the purple dress.

James speaks from behind the fire once more, "Ni raibh a fhios ag an mbeirtin cerbh i indairire achrinme an ri. Agus ba e sin go leir a bhi tabhachtach i indairire."

"The bride-to-be did not know who she really was, but the king did. And that was all that really mattered."

James steps out from behind the fire and stands next to the violin player, who I now recognize as Raham's own mother, and they bow. The kids scream in delight and clap, as do I.

"Another, please another!" several children shout.

"No. No children. It's time for bed. We have a long day of travel tomorrow."

The children grumble and complain, but very soon, most of them leave for their family's tent. I look down at Johnny, who is still sitting at my feet.

"What do you think, Hannah? Wasn't that great?"

"Yes, it was," I answer and then look at Raham, "Do they do those plays at the fairs?"

"Yes. Mom and Da do many of them. Sometimes, we all have parts in them, but usually, only the two of them do that," she answers proudly.

Someone yells across the camp for Johnny, and he quickly stands up, "Good night, Miss Hannah. I hope you sleep well tonight," he says and bows like such a little gentleman and runs off to his mother.

"He definitely is in love with you, Hannah," Raham remarks with a smile.

What a fine little boy, I think. I sit for a while with Raham, and we talk more about her family. Soon, only Raham, the grandmother, and I remain by the fire. After a while, we grow quiet and stare into the glowing fire as I think again of the strange play performed. I think of what Mother had told me about being the bride of a king. I think of my dream of the night before, of the visions of my mother, of the horrid dragon and the green-eyed witch woman in the forest. What is going on? What am I to do? The play seemed to talk directly to me, but how could that be? There are too many questions, and now I have a headache.

I glance away from the fire and notice the grandmother staring at me. She says something in her own language, and Raham responds and stands up. "Grandmother wishes for us to help her to her tent," Raham informs me, and I stand up as well.

We walk over to her, and Raham takes her hand and helps her up. Her blanket falls to the ground, and as I bend over to pick it up, she takes hold of my hand. I look up at her, and she smiles. Her hand is wrinkled with age but very soft and warm. Her bright green eyes are youthful despite her age, and she looks deep into my soul, it seems, with her piercing eyes.

I think that she wishes very much to say something to me, but she knows that I cannot understand her language and she does not know mine. When she has fully stood, she stands over a foot below me, her body frail and shaking a bit. She takes my other hand in hers and pulls me closer to her, looking at me as if searching for something. Raham stands to the side quietly.

She lets go of one hand, reaches out, and places the hand flat against my chest over the amulet Mother had given me. I do not know if she feels the jewelry or not, but her hand rests softly over it. She looks at Raham and says something to her, and Raham shakes her head yes.

"Is tusa an bride a bheidh," the woman says and I step back. I remember from the play what one word means.

38

"Is tusa briathar an ri," she finishes her sentence and shakes her head and smiles and takes a step away from me. Raham leads her away, leaving me to stand next to the fire all by myself in total awe of what she said. I only recognized three of the words, but enough to understand what she was trying to tell me. How can that be? I am nothing. How could what she said make any sense? I am scarred. No man would want me. I walk slowly back to my tent.

CHAPTER EIGHT

After a fitful night of sleep, I wake up suddenly in the half-light of early morning, just before the sun emerges under the fir covers in the tent that I share with Raham and the younger girls. I am the only person in the tent. I lay for a moment, remembering the previous night, the wonderful drama, the grandmother's words spoken over me.

Outside the tent walls, I hear people scurrying around, mothers scolding their children to hurry, men calling for the horses, dogs barking, the noises of a nomad Faireadoiri's camp coming to life on a morning when they are packing up to move once more. I look around me and realize that everything is missing from the tent except for my belongings and the fir covering over me.

After a hearty breakfast, I find myself riding in the front seat on the last wagon in the small caravan with Raham at my side. I have never ridden a wagon so large that it required two horses to pull, and I am amazed that Raham has no problems controlling the great beasts. Several of the smaller children and the younger mother with the baby ride in the back. The other wagons are driven by the woman. The three brothers each ride a horse, and I see that they are all armed with curved swords and crossbows. Each horse has a round, wooden shield attached to the back of the saddle, along with a scabbard filled with arrows.

James rides to the front of the wagon, and the two younger brothers ride just behind the wagon that I am in. The day is unseasonably hot, and we travel over a great, open savanna that is barren of any shade. There is no breeze, only the constant dust and burning sun.

There is no sound but the constant shuffle of the horses and the rhythmic clanking of pots and pans tied to the sides of the wagons. Every now and again, a child will cough or complain of the heat; a mother will offer soft, comforting words to her children.

Suddenly, the dogs both bark in unison and growl. I look up at the noise and see James standing in his stirrups and looking off toward the distant sun. The younger brothers spur their mounts forward as Raham suddenly pulls hard on the reins and all three wagons stop.

Dust blows in on me from a sudden, ominous breeze that comes up from the ground as in a warning.

I strain to see what had alerted the dogs, and at first, I only see the desert grass and the sun on the horizon, but then I see a single horseman riding out of the sun's glare. And then, behind the horseman, six more emerge from behind the low swell of land and fall in line with the first one. My heart stops for a moment, and I gasp at the sight of the warriors. Raham looks at me in alarm. They are the men who had chased me at the ferry crossing.

I look frantically around me in panic and then Raham takes my hand and holds her finger to her mouth to quiet me. I notice for the first time, that she has pulled her own crossbow from beneath the seat and lays it in the folds of her dress to hide it.

There is movement behind me, and I turn to see the young mother lay her sleeping baby in the arms of one of the other children and retrieve a curved sword in a leather scabbard and lay it beside her.

Mother had once told me a story of the Faireadoiri warriors and said that many of them were women. She had told me that before a man could take a Faireadoiri woman as his wife, he had to first best her in single combat. If the woman wished to be his bride, she would submit in combat otherwise she would fight hard to show that he was not her mate.

I think of my own short sword that I hid under my cloak, but what use could it be? Mother taught me how to use the sword, but I am unsure if I can use it properly to protect myself. Holding the hilt in my hand offers some comfort.

The warriors stand silhouetted by the sun along the ridge in front of us. James turns and says something to his brother, and the man turns his horse and trots back to our wagon. He says something in his own language to Raham, and she turns to me.

"Are those the men you told us about?" she asks.

I cannot answer her, for I am gripped with a fear that I cannot control, but I shake my head, yes.

The brother rides back to the front.

"Hannah, very slowly slide back into the wagon," Raham orders, "Anna, hide her; children, don't say anything. We need to hide Hannah from those men, okay."

I carefully slide back into the wagon, trying to keep myself hidden as Anna quickly removes a pile of clothing and pulls on a trap door, revealing a hidden space under the wagon itself.

"Dean deifer!" Anna says and I understand that she wishes for me to be quick. I lower myself into the hidden compartment and pull my small pack and sword in with me as Anna closes the door over me.

I turn myself in the hiding place to the point where I can see out through a crack under the wagon seat. I see Raham's hand reach down and slowly pull a short arrow from the hidden scabbard. I carefully slide back into the wagon, trying to keep myself hidden as Anna quickly removes a pile of clothing and pulls on a trap door, revealing a hidden space under the wagon itself.

"Dean deifer!" Anna says and I understand that she wishes for me to be quick. I lower myself into the hidden compartment and pull my small pack and sword in with me as Anna closes the door over me.

I turn myself in the hiding place to the point where I can see out through a crack under the wagon seat. I see Raham's hand reach down and slowly pull a short arrow from the hidden scabbard. Anna whispers something to the children above me, and I feel her as she moves closer to the back of the wagon.

The dogs continue to bark at the strangers until James shouts, "Maoth!"

The dogs immediately stop barking and sit on the side of their master's horse. The first rider spurs his mount forward as the two brothers sidestep their own mounts to one side of their older brother. The sun glares directly behind the warrior as he rides forward, and I cannot see him clearly, but I can tell that he wears chainmail and is armed with a broadsword that rides at the side of the saddle. The other warriors stand silent along the ridge.

The two dogs stand again; their hair bristled up the back, and growl. They are massive dogs, full of fir and muscle.

"Maoth!" James orders, and they both stop growling but remain standing, their heads low, their teeth showing, and their muscles tense.

The warrior reins in his horse in front of James, turning himself to face the two dogs, and there is a moment when it seems time stands still as the two men face each other; the brothers hold their loaded crossbows before them, silent. Raham holds the arrow just below her dress, and I forget to breathe.

The warrior salutes James, and he returns the gesture, and they talk among themselves. However, I cannot hear what they are saying. The warrior points behind him and then across the desert to the forest behind us from where we came, and James shakes his head no.

James pulls a paper from his breast pocket and hands it to the stranger, who looks it over and gives it back to James. The warrior then waves his men forward, and James backs his horse away and back to the first wagon where his wife and grandmother are. I think how they both must look, sitting on the wagon seat with weapons hidden under their long dresses.

James rides down past the three wagons, speaking in the Faireadoiri language, and I hear Raham whisper above me.

"Da says they are the sheriff's men looking for a runaway prisoner. A young girl. They will search each wagon."

I hold my breath and look back through the crack. The other warriors ride down from the ridge toward the first wagon as the two brothers pull their horses back away, one on each side, and James positions himself next to the leader. Two riders stop at the front, one facing each brother, and the other four dismount at the first wagon. They don't seem dangerous at all, just men doing their job, but under the surface, there is a tangible level of intense stress and uncertainty mixed with distrust and fear. I notice that Raham still holds the arrow behind her leg and under her dress. The crossbow is on her lap under her shawl and can be quickly loaded if she needs to do so.

The men look through the first wagon as Grandmother scolds them in her own language like a mad woman, ranting and swinging her arms wildly about her. The men dismiss her as if she is truly mad and quickly look through the first wagon and turn to the second. I see a flash, a glimmer of steel, and realize that she holds a short sword in the folds of her long dress, and she turns away from them.

They search the second wagon and then approach the front of my own hiding place. Through the crack, I can only see the legs of the two horses as James and the stranger stop their mounts just to the side of the wagon. The warrior turns his horse, and I see the broadsword. I hold my breath as I feel the heavy men climb onto the wagon and look inside. Anna's baby suddenly begins to cry, and thankfully, the men climb back out of the wagon.

A few moments later, the men ride off into the desert.

CHAPTER NINE

I lay completely still, not knowing if I should move from my hiding place or not. Anna stirs above me, and I see Raham place the arrow back and lay the cross bow at her feet through the crack in the wood.

James dismounts and walks up to the side of the wagon. I hear his voice next to me order something in his own language, and then he says to me, "Hannah, you can come out, but stay in the back of the wagon for a while in case they are watching."

Anna opens the trapdoor, and I climb out of my hiding place and sit among the pile of firs just behind the wagon seat. One of the younger brothers appears on horseback behind the wagon and leans inside without unmounting, kissing Anna before riding off across the savannah in the direction the warriors had taken.

I look at Raham, questioning as she lightly taps the horses with the reins, and the wagon jumps forward.

"Da told Collen to trail the sheriff's men to see if they double back. We are riding to the river and set up camp for tonight," she answers my questioning look.

Anna places her sword back in a small compartment below the wagon rails and retrieves her crying baby from the girl who held her, comforting the baby, who soon falls silent. She smiles at me, and my heart slows as I calm myself.

We ride toward the setting sun until I see a grove of trees with flowing water behind. Raham pulls back on the horses that smell the water and wishes to rush forward. James rides into the river with a splash of water and walks his horse across the river and onto the other side. He reins in his mount on a low rise on the opposite shore and waves the caravan across. After a few moments, we are all safely on the other side, and the three wagons are turned to the side to form a small half circle with the river to one side.

I sit for a moment in the wagon as the others climb out, and the baby is carefully carried by his mother as she, in turn, steps out of the wagon. The family risked everything to assist me, and they have only known me for a few days. If I had been found, someone could have gotten hurt. Even now, Collen was out there across the river, watching the riders we had encountered. I would never forgive myself if this wonderful family was hurt in any way.

I will tell them that I will carry on to the village myself if they will only show me the way and give me a bit of food. The thought of leaving my new friends saddens me, but I know that to leave them now, before any harm comes to them because of my presence, is the right and honorable thing to do.

I hold my sword tight against me, pull my dress up a bit, and climb from the wagon with my decision made. I will ask for directions and food and make my leave first thing in the morning.

"Don't be foolish, girl. You will do no such thing," James tells me by the light of the cooking fire after I told him my decision to leave in the morning.

"But I do not wish to harm your family. Those soldiers who are after me have killed before, and they will do so again," I plead.

James walks up to me as Raham stands to one side. He stands over me and looks down with a smile. He is so much taller than I am, I think, as are most of his entire family except the smaller children. His eyes are blue, his hair brown and streaked with gray.

"Child, we do not fear those men. They are of no consequence to the Faireadoiri who are in your presence."

He places his strong hand on the side of my face. "Besides, Hannah. You are the Bean an Ri. It is Faireadoiri's job to protect you on your journey. Even if you do not know who you are, you are still the Bean an Ri. We will see you to Glenmorrow as we said we would do."

I stand, stunned by his words, as he smiles, pats my head, and turns back toward the fire. I hear a horse approach out in the darkness beyond the firelight from across the river.
I turn to the river but see nothing in the darkness. But I hear the splash as a horse enters the water.

'Dia duit an campa!" a voice shouts from the darkness.

"It is Collen," Raham tells me, "He calls to the camp."

I see the horseman now emerging from the riverbank and into the fire's light. He dismounts and walks past me, leading his horse to where James stands waiting, and they talk in their own language.

I can see by the expression on James's face that the news his younger brother has told him is not good news. He looks over to me and then back over to the camp where the children sit by the fire. For a moment, he lowers his head and runs his hands through his thick mane of hair. I can see that he makes a quick decision and speaks again to Collen. The brother acknowledges the decision and takes his horse to where Anna is waiting for him with a plate of food. He trades the reins for the plate and sits by the fire to eat as his wife takes the horse and leads the animal to the makeshift corral.

"What's going on?" I ask Raham.

"I'm not sure, but I will find out," she answers, and we walk over to the fire where the others gather as well.

James speaks to the family in his own language, several times pointing toward me and then out into the darkness. Whatever he says, the family agrees. I look to Raham for her to tell me what is going on. I see concern, maybe even fear, in her expression.

"Collen said that the men rode back to another group of their kind that were searching for you. He was able to hear their conversation. It seems that they think that you are with us. They also think that we are Faireadoiri."

She smiles at that statement, "They did not want to take the chance when they first encountered us, so they are gathering more men and are on their way now. They plan to take you, Hannah. They plan to kill you."

I stand in shock, "Why do they want to kill me?"

"Because they believe you are the Bean an Ri," James speaks behind me and I turn suddenly to face him.

For the past several days the Faireadoiri has called me that. Ever since the first night when I witnessed the spectacle of the dragon in the fire, they have called me those words. How can that be? How can I, scarred and alone, be the wife of the king? What does that even mean? People wished to kill me. Those same men killed my mother and drove me from the only life I knew. I am no wife of the king. I'm just an orphan girl, lost in an ugly world, scarred, and shamed by my disfigurement.

"I don't know what you mean!" I shout.

I step back away from him, "All I know is that they killed my mother! They took everything away from me! How can I be a wife to anyone? I just wish I could go home and go to my mother!"

The thought of her fighting to save me, the picture of her bloodied dress I saw through the crack in the door, her body slumping in death is too much for me. I cry now, the deep cries of a soul that seems lost, a child that has lost all she knows.

I feel a presence close to me in my despair.

"Hannah,"

I never knew a father. No man has ever touched me in any way except, I suddenly realize, until James touched the side of my face a few moments before.

"Hannah," He speaks again, and I look up to him through my teary eyes.

He reaches down and softly wipes the tears away, and I feel a strange, unknown feeling of a father's loving touch.

"You know that in our Lord's language, your name means Favor or even Grace," he says.

I shake my head no. I never knew that.

"Well, it does. There is more to you than you will ever know, this side of the veil. I cannot explain what has happened. I do not know what will happen. But I do know that you are indeed the Bean an Ri. I know that must be a strange thing to you. It is to us as well."

I totally trust this man; I think to myself. I cannot explain why I feel that way, but I do. I place my hand over the amulet around my neck. Is he the person that I am to show the necklace to? Mother said that I would know who to show it to when the time came. For a moment I hold the necklace in my hand and then know beyond a shadow of a doubt that he is not the one. But I do trust him.

Suddenly, I jump forward, wrap my arms around his massive form, and bury myself into his chest, crying still but no longer afraid. James jumps a bit in surprise, and I feel him embrace me as well.

After a moment, he gently pushes me away, "You okay, child?"

I shake my head, yes.

"Good, now we have much to do to prepare."

The entire camp is suddenly alive with activity as the family prepares to resume our journey. Raham shows me the horse's tackle, and I help her hook up the two horses that pull the wagon we ride in. In just a few moments, the wagons are ready, and the children are loaded.

The men erect a tent by the fire, and another covering is placed over the cooking fire and on the table. More wood is placed on the fire, and I begin to understand their plan.

I walk to my wagon but see Anna sitting on the seat, holding the reins. Where is Raham? I turn in confusion and see Raham walk to me, a saddled horse between them. James leaves the horse with Raham and stands before me.

"Raham will ride with you to Glenmorrow. She will stay with you in your journey, Hannah," he orders as one in authority and I immediately shake my head, no. I did not wish any of them to risk their lives to help me.

"Yes, Hannah, Raham has agreed."

I step past James, "No, Raham. It is too dangerous. I will go alone."

Raham mounts the horse, "Then you will walk the rest of the way."

She looks down at me defiantly, and I see that my small leather pouch and sword are tied to the side of the saddle.

"I regret that we only have one extra horse," James remarks, "But he is strong, and you both are small."

I stand a moment, still not wishing for Raham to go, but realizing that I did not wish to go alone. My new friend holds a gloved hand down to me, and I take it, and with one quick jump, I am astride the horse behind her in the saddle.

"Good," James shakes his head and reaches up to clasp his daughter's hand. The horse steps back and to one side, and I hear other horses out in the darkness across the river. The wagons lurch forward.

The two say a silent goodbye, and I realize the sacrifice that they made to help me. I could never let them down, but what could I do? There are no words between them, only the love of a father for his daughter, the love of a daughter to her father.

CHAPTER TEN

Raham pulls the reins, I clasp hold to her waist to keep from falling, and she kicks at the horse's flanks, and suddenly we are off into the darkness, riding away from the fire and the three wagons. I turn to look back, holding tight as Raham leans forward in the saddle. The three brothers are mounted by the fire's light, and the wagons are turning to one side. A horn blows out over the darkness, and I hear the Faireadoiri war cry of an ancient time answer in return.

I realize suddenly that the Faireadoiri are not running away. They are turning to fight!

"No! Raham! No!" I scream, "We must go back!"

I see darkened shadows across the river, and then more horsemen flash in front of the fire's orange glow. Raham disregards my scream. The brothers fire their crossbows, and horses scream; men fall through the fire. The glint of a broadsword flashes, then others. There are several horsemen at the wagons, and Anna is pulled from her seat, but she is armed with her curved blade, and a soldier falls at her feet after a brilliant flash of the sword.

"Stop!" I scream again but Raham continues, so I release my hold and fall away from the horse, hitting the ground hard and roll through the tall grass.

I stand, but the tall grass before me partially shields my view of the fight. The wagons continue to turn to one side in a line across in front of the fire. The brothers ride to one side, their swords upraised. A woman stands before the fire, and then another, and then a third. Their swords shine in the fire's glow, and I stand totally mesmerized by the sight of the Faireadoiri female warriors. If only I could be like those women, I think. And then a strange white light shines before the women. What could that be?

I turn to run toward them, but a horse suddenly comes in front of me, knocking me to the ground.

"Foolish girl! Get up!" a voice calls.

Mother?

Raham grabs me by my hair and pulls hard. She grabs my arm and pulls me back up behind her and spurs the horse onward. I look back to the fires, expecting to see the battle, but there is only the glowing fire and bright embers blowing in the wind across the meadow. Where had everyone gone?

I lean into Raham, "What happened? Where did everyone go?"

"The Faireadoiri fight in many ways, Hannah. We are masters of the illusion. Now, please hold on. We must make it to Glenmorrow before morning."

I hold tighter and turn my head to one side. I realize then that Raham's untamed hair is longer than my own.

We ride fast across the dark grasslands until we finally reach a rise in the ground, and Raham reins in the horse next to a craggy boulder field among tangled brush and scattered trees. The broken rock glows brightly in the moonlight, and the trees cast eerie shadows of darkness that sway in a strong breeze. Far off to the west, I hear distant thunder and see flashes of light. A storm approaches.

The horse heaves under us and I swing my leg from the saddle to dismount, but my legs do not work properly, and I fall to the ground instead. Raham laughs and dismounts as well. She reaches to assist me, but it seems the hard ride affected her as well. She falls next to me as the horse gives us one disapproving glance, steps toward the lush grass, and begins to eat.

I laugh as well for a bit as she collapses next to me, but only a second before the enormity of what we had just done sinks in. I worry about her family. I had seen them fighting among the fire and then a bright light, and then they were gone. Were they safe? What magic had I witnessed?

Raham says nothing as she stands up and then reaches a hand to me and helps me up as well. She gathers the horse's reins and walks a few feet to the very top of the ridge. She points toward the distant flashing light, and I see in the plain below near a black line of the forest, the watch fires lighting several towers. They are still a far distance.

"That's Glenmorrow, Hannah. But it is too late for us to continue tonight. They would have closed the gates and they never let anyone in at night. There is a place below the ridge where we camp for tonight. We can be in town by breakfast tomorrow." She remarks.

I realize how hungry I am at her words. I turn to look far off into the plains from where we had come. The ground is washed in the full moon's light, and closer in, I see the grasslands and scattered trees and white rocks; however, the distance is totally under a mantle of darkness. There is nothing but the black of night against an invisible horizon, but then I see a tiny speck of orange light that dances in the darkness.

I point at the light and ask, "Is that the camp?"

Raham steps up beside me, "Yeah, I believe so," she answers.

I stand silent for a moment, staring at the small light and worry of my new friends.

"Don't worry, Hannah. The family is fine."

"How do you know? There were so many horsemen. I saw them pull Anna from the wagon."

I turn and look up into my friend's face, and she smiles at me. It's a strange thought, the fact that I have a friend. It has always only been Mother. Raham points far to one side of the panoramic landscape below us, the close plain washed in the moon's light, the far plain covered in a mantle of darkness.

I look toward her raised hand and see another light, smaller than the first, but a campfire.

"I think maybe that is the family's camp," she remarks.

But how can that be?

"How? There is no way the wagons could outrun men on horseback. They were already riding among the wagons." I question her answer.

"What did you think you saw, Hannah?" she asks.

"I saw horsemen riding across the river. Your father shot one with the crossbow. Anna was pulled from her wagon, but she fought them. I saw several fall from their horses as the wagons turned and moved across the front of the fire. Your father and the brothers rode off, and then the women stood before the fire, and then there was a brilliant flash of light."

"What you saw was the "dara daoine draiocht"."

"The what?"

Raham laughs. "The "draiocht faireoir". Magic of the Faireadoiri."

"But what happened? How could the wagons go without the horsemen following them?"

51

"Hannah, there are Faireadoiri women who can do great magic. They can create an illusion, can create...." She stops and thinks for a moment, "duplicates of themselves. What we saw were duplicates. While the horsemen fought
and chased them, the wagons quietly escaped into the night."

Raham laughs again, "Most likely, the duplicates are leading the horsemen off into the desert until the magic fades and they simply disappear."

I stood astonished at the explanation. I had never heard anything like the story.

"So, don't worry about the family. They are safe, and so are we. Let's find a place to camp and see what Mother packed for us to eat."

We climb down the rocky ridgeline to a grove of trees below us near a small stream that flows cheerily in the night as I still try to figure out all that has happened to me.

Raham unsaddles the horse after handing me our belongings, including two bedrolls and a bag of food. In addition to my sword, I see Raham's crossbow and short sword as well. She ties the horse to a tree nearby, next to the creek, among a lush stand of grass, and we begin to gather wood for a small fire. In but a few moments, I am sitting on my bedroll next to Raham by the fire. Her mother had provided for us well and we eat sandwiches of meat and cheese and drink from the cold stream water.

We sit quietly by the fire. I should be asleep, but so much has happened this night and I cannot sleep. I want to talk to Raham, ask her what has happened, and ask why her family has saved me. In just a few days, my life has transformed. My mother is dead, my life destroyed. So many dreams, so many nightmares. But are they dreams? Or are they real? I did not know the answer. Why do they call me the Wife of a King? Why do soldiers search for me? Why do they wish to kill me? So many questions. My mind spins out of control at all that has happened. I need to get a hold of myself. I need to slow the spinning thoughts in my head.

I realize I am sitting by the fire, my eyes closed, my hands on my chest, holding the amulet. Another mystery that has no answers. I open my eyes and see that Raham is staring at me. I see the worry on her face. What am I to say? What can I do?

She smiles at me, and I gain strength from her smile. She points at my sword. "Such a beautiful weapon. Where did you get it?" she asks.

I pick the sword up and pull the weapon from the leather scabbard. The metal sparkles in the fire's light. I smile mischievously at the thought of how I came to be the sword's current owner. I think of the man by the ferry. What a beautiful man. The thought of him causes me to blush, and I shake my head.

"Oh, you must tell me, Hannah. You must tell me about the sword. Your smile hides good secrets," Raham remarks, scoots closer to me and holds out her hand.

"Can I see it?" she asks.

I place the sword back in the scabbard and hand it to her. Why did the memory of the stranger make me blush so?

Raham pulls the weapon from the leather and holds it up before the fire, admiring the beautiful craftsmanship, the wooden handle, the emblazoned winged coat of arms, and the razor-sharp blade. After a moment, she places the sword back and hands it to me.

"A beautiful weapon. An expensive one too. You must tell me how you got it."

What could I say? I have not shared anything with them except that the soldiers had been chasing me and my mother was dead.

I place the sword next to me on the bedroll. I would tell her the truth.

"I stole it," I state.

"You stole it," she exclaims.

"Yep."

I say nothing more as she leans forward, waiting for me to tell her more. Finally, she speaks, "Okay. Hannah. You got to tell me more. Whatever you thought a minute ago is worth the telling." She points at the sword, "That's a gentleman's secondary weapon, a sword that only a knight or nobleman can afford. Must have been quite a handsome man for you to blush so at the thought of him."

How did she know? I think. I blush again.

"See, you have to tell me," she says.

I look up at her and smile, "Okay, okay. I'll tell you. A few days before you found me, I was across the river near a ferry. The soldiers were chasing me and all I knew was that I needed to cross the river. When I got there, a man was standing by the river waiting for the ferry. I hid in the trees and watched him. He seemed strange to me. He wore black and rode a great, black horse."

Raham interrupts my tale, "What did the man look like?"

I think a moment, "He was tall like your Da but much younger. He had long, black hair past his shoulders. His arms were tattooed."

"Was he handsome?" Raham smiles at the question.

How could I answer? He was not handsome. He was beautiful.

"Yes, very handsome," I answer and blush again.

I continue as Raham giggles and pats my leg.

"I needed to get to the ferry, but how could I? As I tried to get closer, the man must have seen me because he and the ferryman were searching for me. I ran as fast as I could until I reached the ferry, but I could not untie the ropes, so I took the sword from the horse and cut the ropes."

"Such a grand story, Hannah. You were so brave. And think that you stole a gentleman's sword from him as he searched for you," she smiles again, "and a handsome gentleman as well. Did he see you, Hannah? Did he know that you stole his sword?"

I smile at the thought, "Yes, he did, Raham. They shouted for me not to run. I think that the gentleman was trying to help me, but I was afraid of him."

I think of the sight of him standing across the river, staring at me as I stood on the ferry. He was indeed a gentleman, I think. A beautiful gentleman.

"What else happened?" she asks.

"He bowed to me, Raham. The man bowed to me as the ferry pulled me away." I answer proudly. No man had ever bowed to me before.

"Oh, how romantic, Hannah. You surely won his heart for him to do so."

I look down, blushing. How could that be? I place my hand over the side of my face to cover my scars. What a thought. How could I ever win a man's heart?

"No, surely not. I stole his sword, after all."

54

"Oh, surely you have stolen a gentleman's heart. And I think, just maybe, he searches for you even now."

"Yea, to get the sword back," I laugh.

"You never know, Hannah. He bowed to you. Maybe he searches for you," she answers.

"You jest, Raham."

We are silent again as I think of her words. I have often dreamed of dancing at grand balls and gentlemen bowing to me to ask for my hand for a dance. But they are only dreams, I think. I know nothing about men. But I remember well my gentleman bowing to me as I stood on the ferry, his sword in my hand.

I ask a sudden question, "Raham, have you ever had a boyfriend? How do you know if a man likes you?"

"Well, he bows to you, for one thing," she answers.

"Stop. You are teasing me. Seriously, have you?"

"No, Hannah. I am way too young for that. I am only fourteen years old. I have not met a man that I wish for."

I am shocked by her answer. How could she only be fourteen years old?

"No way! You must be older than fourteen. Oh, my lord. I am older than you,"

She shrugs her head, "Yep, only fourteen."

Raham suddenly stands up, "We need to sleep. It is not far to the village, and I know a family that will let us stay. You will be safe with them."

She is right. I am sleepy, But I still cannot think of her as only fourteen. She seems so much older than that. But she is Faireadoiri, after all.

CHAPTER ELEVEN

One warrior lay dead, an arrow through his throat. Dark blood covered the ground around him from the wound. A horse screamed in pain as it fell into the fire, the rider falling backward from another arrow. The man turned, wounded, and retreated into the brush by the river as other mounted warriors emerged from the water and charged among the wagons.

"Kill them all but the girl!" the captain ordered as he stopped briefly to survey the scene after crossing the river.

The wagons were moving off to one side, trying to escape. A large fire burned before him. Scattered camp furniture, pots, pans, and scraps of food lay all around him. To one side of the fire, his men engaged several mounted nomads with swords. The war horses crashed against one another. Swords flashed in the dark by the fire's light. Men shouted; horses screamed. He had caught them by surprise!

Where was the girl?

The nomad men were fighting desperately, drawing his men away from the wagons into the darkness, away from the fire. The girl must be in the wagons. He kicked his horse and pulled hard on the reins with one hand as he drew his sword with the other.

Two wagons had disappeared into the darkness, but the third was slower, and the woman driving was having trouble with the horses. One of his men grabbed the woman and pulled her from the wagon by her long hair. She fell hard on her back on the ground and lay there for a moment before suddenly jumping up before him as he rode up. He briefly saw a brilliant flash of bright light and looked toward the blinding light for a moment and then back to the woman. She now stood before him, brandishing a curved blade that flashed in the fire's light.

The warrior who had pulled her from the wagon lay at her feet, his horse trotting off into the dark. How had that happened? Her blade now glowed dark with blood, and the captain turned back from the swinging sword and drove his horse into her, knocking her over the fallen warrior. She fell as he dismounted.

56

He looked around him, confused. A moment before, his warriors were fighting among the wagons and then a brilliant flash of lightning crashed around him, momentarily blinding him. And now he stood alone before the woman, one of his warriors dead at her feet. There was no one else around now. The fire had spread outward in the grass, slowly burning away from the river. Off in the distance, horses galloped across the darkness.

The woman glared at him, showing no fear, holding the weapon above her as she struggled to stand up again. He respected her bravery, which was a very rare thing for a woman, or a man for that matter, but he would show no mercy. She had killed one of his men. He thought of the cabin from before. A woman had killed three of his men then. He would have to be wary of this one.

She panted before him like a wild animal, holding a short, curved sword covered in dripping blood before her. She stepped to the side to get further away from the dead man at her feet and braced her feet in a defensive stance. He admired her training. He had heard the Faireadoiri women were trained for combat but had never actually seen one fight before. What a shame to meet such a beauty in this way, he thought as he, too, stepped away from the dead man. If such a woman as this could be tamed?

It was a shame to have to kill such a beautiful creature, he thought. He held one hand up before him. "All we want is the girl. Just show me where you have hidden the girl, and I will let you go," he said.

"Breag tu!" the woman shouted.

"What? I don't understand," the captain answered.

The woman stepped forward, and the captain stepped back in alarm. Her presence unnerved him somehow. He had fought many men. He had killed many. But something about this creature, for some reason, that word described her better, giving him a sense of something unnatural. Was she human at all?

"You lie!" the woman screamed and attacked with her sword.

The sudden attack surprised him, but the captain parried the blow and stepped to the side, striking forward. She parried his first blow with surprising strength, but his broad sword slashed again.

She swirled before him in a low circle, her hair flowing out from her, her dress swirling as in a dance, and again she thrust forward, slicing through the chainmail at his stomach. He felt the distinctive, sharp pain of the blade cutting him, and he backed away as the woman stood crouched before him, He felt down to the cut with his free hand. Her blade had broken through the chainmail in one place, cutting him. Warm blood flowed across his hand.

Her long hair covered most of her face, her dress muddy and covered in blood. He stood a moment as she wavered, and the captain realized the blood was hers. His second thrust had cut her deep across her chest.

What a marvelous woman, he thought. She stepped back from him. She did not seem to notice any pain from the deadly wound he had inflicted. She fell to one knee, still holding the sword in defiance. She took one hand and pulled the hair from her face, and the captain saw that she was a very young, pretty woman. Her eyes glowed in the dark, staring straight through him, and he backed away in fear of her eyes. She fell over then, the sword clanging overly loud across the rocks below her.

The captain stood transfixed by the sight before him. How had her eyes glowed in the dark? What kind of magic was this? He checked the wound in his stomach. Thankfully, it was only a small cut. He had scars from far worse. The captain glanced around him and realized he was now alone. He heard horses out in the darkness. He left the woman where she lay and ran over to the wagon. He frantically searched but found no one. He saw the other two wagons a little further back from the fire, and both were empty as well. The nomads had escaped by horseback.

He mounted his horse and rode off into the darkness after the sound of the other horses. His men were on the trail, he thought. It was only a matter of time before they caught up to the nomads again.

Anna ran as fast as she could away from the fire and the three wagons as the captain fought her magic behind her. She stopped a moment to listen but heard nothing. The plan had been to perform the dara daoine draiocht as the family retreated away in the opposite direction. Her magic was the strongest of any in her family, and she had to stay longer than the others, but the illusion was harder than she remembered it being, and she had to remain far too long.

She stood in the darkness, watching her duplicate being pulled from the wagon before running away. The plan had been for her to have a horse, but the horse had retreated without her. Now she stood in total darkness in a wide grassland, not exactly sure of which way to go. If she was riding the horse, all she had to do was let him run because he would follow the trail of the others.

She knew that the family would travel to the north as the magic ones traveled to the south, so she found the north star high above and resolved the fact that she would have to walk the entire night to find her family. And then she heard a horse somewhere to the north. She listened carefully and heard the horse again, closer, and then silence.

A shrill hawk's call spoke from the blackness, and she returned the call. A few moments later, the darkness revealed a horse, and Collen jumped from the horse before it stopped and gathered her into his strong embrace.

"Thank God! What happened?"

"That stupid horse left me."

Collen mounted his horse and pulled his wife up behind him.

"Did the dara daoine draiocht work?" he asked.

Anna chuckled, "I believe so. Before I left, they all were riding after ghosts to the south."

CHAPTER TWELVE

I lay on the ground in a meadow of beautiful, multicolored wildflowers that dance under the caress of a gentle morning breeze. The sun shines brightly, warming my skin, and I look down at my body and see that I am naked, but I feel no shame in being so. I see flowering trees off in the distance by the edge of the meadow. The pink, purple, and red flowers float off the trees and glide over the meadow before turning into butterflies that flutter and turn and play on the breeze above me. I reach up to touch them and laugh as they tickle my hands with their delicate wings.

What beautiful place is this?

Birds sing from the trees. A few flies over and circle through the lower fluttering butterflies, scattering them down to me, where they find refuge among the flowers. A few land on my stomach and look up at me with tiny eyes, the brilliant crimson, yellow, and blue wings bending back and forth slowly. I reach down and touch one, and both suddenly explode away in a flurry of colored, erratic flight.

I sit up and look around me. I am in the middle of a meadow surrounded by a majestic forest of tall, stately trees that grow hundreds of feet toward the bright sky. Many of them are covered with fruit of all types. Birds fly overhead in flocks that wave back and forth in a swirl of motion before landing among the branches. Many of the trees are fully alive, with thousands of birds moving the leaves with their presence, making the entire tree crown seem to move in unison with the birds.

I stand up and turn and look in all directions, perplexed with the question of where I am. Something about the meadow seems familiar to me, but I cannot remember how or why.

I hear movement behind me over against the tree line and turn quickly but see nothing. When I turn back, I am startled by the sight of a wooden structure standing only a few feet from me that I have seen once before, but where? I cannot remember. The structure stands over ten feet tall and is made of some type of dark wood that glistens with crimson and casts a huge shadow across my body, totally shielding the sun. The shadow feels warm across my body and soothing to my skin.

Where have I seen this structure before?

The meadow is now totally silent. There is no wind, no butterflies, no birds. Everything around me is suddenly frozen in quiet silence. The structure pulls at my soul as if the wood is alive and calls to me. I take one hesitant step forward and then another. The closer I walk to the structure, the more power it has over me. In just a few steps, I stand within reach of the stained wood and look upward and see that the structure reaches far above and out of sight past the sun itself into the far heavens. The wood pulsates with pure energy. The wood breaths with a life of its own with the rhythm of my own heartbeat. The red stains have a life of their own and flow down and across my own body, covering me with a red liquid that smells of honey and flowers.

I stand totally in awe of what is happening to me, and one word comes to mind that totally encompasses the power that the structure emanates.

Love.

I hear something crash against the trees on the far side of the structure and turn to face the sound, even though my heart tells me not to do so. The trees scream in mortal agony and crash all around as something moves beneath them. Several fall directly toward me and I turn to run even as I hear the wooden structure seem to scream for me to stand and not run.

But fear and unbelief take over, and I run away from the falling trees. One by one, they crash violently around me as I run, tearing at the soil and destroying the beautiful meadow. I hear a scream in the sky above and the sound of great, flapping winds. A massive figure flies overhead, totally covering the sun, and the meadow suddenly turns totally black like a night with no moon.

I slip and fall as another giant tree crashes down, shaking the ground. I fall on dead ground, totally void of the lush bed of flowers that covered the meadow just moments before.

What nightmare is this place changing into?

I scream at the sight of the hideous flying monster that hovers in the dark sky above me with glowing yellow eyes, scales, and flapping wings like metal.

I hear a voice call from some distant place, "Hannah, you must make up!"

I scramble back away from the monster that smells of death and sulfur. I am stuck in a nightmare, my mind tells me. I must wake up, but I cannot!

The ground shakes around me, and I see a glimmer of light far off in the distance, and a girl stands in the light. She stands totally naked before the structure, her raven black hair flowing across her back in the wind, her body covered in a red, flowing liquid that looks to be, of all things, blood.

In contrast to the chaos immediately around me of death, destruction, falling trees and flying monsters, the girl stands in total peace. The area immediately around the structure is in full daylight, the meadow full of flowers, the butterflies fluttering merrily around the girl, oblivious to the destruction happening all around her. For a moment I stare at the scene before me, and suddenly realize that the girl is myself. How can that be?

But close to me, there is a massive fire that engulfs my body, and I scream.

I wake up suddenly, thankfully, and immediately pull away from the arms that hold me until I realize that I am truly awake, and the arms are those of Raham as she attempts to wake me from a horrible nightmare that seems all too real. But how could that be real at all?

Raham holds me tight like Mother used to when I would have nightmares. But the nightmares of my youth never followed me into the waking world. But this dream did not retreat into the sleeping part of my brain. It burned a lasting memory that to me seemed to be a living memory of a past event. How can that be?

"Hannah, it's only a dream. You're okay. It was only a dream," Raham says, and I shake my head in agreement. But I know differently. The dream is real, somehow.

"I'm okay, Raham. Thank you, I'm fine," I answer.

But I am not fine. The fire was too vivid. The scars I have are real. But so is the structure, I suddenly realize and remember where I have seen that structure before. I grab the talisman at my chest. The charm Mother gave me is the same as the structure.

CHAPTER THIRTEEN

Raham sits back against the tree she had been sleeping against and pulls the blanket up to her. There is a bit of light glowing from the soon-to-be-rising sun, and the morning is a bit cold. I see the worry in her young face.

"You scared the fool out of me," the girl remarks.

"I'm sorry."

"You sure you're okay?" she asks.

"Yeah, just a horrible nightmare. Sorry, I woke you up," I answer and pull my own blanket up against me. It is cold, I think. Thankfully, the vividness of the terrible nightmare fades away as I totally wake up. I crinkle my nose at the horrible smell of myself and the blanket, "Oh God. I stink, Raham. I smell like horse crap."

Raham laughs, "Yeah, I do, too, but I know a place that can help with that. Glenmorrow is only about an hour from here. If you smell as bad as I do, they will never let us in."

She stands up and kicks dirt over the gray ash from last night's fire to make sure it is totally out. She grabs her blanket and belongings.

"Come on, we can walk from here. It is only a short distance back behind the rocks. There is a place where we can bathe." She sees the concern in my expression, "Don't worry. We are the only people here this early."

She takes the reins of the horse and walks up toward the rocky outcrops near the stream. I quickly pick up my own belongings and follow her. She leads me down a wooded path through a field of boulders in the half light of dawn. The stream bubbles along merrily below me and I see a series of small waterfalls and am surprised by the steam that rises from behind the boulders. Hot springs, I think.

We climb across a rock, and Raham leads the horse a bit further in the trees just above a pool of water covered in drifting steam that rises in the early morning light. She ties the horse to the nearest tree and begins to disrobe in front of me unashamedly. For the first time, I see that she has the figure of a full-grown woman, even though she says she is only fourteen years old. She unbraids her hair, and the red locks fall to her waist and hide her freckled shoulders.

"Come, Hannah," she says and dives into the pool headfirst.

I stand in total shock and watch as she disappears into the depths before emerging on the other side of the deep pool.

"Come on in. You can swim, can't you?" she asks.

I shake my head, yes.

"It's deep on your side, but over here, the water is shallow." She stands up, revealing herself above her waist. Her hair floats in the water around her. She is so beautiful, I think. How can I disrobe in front of her. She will see my scars.

Raham seems to understand my fear, "It's okay, Hannah. We are both girls, and there are no men anywhere around. The water is so soothing and warm, "she smiles, "and plus, I will not let you ride with me stinking as you do."

I laugh. This is stupid, I think. She is right. I pull the dress over my head, lay it down next to my blanket and sword, and quickly dive into the warm waters. A moment later, I emerge next to her on the shallow side. Raham had walked over to the edge of the rocks at a place where she could lean back in the water on a rock bench. I walk over and do the same.

I am immediately soothed by the warm water as steam rises upward around us. I look around the water and realize just how filthy we both are as the dirt flows off our bodies and tints the clear water a dirty brown.

"Goodness, we are a sight," Raham remarks.

I laugh and lean further back into the water, taking my own water-heavy locks of hair and scrubbing the matted dirt away. Shafts of sunlight suddenly slant across the forest, glade, and glisten over the warm water. The horrors of my nightmare and the stress of the past night seem to melt away into the deep pool of water and I sigh.

"Told you so. My family camps here every time we come this way. The hot springs are wonderful." Raham remarks.

I agree. This is a beautiful place, so different than the forest of my home. What home? I think. I no longer have a home. I immediately push that thought away. I would not let the thought of my past haunt my present, but as much as I try, it still does.

I look down across my body and see the red burn scar that covers my right breast and side down to my waist. I know that I have a scar across the right side of my face as well, but there is nothing I can do about the disfigurement. I have known it to be so my entire life. My mother always told me not to worry about the scars. She told me that I was always beautiful, but I did not believe her. And when we went to the village, I always hid from the people. I always thought Mother was ashamed of me, but now, with everything that has happened, I think maybe she was only trying to protect me.

I suddenly realize that the charm lay between my breasts, shining brightly in the sun's light, and I place my hand over it and look at Raham. Did she see it? She lay beside me, only her head above the water, her eyes shut. She seems so much older than her age, but then she is Faireadoiri, after all.

I had heard stories of the Faireadoiri told to me by my mother, but until now, I had never seen one. But maybe I have, I think.

A horse snorts suddenly from somewhere in the forest, and Raham immediately opens her eyes and sits up in alarm. Our horse eats the grass where she had tied him earlier. He jerks his head up and turns toward the sound. Raham grabs my shoulder and points toward the shining sun. Another horse moves in the shadows of the deep forest.

She places a finger over her mouth for silence, slowly rolls off the bench, and drops quietly below the water. I follow, and we swim across the depths to the other side, where we both emerge near the rocks. I scoot as far back against the rock ledge as I can, and Raham pushes back against the rock ledge as well to hide from whoever is out in the forest. Our clothes lay just a few feet away, but to get them, we have to climb from the pool. What a mess we have gotten ourselves into, I think. Raham leans out of the water and is barely able to pull her crossbow and one arrow to her. She loads the weapon and leans back against the rock.

We are hidden from the far side of the pool, but the horse is not. I peer over the rock and see a man tie the horse to a tree. He moves around the trees partially hidden and then suddenly appears near the edge of the pool, having disrobed all except for a loin cloth. He reaches down to remove the last bit of clothing and then stops, realizing that our horse stands across the pool from him. He looks around in alarm, and I gasp at the full sight of the man.

I whisper in Raham's ear, "That's him."

"Who?" she mouths back to me.

"The man at the ferry," I answer.

She stares for a moment as the man steps back to the horse and returns to the pool, a sword in his hand.

"Oh my God," Raham mouths the words silently, "He is handsome."

She turns and looks me straight in the eyes, a mischievous, devious smile on her face, "He is searching for you," she whispers. "We need to say hello."

I cringe away from her, "No!" I mouth the word to her.

"Well, we got to do something. We can't just stay here, waiting for him to leave."

"But he cannot see me like this; please, Raham, he must not," I say, pleading.

"Hello, is anyone here. I just came for a morning swim," the man speaks. Raham thinks a moment and then shakes her head in agreement with my wish.

"Stay back behind the rock," Raham orders and steps away from the rock ledge, holding her weapon beneath the water.

I could never do such a thing; I think to myself. I look behind me. My clothes are too far away to reach without exposing myself and the sword lay beneath the blanket, further still.

I peer around the rock and can see him better.

The man sees her then and steps back in astonishment. "Oh my," he states, looking around again, "Are you alone?"

"I was until you showed up," Raham answers, "And I would like to be alone again if you don't mind. You can leave and come back when I have left."

I place my hand on the small of her back under the water. How can she do this? She steps further away from the rock. The man kneels by the pool's edge, holding the sword to one side of him. I see that both his arms are covered in the brightly colored tattoos I had seen before. But now I can see beautifully painted trees, flying birds, a lion, and a warrior. His hair is shorter than I remember, but it still touches his shoulders. His skin is bronzed, his face clean-shaven. I blush at the sight of him, and my heart beats hard. Oh my God, I think. Why does the sight of this man cause me to do such things?

"Well now," he says and twirls the sword in one hand, "we do have a problem because I wish to soak my sore muscles in the pool just as you do, my dear."

"Well, sir, that is out of the question. As you can see, I am alone, and if you are a gentleman, you will not compromise my honor by being here while I bathe," Raham responds.

"Who says I am a gentleman, my lady?" he answers.

He stands up and takes a step closer to the pool, peering over the rock ledge into the steaming water, "I think I will bathe on this side of the pool and you on the other. What do you say?"

"That is totally unacceptable. I say that you need to leave and let me finish. Then you can have the pool to yourself," Raham answers.

What a mess we have gotten ourselves into. I look at Raham as she turns slightly and notice a half smile on her face. How can she smile? But he is so handsome. And I truly believe that he is a gentleman. Oh my God, Hannah, get a hold of yourself. I scold myself silently. We are both totally naked in the water with a man in our presence.

He shakes his head slowly and takes another step, looking over to the horse, "No, I think that an even better idea is that I'll bathe with you, my dear," he says, a smile on his face.

Is he serious, or is he just playing with her? I question.

Raham pulls the drawn crossbow from the water, "Then dear sir, if you choose not to be the gentleman that I believe you are, then you will find that I am a very good shot with this bow."

Raham shakes her hair away and takes a step further away from the rocks into more shallow water, her body further out of the water, and I melt further back against the rock. I could never let him see me.

"I am Faireadoiri," she states proudly.

The man steps back, and I can see the initial shock on his face, but then he smiles even wider.

"Then, my dear Faireadiori warrior, you should know that the crossbow you point at me loses its effectiveness when in the water as long as you have held it. Go ahead, shoot me. I bet the arrow will not even clear the water."

Raham looks down at the weapon and then back to the man, "Ifreann fuilteacha!' she exclaims.

The man laughs, "Bloody hell, indeed, my dear."

I hold my breath for a moment, in panic of what will happen now. Breath, Hannah, you have to breathe.

Raham sighs and places the useless weapon on the rock above her, "You know my language?"

"Just a bit. I know the more colorful expressions."

"No matter," Raham acknowledges, "you should leave. At least give me a chance to dress and I will leave you to the pool. Sir, if you are indeed the gentleman that I know you to be, you will do so."

The man steps a step closer to the horse and looks around the area. He must see the clothes, even from across the pool from us.

"Again, I ask. Who says I am a gentleman?"

"I know the crest on the sword, my lord. Unless you stole that sword, then I know your family even though I do not know you. You are indeed a gentleman, my lord." Raham states.

The man shakes his head in agreement and sighs, "Yes, my lady. I am a gentleman, and you can rest assure that I mean you no harm. I was only jesting with you. But even a gentleman would not lose the chance to witness such a beautiful woman, a Faireadoiri woman at that, emerge naked from a pool of water."

My heart explodes within me. He is a gentleman! A gentleman bowed to me! I look over to Raham and realize that she blushes as well at his last statement.

He continues, "Oh, what stories I would tell. I am a lowly servant of God, a lord of the Bene Elohim, a knight of the realm, a man who has taken an oath to never harm a woman, to never yield in battle to less than nine warriors, to honor God, to," he stops. "If you know my family, then you know the rest."

He smiles, "But what a story I will have to tell in the halls of Bene Elohim to have seen a Faireadoiri woman naked before me."

68

"You would not dare!" Raham exclaims, "Now go back to the other side and turn your back, sir and I will leave you to your pool."

He stands for a moment in deep thought, shaking his head from side to side as if to decide, and then suddenly, he sees something that confuses him: "Wait a minute. There are two dresses. You said you are alone?"

"I travel far. A lady can have two dresses, can she not?"

He shakes his head yes and then turns away. And I do a stupid thing. I lean too far out from my hiding place and lose my hold, falling out into the water with a splash behind Raham.

The man whirls around as I stumble against Raham, and we both fall backward into the water. I struggle to get up and stand in the shallow water, my hair covering my face as Raham falls into the deeper water. I pull the hair from my face and see that the man is staring directly at me, his eyes wide with a sudden recognition of who I am.

"Oh my God, it's you!" he exclaims, and I scream.

I stumble out of the water and run to the blanket, throwing the blanket over my body and face. He could not see me like this!

Raham emerges from the deeper pool, astonished herself, sputtering and coughing up water. She looks over to me and then back at the man as he stares at me, his mouth open in shock.

"I have been searching for you for weeks, ever since I saw you at the ferry. Please, I must know who you are. I must see you. I began to believe you were not real. But you are!"

He steps forward, leaving his sword lying by the rock where he had dropped it when he first saw me. I huddle under the blanket, only my eyes above its barrier. I see him through the thick mantle of hair that hides my face from his view. He saw me! Dear God, he saw me naked! How could he wish to meet me?

Raham boldly steps out of the water in full view of him, and he turns to face her. I see that he is totally struck by her beauty, but she grabs her dress with one hand and her curved sword with the other. She bunches the dress in front of her to partially hide her nakedness from him and extends the weapon.

"You are mistaken, my lord. There is no way you have seen this girl. She is my…." Raham stutters, "She is my maid."

She steps toward him as he suddenly retreats away from the blade, his hands up.

69

"And I assure you, sir. That this weapon in my hands is totally effective," she declares.

"But I know it is her. She was by the ferry. I would know her face anywhere."

I pull myself back under the blanket. He has seen my scars. That is why he searches for me. He has seen my disfigurement. I am totally crushed, but how can it be any other way?

"You are a brute, sir, and you have frightened her. She is but a child who knows nothing about men. And you look at her with such manful lust. How dare you, my lord!" Raham scolds and steps toward him again.

I am not a child, I think. How can you call me a child, Raham? I am older than you. But she is right. I am frightened, panicked, in fact. I cower under the blanket while Raham threatens a gentleman with her sword, naked before him with no fear or shame at all.

She turns her head, "Hannah, dress yourself and take our things. Take the horse back up the hill through those trees and stop by the trail. I will be along shortly."

She looks back to the man, "Now you turn away, my lord and leave us be. We will leave you to this pool."

I place the dress over me and tie the leather shoes about my feet and stand, gathering our belongings, all the while staring at the man who turns his back to us. What is going on? Raham takes a step closer, her extended blade touching the middle of his back.

"I apologize. I have behaved poorly. I do not stare in lust. The girl I saw by the ferry is the most beautiful woman I have ever seen. Your maid must be the same. I would know her anywhere."

I am shocked by his words. He thinks me beautiful! But how? Raham looks back at me, a wide smile on her face.

What?

I throw the blankets over the horse and lead him up the slope but stop halfway up and turn back to see what Raham will do next. I have seen that smile before. She takes the blade and suddenly cuts at the loin cloth and kicks the man into the water, holding the clothing above her with the sword.

He falls headfirst into the water, his arms flinging wildly about him. Both Raham and I laugh loudly as he struggles to right himself in the depths of the pool. He springs upward and grabs the rock ledge, coughing.

"Woman!" he exclaims as he regains himself.

Raham clothes herself and walks over to retrieve her crossbow from the rocks. I stand in shock at my friend's tenacity and laugh again, quietly this time.

The man looks up to me, and for the first time ever, I do not look away or hide from a strange man. I stare back at him. He thinks I am beautiful! From this distance, I think he has blue eyes, but the only thing I know for sure is that they stare through my very soul, and my heart skips a beat. I turn quickly and scamper up the hill.

"Not the horse!" I hear the man shout.

I hear Raham respond, "I will leave him by the trail at the rocks with your clothing. You enjoy your bath, my lord. And I leave you your sword. It is not wise for a man to be naked without a sword to protect himself. You will know now not to treat Faireadoiri women as you have," she laughs.

"Ifreann failteache!" he shouts.

"Bloody hell, indeed," Raham replies. I hear the horse walking through the brush below me on the trail.

CHAPTER FOURTEEN

Dust marked the position of several horsemen off in the distance to the south, the floating particles sparkling in the early morning light from the rising sun that glowed a brilliant orange over a distant tree line. The captain reined in his mount on a low rise. Several of his men slowed their own horses behind him. They had been trailing the wagons for the entire night but never seemed to be able to catch up to their quarry, which confused the captain.

At first, earlier in the night, they had sprinted across the grasslands after the sound of wagons moving fast and should have caught up to them in the dark. And then there was a time when they had totally lost their prey and thought for a moment that they had ridden past the wagons. But then they heard the horses again at a stream crossing. There had been a brief fight by the stream, and one of his men was wounded.

A few hours later, they had been attacked by a charging warrior, screaming in some foreign tongue that no one could understand. He had ridden among them out of the blackness of the night, slashing his sword and knocking one warrior from his horse before disappearing back into the night.

After that unnerving attack, his men rode slower and more cautious through the rest of the night, within the sound of the wagons but never within sight of them. The captain pushed his men on. They were well trained and experienced in battle, but something about their quarry this time affected everyone with a deep feeling of eventual doom. Something about the warriors out in front of them was totally unnatural, just like the woman encountered by the wagon at the river crossing. She had been flesh and blood, a beautiful example of a Faireadoiri warrior woman in her youth, but something about her had been totally primeval, unreal even. She had killed one of the men, so she was real enough to kill, and she was real enough to bleed and die. But at the same time, she was like a phantom.

But they continued, even though tired and a bit unnerved by the sounds of horsemen riding in the dark. The captain had to bury those thoughts deep under his training, experience, and orders, and his men would have to do the same.

But as the night progressed and the constant sounds of the wagons and horsemen just out of reach continued, it became increasingly harder to maintain their vigilance, to maintain their vigilance, to maintain their discipline. The one constant in all their thoughts was the fact that eventually daylight would come, and they could see their prey and so they continued.

Now, with the rising sun, they saw the dust and several horses, but where were the wagons? The captain pulled out his eyeglasses and looked across the plain.

"You see them?" one of his men asked.

The captain counted three warriors on horseback, and then, a bit further near a grove of trees, he saw several wagons.

"Yes, the wagons are by the trees beyond the horsemen," he answered as he placed the eyeglass back in its case. He took his canteen and drank. The water was hot and sandy. He replaced the cap and placed the canteen back in the leather pouch to the side of his saddle. His men needed fresh water, he thought. But first, they needed to finish the job at hand.

"I knew they had to stop sometime. We have them now. I see only three horsemen. The women must be at the wagons," he remarked and then thought of the woman he had killed the night before.

He looked over at the soldier next to him, "The women fight as well. So be wary when you approach the wagons, for they will not hesitate to slit your throat given the chance."

All his men now sat mounted on their horses in a line across the low ridgeline. The captain looked to the right and then left. There were two dozen warriors, two of whom were slightly wounded. He had lost one dead at the river crossing. He could tell that they were tired. Several drank from their own canteen. One seemed to be eating a bit of dried meat.

73

Let's finish this, he thought to himself. He did not fully understand why his queen wished for the girl, but he had his orders. Ever since they had come upon the pitiful thatched roofed cabin through the mountain gap, they had pursued a shadow that he did not even know was real.

She had disappeared at the cabin, and his men had been attacked by what he now thought was a witch. They had briefly seen her on the ferry, and then they encountered the Faireadoiri after following the trail of a young girl across the prairie lands. He knew she had been hidden in the wagon. He had caught just a glimpse of a black-haired girl beneath the seat, but he had also seen the hidden weapons of the women and the presence of three strong warriors. So he had smartly regrouped and now had finally caught up with them again.

He drew his sword, "Kill them all but the girl. She has scars across her face. She must be taken alive," he ordered and spurred his horse onward.

The warriors charged out onto the lower plain, the horses kicking up a heavy dust cloud that followed their progress in a strengthening morning breeze. The captain could see the three mounted warriors in the distance turn, and to his surprise, they charged as well. He admired their courage, but it would lead to their death. There was no way three could defeat two dozen.

The captain instinctively lowered his body closer to the horse, fully expecting the oncoming arrows, several of which passed close overhead but did no harm. In just a few seconds, the first warrior charged toward him. A sword glistened in the morning sun. The man was huge, his bare chest covered in tattoos, his long black hair blowing outward away from him. The man leaned forward on his mount, holding the broad sword high and to one side. The captain prepared himself to parry the expected blow with his own sword. Other warriors rode past him in the dust storm.

Time seemed to stand still. He heard nothing but his own labored breathing for just a second before impact. Then, there were the distinctive sounds of screaming warriors, pounding hooves, and clashing swords, and the warrior was suddenly directly in front of him. He swung his own weapon in an arch toward the man's head, fully expecting to be crashed upon by horse and warrior, but there was suddenly nothing before him. He looked back in alarm and turned his mount around, almost hitting one of his own men who was immediately beside him.

Where did the warrior go?

The captain circled, desperately searching for the enemy, but only seeing his own men. Many of them rode fast past him toward the wagons, but several were turning their own mounts and began attacking each other in the blinding dust.

He turned just in time to parry the blow from a charging tattooed warrior, but once again, the man disappeared in the dust, and he circled his horse again. His men pulled in their own mounts and realized that they were attacking their own.

The dust settled a bit, and the captain saw only six of his men directly near him, all dazed by what had just happened to them. The others were charging into the group of trees where the wagons had been, but now, with the settling dust, the captain saw no wagons.

Their prey had simply vanished.

"Where did they go?" one of the men asked the captain.

The captain sheathed his sword, "I don't know."

"What magic is this?" another asked, but the captain had no answer.

They were all there just as the sun came up, but now they were gone. He swore to himself. He had followed phantoms all through the night, only to watch them disappear before his very eyes with the rising of the sun. He and his men were worn out and hungry. He had lost one dead and two wounded, chasing after ghosts, while the girl had escaped and was most likely miles away now. If she had ever been there to begin with? He questioned.

"What do we do now?"

The captain swore again, "We rest a bit, get something to eat and head back. We have been tricked by some type of Faireadoiri magic."

75

Miles across the plains to the north, Anna stood staring toward the south as the sun rose. She silently sang the ancient dara daoine draiocht chant and visualized the three charging warriors, but the magic had run its course. The rest of her deception had already vanished. They made one heroic charge, and she hoped that the magic was still strong enough for them to fight, but it was not to be. She was too far away, and the spell had been active for the entire night. One by one, her creations disappeared in a cloud of dust and horses.

When the last warrior disappeared suddenly, just as it was about to attack, she stopped her song. She was very tired and needed to sleep. James walked up behind her and placed his hand on her shoulder. She turned to him.

"They are all gone," she remarked.

"You did good, Anna. That was a hard thing, but you did great." James commented.

"Thanks," Anna said, "It's funny. I know they were unreal. Just a creation of the magic. But when they disappear, it seems that they are real. It makes me sad."

James turned his head at her comment and agreed. Anna could perform the dara daoine draiocht better than any of the other women, even though she was so young. All the Fairieadoiri could do some parts of the magic, but she was the strongest. Her magic had saved them all. He looked off to the west and thought of his daughter. Hopefully, she had gotten Hannah to Glenmorrow. He missed her already but knew that Raham had a mission to do. When the time came, he would see her again. He turned and followed Anna back to the camp.

CHAPTER FIFTEEN

Raham walks up the trail toward me, the gentleman's horse in tow, a wicked smile on her face.

"What did you do?" I ask.

She laughs. "Took all his clothes," she replies.

I stare at her in disbelief as she walks past me as if nothing had happened.

"Come on, Hannah. We'll leave his clothes by the trail, but we'll take his horse with us a while and let him go when we get closer to Glenmorrow. The horse is well-trained and will come back to him, so don't worry. Your new love will be fine," she teases.

I hit her lightly on the shoulder as she walks by.

"Not kidding, Hannah. I saw the way he looked at you. That man is in love with you."

But how? I think He does not even know me.

"That's crazy, Raham. He has never seen me before. And I don't even know his name," and then I remember what Raham had said by the pond, "But you know him. Who is he?"

"I will tell you later, but now we got to hurry. I think I hear him coming up the trail."

We quicken our pace, and when we leave the forest, Raham mounts her horse, and I throw our belongings over the saddle. I then throw his clothes in a pile by the trail. The man's horse pulls back at the reins.

"Take the reins, Hannah. You will have to lead him as we go. I don't think he will let anyone ride him."

I grab the reins and mount Raham's horse behind her. I tie down our bedrolls and food tighter behind me after placing the sword within my bedroll.

I hear the gentleman now crashing through the forest along the trail and grab Raham by the waist.

"Hurry, he is here!" I remark, and Raham spurs her horse onward. I pull strong against the man's horse, and thankfully, he follows. The last thing I see as we ride away is the man emerging from the brush, holding only his sword.

"Don't take my horse!" he shouts.

"Only until we are safely away from you, my lord," Raham shouts back as we ride away.

He sits by his clothes on the trail, and I smile at the thought of how we had bested a brave gentleman of noble birth.

After half an hour of hard riding, Raham slows to a slower pace. I adjust the reins. So far, thankfully, the other horse followed behind us willingly, or else I do not think I could have kept him from bolting away.

"Now tell me, Raham. Who is that man?" I ask.

Raham turns her head to answer and slows the horse to a walk. I see a tree line ahead and several smoke columns, which are signs of a small village. We must be very close to Glenmorrow.

"I don't know who that man is, but I know the family. They are a royal tribe called the Bene Elohim, the sons of Elohim. Legend says that they are warriors sent to all realms to fight against evil wherever it may be. Their king is said to be the king of all the worlds."

"King of all the worlds? What does that mean?" I ask.

"Don't know. That is just what the legends say. The Halls of Bene Elohim are within the king's city by the sea. I have only seen them once from afar. They are so beautiful, Hannah. Glorious spires, great halls, beautiful statues. The glory of God Himself shines from the ramparts."

"But why would one of them be here, in a backwater place like the plains of Glenmorrow?" I ask.

She looks over her shoulder again at me, "Searching for you, my dear," she remarks.

"Oh, shut up. You tease me." I answer.

She stops the horse. Up ahead, I see a small cabin and barns. Children run across the fields, chickens scattering before them.

"Nope, I do no such thing. One of them is searching for you, Hannah." She remarks.

"How can that be? He does not even know who I am. Plus, why would he love me? No man could ever love me, Raham. You see my scars. You see the ugliness."

Raham turns further in the saddle. She takes her gloved hand and glides her fingers across the side of my face over my scar.

"I see the scar, Hannah. But there is no ugliness there. Your gentleman says the truth when he says you are beautiful. You must believe who you are, Hannah."

She turns back, "We'll let the horse go now. The village is but a short distance away."

I dismount, as does Raham, as the children stop their playing and stand, staring at us. I turn away from them, instinctively hiding my face from them. I remember all too well the children laughing at me, pointing at me. The men and women looking disapprovingly. How could Raham say I was beautiful? How could the gentleman say I was beautiful? However, I think both did.

Raham stretches and takes the reins for the horse.

"Raham, hold on a minute. I need to do something."

She looks at me, questioning. I still had the man's sword. Should I give it back?

I think that I should.

I take the sword from the bedroll and hold it in my hand. It is a beautiful weapon, but it is not mine. Then I think of something that I would do. The man said that he was searching for me. He said that I am beautiful. He questioned whether I was the girl by the ferry or just Raham's maid or maybe both. I would answer him. I take a length of my hair and cut it with the sword, braid it in a tight braid, and tie it to the sword. I place the sword back in the sheath and tie it to the saddle. If it is meant for him to find me, he will find me again, I think.

"Okay," I say and step back.

Raham hits the horse hard on the rump, and the animal runs off down the trail from where we had come. Raham steps up beside me, removing her riding gloves. She stands a few inches taller than me and seems to be older than me. How can she only be fourteen years old?

"So, you send the gentleman a lock of your hair, do you?" she remarks and smiles widely.

"Oh hush," I scold her and turn away.

How foolish a thing to do, I think. What good would ever come of it? I will probably never see the man again, I think. But would it be such a wonderful thing? To have a gentleman who searched for such as I find my braided hair on the weapon that he knows that I stole from him.

I sense that Raham is staring at me, but I do not return her gaze. I stare at the wonderful, colorful litter of children standing by the road, staring at the both of us in wide, childlike wonder. And suddenly, I remember the whole point of this journey. I am to go to Glenmorrow and seek the carpenter, who hopefully can tell me what to do next.

Is the carpenter the one I am to show the amulet to?

I have no clue.

This past morning had been a truly remarkable interlude, but now reality sets in, and I look over to Raham as she places her riding gloves in her saddlebag and retrieves her crossbow and sword. What is she doing?

She smooths her dress, pulls back her long, red hair, and begins to braid the locks into one long braid that hangs down to the middle of her back. She fastens the crossbow and quiver of arrows to a sling and positions the weapon over her shoulder, and after a bit of adjustment, the weapon hangs freely by her shoulder over her back. She looks over at me as if to show me something, and with one swift movement, the weapon is in her hand. She only must retrieve an arrow from the quiver, and she can fire the weapon. She reverses the movement, and the weapon hangs from her shoulder again. Satisfied with the weapon, she belts her sword around her narrow waist, and the weapon is almost totally hidden by the folds of her dress.

She stands proudly before me, "How do I look?" she asks.

I have no answer.

"Da always said that a Faireadoiri warrior should enter a village in such a way that friends will immediately recognize you and enemies will leave you alone."

Who can argue with that logic? I think. I now wish that I had not returned the weapon. I take my cloak throw it over my shoulder, and pull the hood over my head. Unlike Raham, I enter a village and try to be as invisible as I can.

Raham takes the reins of the horse, and we begin to walk down the lane by the farmhouse. The chickens flock before us, and the children continue to stand by the road and stare at us. A woman emerges from the small cabin, holding a basket full of clothes, and calls to the children as she watches us walk by her on the trail. The children scamper to her, and they all watch as we pass.

After a few minutes, we are around the bend in the road among a grove of pine trees, and I see before us a wooden gate between two watch towers that open. I remember the gate from the last time I had visited the town, but that was many years before.

Raham holds the reins to her horse and walks immediately beside the great animal. I walk a pace behind her. She had told the Bene Elohim warrior that I was her maid. And now as we enter the gates of Glenmorrow, I feel far more comfortable playing that part to be as invisible as possible. Plus, I see immediately that as we enter the main street of the village, all eyes are on Raham.

I hear a woman whisper a question and a second answer, "Yes, that is a Faireadoiri."

I look at Raham with more admiration. Her tribe is so well-known and respected that one young woman can be recognized for who she is and respected as such by common people. Who really are these Faireadoiri that I have spent the past few weeks with?

After a moment, the villagers continue their daily routines, leaving us to stand in the middle of the road. We are standing at an intersection of three different roads just inside the village gate. The road forward is wider than the two side roads and travels between varied wooden and stone buildings that line both sides. Street vendors fill one side of the lane, their multicolored tents filled with fruits, vegetables, meats, and breads as well as leather goods, tools, farm implements, and household items. Both women and men meander through the streets, visiting booths, trading, buying, and selling. Children run among the adults. Dogs run, darting in and out among the people. The street is muddy in places or covered in refuse in other places.

The two side streets are narrower and filled with homes, gardens, out buildings and sheds. The homes on the right seem larger and better kept than the homes on the left with many small, beaten down enclosures, some smaller than the cabin of my youth. It is very apparent that the main street through the village divides the village by social and economic class.

Just ahead of us in a small-town square stands a well where several travelers are watering their animals.

Raham points at the well. "We need to water the horse," she states.

I say nothing but follow her as we cross the intersection, waiting a few minutes to allow a wagon loaded with hay to pass by.

As she draws the water from the well in the bucket, I stand back against the horse and hold the reins, nervously watching the people all around me. So many people make me apprehensive. I feel my heart tighten, my breathing quicken, and I feel like I need to run away from this place and back to the safety of my cabin in the mountain meadow. But I cannot yield to the fear of this place, to the throng of villagers going about their business. Also, I know with continued sadness that my old home is no longer a place I can ever go back to.

I watch the people, and after a moment, I collect myself when I realize that they don't even see me. They have no clue that I am even present, which gives me assurance. However, I stay hidden by the horse next to the well, my hood covering my face.

I think of the Bene Elohim, the thought of which drives my fear further away. He had thought me beautiful. I had stared him down from the trail, which was a great achievement for me. I smile at the thought of the man in the water looking up at me in admiration. Who is he, really? Why is he taken by me so?

"Hannah."

I turn to see Raham staring at me.

"You, okay?" she asks.

I shake my head, yes.

"You said your mother told you to find the carpenter who would tell you what to do. Is that right?"

I shake my head in agreement.

"Okay. As far as I know, Glenmorrow only has one, a giant of a man who always smells of wood and sawdust. I don't know where the shop is, but I'll ask."

She takes the reins from my hand as the horse continues to drink from the water in the bucket that she filled.

"But first, we need to get something to eat. I know a small place owned by a friend of my father. We can leave the horse in his stable while we search for the carpenter," she remarks and then looks down at me.

"You sure you okay, Hannah?" she asks.

I shake my head. I need to overcome the fear of this place, of all the people. "Yeah, I'll be fine. It's been a long time since I've been in a place with so many people. The last time was not a good time for me."

"It will be fine, Hannah. We'll in this together. Let's get a bite to eat and stable the horse and then we'll find the carpenter. Hopefully, he will know what we are to do next."

CHAPTER SIXTEEN

Raham pulls the horse away from the water, and he resists her a bit. "Okay, you brute, come on. We'll get you more in a bit," she scolds him.

We cross the intersection and head down the main street of the village among a throng of people who are attending the mid-morning village market. I instinctively keep the hood over my face and focus on Raham's bright red hair as we walk. But I still take notice of all the people, the crowds of small children playing among the storefronts, the tantalizing smell of freshly baked bread, overwhelming scents of heavy spices, the drifting scent of fish and raw meat, and then suddenly an overbearing, almost sickening mixture of beer, horses, and sweat.

I almost step into Raham as she suddenly stops. Foamy liquid runs past my feet.

"Now look what you've done, you goof!" someone shouts.

I look over to see several boys trying to unload large barrels from a wagon. It seems one had fallen and burst open, the beer pouring out over the ground. I step back from the flowing beer. Our horse snorts and jumps backward as well from the rolling barrel. I push back against the horse, and Raham turns, pulling back on the reins as our horse pushes both of us away from the exploding barrel and further into the street among the playing children.

"Watch out! Or you will drop another one!" the man shouts again from the porch of the structure just across the horse from me.

Raham is finally able to get control of our horse.

"Sorry, Mr. Spivey." A boy's voice speaks from the other side of our horse. At first, I see nothing, but as Raham calms the animal and turns him back toward the boardwalk, I see around him to where several younger boys are manhandling a barrel off a wagon.

"I'll not pay for that one, lad. You tell your dad; I'll only pay for the two that you unloaded. That one will come out of your wages or hide, whichever your dad thinks."

The boys curse quietly among themselves as they place the barrel on the wooden front porch of the building and return to the wagon to get the second one. Raham steps away from the horse.

"Surely, Mr. Spivey, you wouldn't be the cause of three young boys getting a whipping," she remarks to the man.

"Who said that?" Mr. Spivey calls out, looking over the crowd of people.

Mr. Spivey is a short man that is almost as wide as he is tall. I believe that I may even be taller than him. He is mostly bald; however, he has some thinning white hair on the top of his head that he seems to comb over the side to try to hide the baldness but fails to do so. He has bright eyes over a crooked nose. He wears a stained leather apron over a white, short-sleeved shirt that reveals muscular, short arms and overly large hands.

"I did," Raham states.

Mr. Spivey looks down at us, a bit of confusion on his face, and then suddenly, his eyes sparkle, and he smiles widely at the sudden recognition.

"Oh my! What a sight to behold!" he says, and with one step, he jumps from the boardwalk as Raham steps to him.

"My dear Raham, it's good to see you."

He grabs Raham, who is a few inches taller than himself, and, with strong arms, raises her off her feet in a giant bear hug.

"Oh, my child, you have grown," he says as he places her back on her feet, looking up at her, "Where's your family? Are they well? Oh, I would love to see them. It has been over a year. Are they setting up for the market?"

"They are fine. But we are here alone," Raham answers and turns to me. "This is my friend, Hannah. I am helping her to find her way, Mr. Spivey."

Mr. Spivey gives Raham a knowing look and then looks at me.

"Take your hood down, Hannah. It's okay. He is an old family friend. And he, too, is Faireadoiri."

I pull back my hood and curtsey as my mother told me to do, "How do you do, Mr. Spivey."

Mr. Spivey steps closer to inspect me. I know he sees my scars. He can't miss them, but he looks into my eyes.

"Hello, Hannah," he says, "What a beautiful name, young lady. Grace or Favor."

"Mr. Spivey. We need a place to stay for a few days," Raham remarks.

"Of course, of course. You can stay with us. We have plenty of room. Lucy will be so glad to see you. Tie your horse here and come on in. Lucy is working the store today. She's just inside there."

Mr. Spivey turns away, "Okay boys. That's fine. Now you go on back now and bring me another barrel. Tell your dad I ordered another one. I'll let you slide on this one, but you be more careful next time."

The boys mount the wagon, "Thanks, Mr. Spivey."

We wait as the boys maneuver the wagon out into the road and into the crowd of people. There is barely room for them to get by the market stalls, but to my surprise, they do as the people back up away from them and let them through.

"Come on girls. Come on in." Mr. Spivey waves us in, "Lucy. You won't believe what I found out on the street," he yells into the store front.

A young man steps out the door.

"It better not be another stray cat, Mr. Spivey," I hear a woman call from inside.

Mr. Spivey stops the young man at the door, "David, roll the barrels inside and then take that horse to our stall and make sure he is fed and watered."

"Yes sir," the young man says and quickly passes by both Raham and me.

"No, Lucy. It's not a stray cat," Mr. Spivey yells back and then says to me, "Lucy says I bring in every stray cat in Glenmorrow. But that's not true. We only have eight or ten of them. Come on, girls. Let's get you something to eat. And Raham, you tell us all about the family. It's been at least a year since we have seen them."

We follow Mr. Spivey through the door and into the store. The store is one room filled with canned goods, dry goods, tools, clothing, candy, and farm implements. A long bar runs down one side of the room, where two men sit, drinking and talking quietly. There is another smaller bar against the back wall beside an entrance that leads back to another room.

A woman almost the same size of Mr. Spivey stands behind the bar, a towel in her hand. She has long black hair streaked with gray that hangs just past her shoulders and a round face with almost black eyes.

"It better not be another cat," the woman says, and then she sees Raham and I standing by the door.

"Oh, dear lord. Oh, my, if it isn't, dear Raham. I would recognize that hair anywhere. Child, what are you doing here? Where's your family?"

She throws the towel down, runs over to Raham, and gives her the same bear hug that Mr. Spivey had done before.

"Oh, child. It is good to see you. Where's your mom and Da? Are they setting up at the market? Oh, that would be great. It has been a while since I saw their drama plays."

"No, Aunt Lucy. They are not with me."

Lucy puts her down and looks at her very disapproving.

"What do you mean? They are not with you. You are but a child. You wait till I see James."

"I'm fourteen now, Aunt Lucy. I'm not a child anymore."

Lucy steps back and inspects the girl, starting at her face and down her body to her feet. She notices the weapons.

"Oh, you have grown up and quite a young woman, a Faireadoiri warrior, I see," she remarks and shakes her head in approval.

"But you are still too young to be away from the family," she says and then looks over to me for the first time.

She steps back.

"This is my friend, Hannah. She is the reason why Da sent me." Raham says.

I curtsey again.

Lucy looks at me for a moment, and I see some type of recognition on her face. How can that be? We have never met before. She looks back to Raham, then to Mr. Spivey. What do they know of me?

"Hello, my dear, Hannah. What a beautiful name. Oh my. You girls look a fright. When was the last time you ate or had a proper bath?"

She looks at her husband, "Don't just stand there, Mr. Spivey. Let's get these girls something to eat."

"Yes, dear," he says and scurries into the back room.

"Come, girls. Have a seat at the table. You need to eat, and then I'll take you home and draw you both a bath."

She winkles her nose at us.

"You both smell of horses and sweat. That is not fitting for young ladies."

We both sit at a table in the back corner of the store, and Lucy leaves us to join her husband in the back room. I smell myself and look over at Raham. Yesterday, we both stunk, but I thought that now we were clean after our bath in the hot springs this very morning. I blush, thinking of the Bene Elohim, and wonder if he had ever regained his horse. I hope so. And did he find the sword and my lock of hair?

"Is she really your aunt?" I ask Raham,

"I don't think so, but that is what I always called her. And Mr. Spivey has always been just Mr. Spivey. Even Lucy calls him that."

"They are a strange couple," I surmise.

Raham laughs in agreement, "Yes, they are. They have always been friends of my Da and they have always been here at this store. I don't know any more about them, but that they are Faireadoiri. Da says they are from the Faireadoiri from across the eastern ocean."

A few moments later, Lucy enters with two plates of food, followed by her husband, who has two other plates and a pitcher of water. Lucy places a plate in front of each of us and then retrieves four wooden cups from the bar. Mr. Spivey fills each of them with water, and they sit down across from us.

"Now you eat, girls, and then tell us what is going on," Lucy orders.

Our plates are full of fruit, cheese, and bread, and I realize that I am famished.

Mr. Spivey leans forward as I take my first bite and asks, "What are you girls doing in Glenmorrow and all by yourself?"

Lucy taps Mr. Spivey on the hand, "Now, Mr. Spivey, let the girls eat first. They must be starving."

"Yes, dear," Mr. Spivey leans back and drinks from his cup.

I look over at Raham and see her smiling. She looks back at me as she eats, and I hold back a laugh. I see Lucy fidget a bit as she looks at me, over to Raham, and then back to me again.

"What are you doing here? Raham, I can't believe your Da would let you travel with only a girl as a companion. What a crazy thing to do. You could get hurt or kidnapped or anything."

"I thought you wanted them to eat first, dear," Mr. Spivey remarks.

88

"Oh, don't be foolish, Mr. Spivey. What was James thinking?" Lucy responds, and Mr. Spivey rolls his eyes and shakes his head.

Lucy looks at me with dark eyes that shine brightly, a look of recognition as if she had seen me before. I do not know why I think that way about the way she looks at me, but that is the feeling that I have. It is as if she knows everything about me, but how can that be? I take a bite of cheese as she stares at me and reach for the cup. I raise the cup up more to hide my scars than to drink. She smiles at me and then looks over to Raham.

"Who is this young woman, Raham? She is not Faireadoiri, but something more."

I hold the cup before me and look down at my food. She knows me, I think. She knows more about me than I know of myself. But how can that be?

"We found her in the wilderness, running from men who will kill her if they find her," Raham answers and then lowers her voice and leans forward, "Aunt Lucy, she is the Bean an Ri."

Lucy sits back, her eyes wide, holds her hand up to her mouth, and looks back over to me. There it is again, I think. The Faireadoiri all think that I am someone that I am not. There is no way that I am the wife of a king. And then I remember my mother's last words. She told me that I was to be the wife of a king. And James told me that it was the job of the Faireadoiri to assist me in achieving my quest because he said I am the wife of a king. But I do not know anything about a quest. All I know is that I must find the carpenter, and when the time comes, I am to show the amulet to someone that I know is the person to show it to. How ridiculous is that?

To my surprise, Lucy reaches across the table, takes her hand, and lightly caresses my cheek, running her fingers along the outline of the scar that covers the entire side of my face. She pulls back my hair from my shoulder and exposes the red scar down my neck and shoulder. I do not know what to do. She sees my scars. They all do, but for some reason, the Faireadoiri do not react the same way as other people.

When I was a child, other children laughed at me. As I grew up, adults and children would stare at me in disgust. They would point and whisper about me. So, I always covered myself anytime anyone, but my mother was around me.

Mr. Spivey leans in, "How can we help you, child?" he asks.

Lucy sits back in her seat, "We have heard about you, Hannah. We knew that you had been born, but we never knew when you would show yourself. But suddenly, you are here among us. Why is that so? Where is your family child? Surely, your mother would not bring you forward before your time."

I think of my mother and of my last sight of her as she fell, blood covering her dress. She is dead. But she had said that she thought she had more time, but that I had been located. Tears run down my cheek. I take a deep breath, and I begin to tell them my story. I take notice of the two men at the bar as they stand and quietly walk from the store.

CHAPTER SEVENTEEN

I walk through a beautiful meadow full of multicolored flowers, the silky petals brushing lightly against my hands as I walk. Butterflies flutter upward from the flowers at my approach. They playfully fly back and forth across the tall grass, darting here and there erratically as only butterflies can do. The warm sun caresses my cheek. The smell of flowers floats on a gentle breeze. I have been here before, I think, but I cannot remember when. Is it the meadow of my youth?

Up the hill before me, dark trees form a barrier of thick foliage between my meadow and a far mountain range of broken rock, towering spirals, and snow-covered high cliffs. I belong in this place, I think. This garden is where I am supposed to be, where I was always to be, and where I should forever be. What strange thoughts are these?

I am barefoot and wear a long, flowing white dress. The grass is cool against my feet. I wear my hair in braids, purple tassels tied to the braids that hang to my shoulder. I look more carefully at my dress and remember my dreams of my youth when I would dance with gentlemen in a grand ballroom. I turn to one side and see a glitter of gold shining in the sun. Beside the golden doorway stands a man. He waves to me, and I remember him from an ancient time before. But how?

I turn again and see a giant wooden structure extending high into the heavens. It is the same shape as the amulet I wear around my neck. I am startled suddenly because the man standing by the golden door now stands before me. I know this man. He stands over me in the place where the structure had been previously.

Where had the wooden structure gone?

Suddenly, I hear wings flapping, and the man looks up in alarm to the sky behind me. He draws a mighty broadsword and reaches to pull me behind him, but I look over my shoulder instead and see the great winged dragon hovering above me and panic.

91

I know I should stay by the man for protection, but I do not. I turn to run and the dragon breathes fire down upon me, the power of the fire knocking me to the ground and burning the side of my face and down one side of my body to my waist. For some reason I feel no pain, but I cannot see because of the fire and black smoke. I hear men fighting, swords clashing, monsters screaming and then the smoke is suddenly gone.

I lay naked in the field now, my beautiful white dress burned away from my body. The meadow is untouched by the dragon's breath, but I am not. The man stands just a few feet from me, the bright sunshine casting rays of light over his shape. He reaches a hand to me, but I am ashamed. He had wanted me to stand behind him, and I had run away in panic. Now I am naked and scarred. How could I go to him now? I turn and run toward the dark forest.

I wake up in the middle of the night, the dream floating like all the others, just outside my ability to fully grasp it. It is as if I am caught between two worlds. My dreams seem to have a common thread about them. A wooden structure just like the amulet, a winged dragon who is always chasing me, a man who tries to save me, and then I am burned. The man seemed so familiar to me this time as if I had known him in some distant time and place.

For a moment, I forget where I am, and then I see Raham sleeping next to me in a bed, her face and tangle of red hair uncovered. I am in a dark room, only the light of a half-moon shining through the window. I remember now. We talked at the Spivey store until dark, and then we followed them around the corner to their home. After a warm bath, Raham and I had gone to bed with plans to find the carpenter in the morning. Mr. Spivey knew of the carpenter but did not know if he was in the village at this time or not.

I had fallen asleep with the hope that tomorrow I would find out what I was supposed to do. But now I am wide awake. I lay back down and pull the covers up against the cold night. Raham mumbles something in her sleep and turns under the covers. I stare at the ceiling and then out the window to the night sky. I cannot sleep.

Too many things have happened. My dreams of the past few days all swirl around in my head. So much has happened to me in the real world. And then, in my sleep, I am tormented by horrible dreams or wonderful dreams that turn horrible in the end.

92

Just a few weeks before, I had lived in a hidden valley with just my mother. We had very little, and Mother had been sick since the last time we had traveled from the valley. On our way back from that trip, she had seemed so worried. We walked all through the night to get to the hidden entrance to the valley, and several times, we encountered horsemen who had ridden past us. I remember one stopped briefly to look, and I turned away, hiding my face. Mother pushed us even more, even though she seemed to be getting sick as we traveled. Did she know something?

And then the earthquake had shaken our valley, and the cliffs by the crack in the wall that was our entrance had crashed down. That had to have exposed the way in. The very next day, the soldiers came, and Mother died. My mind whirled with all the fear, the strangeness, the unknown. But there had been good times as well. I had met wonderful friends. I had seen places I had never seen before. I had met a handsome gentleman who had been searching for me. Who was he? So many thoughts. I need to sleep, but all the thoughts keep flooding my consciousness.

I am sleepy but cannot sleep. Finally, in frustration, I sit back up in the bed and then walk over to the window. The window is open, allowing the cool, night air to blow in with a scent of wood smoke. I notice a bit of gray light in the east, so at least the night is soon over, and tomorrow is here.

The village is quiet this early in the morning. I see a row of houses across the cobblestone street that extends in both directions into the darker shadows. There is a light in two windows, but otherwise, all the other windows are dark. Something falls, and I look down to my right and see what seems to be a wagon parked by a side lane. A horse snorts in the darkness. How strange that a wagon be parked in the street in the middle of the night, I think. The lighted window across the lane gives off just enough light to show the wagon's outline, and then a shadow moves from beneath the wagon. I lean further out of the window to see what the shadow is.

There is movement behind me, and I turn, but it is too late. Something pulls my hair downward, and strong arms grab me from the shoulders. I try to scream, but a hand clasps strongly over my mouth.

I am forcefully pulled from the window and down to the cobblestone lane. There are several tall shadows standing over me. I fight to get away but cannot break free of the one that holds me by the neck, one hand over my mouth.

"Hurry before someone hears us!" one shadow whispers.

"Are you sure we have the right one? There were two girls at the store."

Someone lights a candle and holds it up to my face. I try to pull myself back, try to break free, but the man is far too strong.

"Yep, she's the one," a voice whispers.

I can see a bearded face in the candle's light just before the man blows out the candle.

I must break free, scream, and do anything to get someone's attention. A second man pulls at my legs, and the first stands up, still holding his hand over my mouth.

"Hurry, throw her in the wagon, Jake, be ready. We got to get out of here before someone wakes up."

They pull me over to the wagon, and I free one leg and kick viciously, hitting one in the stomach. He falls back, the hand slips from my mouth, and I scream as loud as I can. The man hits me hard in the face, and I fall backward into the wagon as the others jump in. My head explodes with a sharp pain, and I feel the blood run down my cheek from a busted lip. I try to scream again, but he hits me a second time and covers my mouth with some type of heavy cloth that swells horridly.

A light comes on in several windows as the wagon lurches forward. My head hurts, and I feel that I may pass out, but I see someone climb out of the bedroom window.

"Hannah!" the shadow calls. It is Raham!

"It's the second girl! Should we take her?" a voice speaks above me.

"And do what? She is Faireadoiri. She would slit your throat first, man. We have the right one. Let's get out of here," a second voice answers.

I struggle to look up, and in the gray light of morning, I see Raham running down the lane after us, holding her sword in one hand. But then the man pushes me back down, and soon my feet and hands are bound, and a gag is tied tightly over my mouth.

The lane is narrow, so the wagon cannot travel very fast. We turn first one way and then the other. At one turn, I see a flash of red hair in the side alley. I think Raham is trying to catch up with us.

We turn down another road and my captors appear to be nervous as the village wakes up around us. They quicken their pace and soon we pull up in a side alley next to a large warehouse of some kind. One of the men jumps off the wagon and I hear a door open and the wagon lurches forward and through the door, which is quickly closed behind me.

They leave me in the wagon. I can only see the timbered, dark roof above me. There are several more men in the building. I hear them talking but cannot see over the rails of the wagon. I try to raise up, but I am tied in such a way that I am unable to do so.

"We got to get out of the village. Pete, the other one saw us. She will have everyone looking for us."

"This is bad! Oh, this is really bad. What are we going to do?"

"Pete, you said this would be easy. All we had to do was grab the girl in the dark and leave."

"Oh, my, this is bad! What are we going to do?" the same voice from before says again. He appears to be the more frightened one.

"Shut up, Clint! Just shut up! "Maybe Pete is talking, but I am not sure, "Jake check the door. I don't think anyone saw us come in here."

Someone walks by the wagon, and I recognize him as one of the men in the store from the day before. He had been sitting at the bar when we came in. The man opens the large door and peaks outside. A small shaft of light slants across the dark room for a moment, and then the door shuts, and the light is gone again.

"All is quiet, Pete," the man remarks.

"Okay. Fill the wagon with the barrels. We can hide the girl between them. Jake, you and Clint take the wagon through the front gate of the village. We will follow closely after you leave to make sure no one follows. When you clear the village, take the road past the hot springs. We'll meet you on the trail, and I'll lead you. The captain has men all over the prairie. All we must do is find one of them and show them the girl. He will pay handsomely for her. I know."

A moment later, I am dragged from the wagon. A few moments later, the barrels are loaded, and I am shoved into the false bottom of the wagon under the barrels. They tie the ropes even tighter so I cannot move at all and cover the opening with another barrel. Please, Raham, you must find me.

I beg, but I do not see how she can. Hopefully, she saw where they had taken me, but I have little hope. If I can only get the gag loose, I could scream for help as we leave.

Suddenly a hand reaches into the area they have placed me, and a wet cloth is forced over my nose. I try to pull back from the horrible smell but cannot. I panic as I realize they are drugging me. I violently fight to free myself, but after a moment, I am suddenly sleepy, and then everything is dark and totally quiet.

I wake up as someone is pulling me out of the hiding place. I struggle to resist, which causes my assailant to pull me from the wagon and drop me hard on the ground on my back. My body hurts, and I lay still, looking around me. We are somewhere out on the grasslands and parked under a grove of trees. The sun is high in the sky, which means we have been traveling for several hours. Several men are talking by their horses. I recognize two of them as the two men at the bar in the store, who must be the ones they call Pete and Jake.

A younger man, almost a boy, even with no beard and short hair, leans over me. His face is dirty, and he smells incredibly bad.

"Now, you need to stop fighting. Pete says I can untie you and give you food and water, but you must not fight or scream. We won't hurt you," he says.

He leans down and unties my bare feet. I am still in my night dress, and as he unties the rope around my ankles, the dress slides up above my knees. He stops and looks upward. I stare at him and see the look in his eyes as if he is contemplating doing something that he knows is bad. He pushes the gown further up my thigh, and I kick him hard in the groin.

"Aargh!" he groans in pain, "you little bitch!"

He recovers and crawls on top of me, sitting on my stomach, and grabs my hands as I try to fight him off, but he is too heavy. He slaps me across the face. My heart is racing in fear. I have never been touched by a man in this way. I have never been close to any man in my life, except for the time James had hugged me. What is he doing?

96

"Now look what you made me do! I told you we didn't want to hurt you. But you keep fighting me, I'm going to hurt you real bad."

I lay still, not knowing what to do, but I did not want him to hurt me anymore.

"Now that's better. I didn't want to hurt you. I just wanted to look at you. I have never seen a woman before this close, never felt one before. You are so soft, and you swell so good," he says as he works at untying the ropes around my arms.

"Now Pete told me to untie you, and I will, but if you fight me again or scream, I will tie you back up and put you back in that hole. You understand?" he asks.

I shake my head, yes.

He takes the gag off, and I breathe deeply and then cough. The boy smells so bad that I feel sick. He looks at my face and then down across my breast. He pulls the sleeve of my dress down a bit and exposes my shoulder.

"I've never seen a scar like this one before. Are you like this all over?"

He pulls the dress further down over my shoulder, and my heart races again. What is he doing?

"You ain't so bad, even with the scars," he says.

"Clint! Get off her!" a man orders, and suddenly Clint is grabbed by his shirt collar and jerked hard away from me.

"I wasn't doing nothing," the boy pleads.

"You get away from her, boy. If I see you do anything to her, I give you a whippen!" the man scolds and kneels in front of me as I straighten my dress, sit up and pull my knees up against my chest, making sure the dress hides my legs. I have not seen this man before.

He looks me over and shakes his head.

"Sorry about the boy. He won't bother you again," he says.

He pulls out a length of chain from the wagon. "What's your name?"

I don't answer him.

He sighs, "That's okay; I wouldn't answer either."

He shakes his head as he measures out the chain and reaches for my leg. I pull back from him in fear. He stops a look of sadness on his face. He holds out his hands toward me.

97

"Look. I promise you I won't hurt you. None of the others will either. Pete didn't think this through. I was told we were capturing a fugitive and would get a reward. I didn't know you were just a girl."

I think a moment as he kneels before me, holding the chain.

"Hannah," I say.

He smiles, "That's a pretty name, Hannah. My name is Travis. Look, Pete would kill me if I didn't tie you. I think you would run given half the chance, right?"

I shake my head, yes.

"I'm going to shackle this chain to your ankle. It will allow you to go as far as the trees so you can have a bit of privacy. But we will watch you. And I have food and water for you. I wish we had something else for you to wear, but we don't."

Travis seems to be kind, and I believe him. I extend my foot out. He places a metal collar around my ankle and locks it. I see him place the key to the collar in his pocket. Without looking up, he says, "I'll watch over you, Hannah. If I can make this right, I will. I promise."

He stands up and walks away. Maybe I have a friend, which means I have hope. He had left a plate of food and a canteen of water. The other men are sitting around the fire, eating. Clint is over by the trees, pacing and looking over at me. I do not trust him and believe that, given the chance, he will attack me again. I take the food and eat. It is dried meat and bread.

The chain gives me enough length to reach just inside the trees, where a small stream runs. I kneel at the water and splash the cold water over my face. My hair is a mess. I wet my hair and try to tame it, but I need a comb. I do the best I can by braiding it, but without a tie, I know the braid will not stay in place.

Finally, I give up and sit by the stream. At least here, I feel safer. I sit by the trees for a long time as the sun climbs higher in the sky. We had left the village at sunrise, and the sun was now past noon. In a few hours, it will be dark again. I fear the dark now. In the day, Clint stays by the fire or occasionally walks by and pulls on the chain, but at night, he can get to me, and no one will see him.

Travis suddenly appears by the trees, and I stand up.

"Hannah, come with me," he orders, and I follow him back to the wagon.

I notice a horseman by the fire, speaking to Pete, who points in my direction. He is a soldier. I stop in fear. He is dressed like the soldiers who had been chasing me. The man dismounts and follows Pete to where I am standing. He does not say a word but walks up to me and looks down at my face. My hair covers most of my face, so he pulls the locks back and reveals my scar. He grunts and turns back to the horse.

"It is the girl. I will take her to the captain," he states.

Pete steps up and places a hand on the man's shoulder, "Hold on now. You bring the captain to us. I was promised payment for her."

The soldier turns quickly and stares at the hand on his shoulder and then at Pete as if he will cut the hand off. Pete removes the hand and steps back.

"Okay, stay here for the night. We will be back first thing in the morning, and you all will receive what is due."

A few moments later, the soldier is gone.

"Travis, If the captain gets me, he will kill me. You must help me," I whisper.

Travis stands a moment in thought and then walks off to the fire. I look around me in desperation. I had to break free and make a run for it. But there is no way to get free unless Travis unlocks the collar.

CHAPTER EIGHTEEN

Raham woke up from a deep sleep. She had heard a scream in her dreams and sat up in the bed for a moment, confused. She could hear a struggle outside the window. Where was Hannah?

She jumped to the open window and peered out just in time to see Hannah being thrown in a wagon. She reached back, grabbed her sword, and climbed out of the window. She needed shoes, but there was no time. She landed on the cold cobblestone below the window just as the wagon turned around a bend in the street. She ran to a side alley and took it, emerging a few moments later just as the wagon turned down another lane. She ran down the lane but heard the wagon pass on another street. She turned down that street, caught sight of a wagon pass between two buildings, and she turned and ran down another road, which was a dead end. In the morning light, the lanes were a maze, and after a few more turns, she frustratingly admitted to herself that she had lost the wagon.

A few people were out beginning their day. She was standing at the fountain at the crossroads at the front gate of the village, breathing heavily from her run. Two men were opening the village gates, and several travelers entered as soon as the gates were opened. There were only two ways out of the village, one through the village gates and one on the opposite side of town. There were no wagons anywhere in sight. Where had they taken her? They had to be hiding somewhere in one of the buildings, or maybe a barn or shed, but where?

Several men were staring at her, and she looked down at herself. What a sight she must be, she thought. Standing in the middle of the road in a thin nightdress, barefoot, hair disheveled, and holding a sword. Raham stared back at them defiantly, and they shrugged and continued with their morning work. She asked several people, but no one had seen a wagon come by the fountain. That means they were hiding, or they were leaving by the back gate.

With nowhere to go and no one to ask for help, she turned and ran back to the house. She had to get her things and horse. The men were in a wagon, which means there were only two ways to go, but which one?

Mr. Spivey was standing at his front door when Raham arrived. He had heard the commotion and knew that something was terribly wrong.

"They have taken Hannah!" Raham cried as she pushed past Mr. Spivey.

"Child, what will you do?" Aunt Lucy asked.

"Please, can you saddle my horse? I need to change and pack. I need to find her."

"No child, you cannot!" Aunt Lucy pleaded as Raham disrobed and grabbed her clothes.

Aunt Lucy pulled Raham to her, "Raham, what can you do? How will you find her? You are but a child. James should have never sent you here with the girl."

Raham stopped and looked at the older woman in defiance, "I am Faireadoiri. I was given a mission, and I will not fail. I will find her, whatever it takes."

She pulled away and quickly packed her belongings and then gathered Hannah's things.

"Please, Aunt. Can you pack us some food? I need to get to the hill trail above the village in time to see which way they have gone," Raham pleaded and walked quickly out the door.

By the time she reached the barn, Mr. Spivey had her horse ready. Lucy ran quickly out the door with a bag of food and handed it up to her after Raham mounted her horse. Raham looked down at the two and saw the worry and fear in their eyes. They were Faireadiori, but they were not warriors. She was, however, and would do whatever it took to find Hannah. Her father would never have told her to go unless he knew that she was the one destined to watch over Hannah in her search.

"What will you do?" Lucy asked.

"I will find her," Raham answered and turned her horse toward the village gate.

There were two roads leading into the village. The one was the road that Raham and Hannah had traveled the day before, which led out into the great grasslands. The second road led back into the great forest and toward the distant ocean.

Raham knew that the soldiers who had been searching for Hannah were searching the grasslands for her, so she took a chance that the road leading in that direction was the one that they would take if they were working for the soldiers. She exited the village quickly as everyone watched her leave. She knew that the villagers would offer no help to her. They really didn't like the Faireadiori; they only tolerated them.

Raham figured that she would ride to the mountain ridge near the hot springs from where she could see the road far across the grasslands. She could see where any wagons were heading. They could not be very far ahead of her, she thought, so she should be able to see the wagons in the road, and then she could check each one until she found them. That was her plan, such as it was, but that was the only thing that she could think to do.

She rode as fast as her horse could go and followed the trail for several miles until she knew that she would have to slow down or else injure the horse. She traveled the same trail that she and Hannah had traveled just a day before. After another mile, she spotted the low ridge covered in trees and the rocky cleft partially hidden where the hot springs were located.

She stopped just below the crest of the hill and dismounted to allow her horse to rest. Raham suddenly remembered the Bene Elohim warrior that they had encountered by the springs. Whatever happened to him? Hopefully, the horse had found its way back to its master, she mused and smiled at the trick she had played on him. He was definitely a handsome gentleman, she thought. She looked warily over to the rocky ledges but saw nothing. After a moment she reached the crest where she could see the trail stretching far off into the vast plain until it finally disappeared.

A single horseman rode slowly away from her on the trail, and then she spotted a single cart with several people walking beside it. Two oxen pulled the cart. Maybe the wagon had not left the town, she hoped. If that was the case, then they would pass her on the road. Or maybe they were so far ahead that she could not see them, or worse yet, maybe they had taken the other road.

The sun glared across the yellow grass, and she had to shield her eyes and squint to see any further out over the prairie. Something lay off the side of the trail by a small grouping of trees, but she could not tell if the object was a wagon or not. If only she had a telescope, she reasoned.

Raham slumped her head in despair. She had been instructed by her father to see Hannah, the Bean an Ri, for heaven's sake, safely to the carpenter. And now she was lost, kidnapped, maybe even dead. She was almost to the point of tears but knew that she had to get herself together. She had to work on the problem. All was not lost, she reasoned. If they were taking her to the soldiers, they had to take her down the trail to the prairie where the soldiers were searching. But maybe they were not taking her to the soldiers, she thought. Maybe they had just kidnapped her for other reasons. The thought of that was even worse.

Her horse suddenly jerked his head, pulling the reins free. Raham immediately turned and retrieved the reins and saw down the trail toward the village a wagon and several horsemen. Her heart leaped. Could that be them?

She pulled her horse further down the hill opposite the trails and then turned his head sharply with the reins, pulling her down until she lay on her side.

"Shh, boy. It's okay," Raham soothed as she stroked the horse gently and then lay across his neck as her father had trained her to do since she was but a child. Now the grass and low rise of the ridge hid her from the trail, but by lifting her head just a bit she could see through the grass toward the oncoming wagon.

Two men rode in the wagon, which seemed to be loaded with barrels of wine just like the ones she and Hannah had seen being loaded at Mr. Spivey's store the day before. Five horsemen rode by the side of the wagon, but Raham did not see Hannah. Her heart failed her again at the thought that this group was not the men who had taken Hannah. But then she recognized one of the men sitting on the wagon as one of the two men who were sitting at the bar the day before. This had to be the same, but where was Hannah?

The wagon neared her position, and she lay her head down, holding her breath and gently stroking her horse, which had been trained to lie perfectly still. The group was about fifty feet away but on the other side of the hill. Thankfully, they were not trained warriors, or they would have most likely caught her. If they had been Faireadoiri, they would have known of her presence, she reasoned. But they were not, so they passed by, not ever realizing that she hid in the brush above them.

After a few moments, she lifted her head above the grass and saw that they had descended the side slope and were out on the flat plains below her, heading away from her. Raham straddled her horse and pulled on the reins.

The horse leaped up quickly with Raham astride, and in one turn, Raham was seated in the saddle. The horse shook his head as if congratulatory. Raham patted the horse and positioned herself more comfortably. As a child, this same horse had knocked her off several times while trying to master this type of mount, but after a while, she had grown rather adept at it.

"Very well done," a man's voice congratulated her.

Raham swirled her horse quickly around to see none other than the Bene Elohim warrior standing by his own horse by the rocks below her. She stared at the man incredulously as her horse sidestepped. How did he sneak up on both her and her horse, she thought.

The man stood fully clothed this time, his short sword in the scabbard by his side, the broad sword and shield attached to the flank of the horse by the saddle. His bedroll and other gear were secured behind the saddle.

"Are you hiding from someone? my lady." The man asked.

"That is none of your concern, my lord," Raham responded. The man flushed her, the same as he did with Hannah, but she would not allow him to do so.

The warrior held his hand up, looking around, "Where is your maid?" he asked.

Raham looked straight at the man, noticing his icy blue eyes. Could she trust him? After all, he had been searching for Hannah as well. But he was a Bene Elohim, a class of warriors that even the Faireadoiri respected and admired. She needed help, so she would have to trust him.

"She was taken last night in the village," Raham stated and immediately saw the concern on the man's face. "I think those men that just passed us on the trail are the ones that took her. I believe they are taking her to the soldiers that Hannah said had been chasing her."

"So, the girl is not your maid." The Bene Elohim remarked.

"No, sir. She is not, but she is a dear friend, and she has been kidnapped. Can you help me?" Raham asked, which was a very hard thing to do considering her youthful pride.

The man shook his head and reached a hand up to her, "Yes, my lady. That is something I will be honored to do," he answered.

He took her hand gallantly and kissed it lightly, and Raham blushed.

"Malak, a Bene Elohim knight at your service, my lady," he said and stepped back, a wide smile on his face.

Raham's heart quickened at the kiss. Hannah was right. This man was the most beautiful man she had ever seen. She regained her composure and pulled her hand back. Her horse stepped back and turned his head to look at Raham as if to say, "What is wrong with you, girl?"

"I am no lady, my lord. Just a girl whose pride has gotten her in trouble. My name is Raham."

"And the girl's name?" he asked.

"Hannah."

Malak shook his head, turned quickly, and mounted his horse, "Then we go down there and save her. Even a Faireadoiri girl whose pride has gotten her in trouble can handle eight ruffians who probably don't know a sword from a broomstick."

"But she may not be with them. Or they are hiding her in the wagon. We need to make sure," Raham reasoned.

"You are probably right. My dear. We will follow them from a distance and see what happens. They must stop sometime."

Malak walked his horse up to the rise. The wagon and horsemen were but small dots on the trail. Raham spurred her own horse ahead of him on the trail to follow them. She needed Malak's help, but she would not let a Bene Elohim take charge of her, she thought. Especially not this one.

105

Both rode down the trail side by side, making sure they stayed totally out of sight, following the trail of fresh wagon tracks. They were silent for the first few minutes as Raham tried to think of how to ask Malak why he was searching for Hannah. Did he know something about Hannah that she did not know? Afterall she only knew that Hannah was the Bean an Ri, the wife of a king and the Faireadoiri had always been tasked with helping her when she was found.

They knew little else except that their stories told them that each generation, a wife of the king would be found, and they were to assist her in her quest. Hannah was the first that her family had ever known to exist. She thought of just asking him but was not sure. But she hated the silence between them.

"I'm glad that your horse returned to you," was the first thing she thought to say.

Malak laughed, "So am I. You know that was a nasty thing you did. Kicking me in the water and taking my clothes and then my horse."

Raham looked sideways at him and shook her head, "Maybe, but you deserved it. You should never have teased us the way you did. I may not be a grand lady, but I am a decent girl who does not like being ogled at while bathing by a ruffian such as you were."

Malak bowed his head to her, "I apologize for that. I have always been one of the rowdier of my tribe, but it is very rare indeed to witness such a beautiful young girl, a Faireadoiri warrior, in fact, and naked. I could not help myself."

Raham blushed and turned away from him, "Stop, you tease me."

Malak reached over and touched her hand. Her heart jumped, and she turned to him.

"No, I do not tease you. You are very beautiful, Raham. I saw you stand before me, holding your sword, your bright red hair wet and matted over your breast. I have never seen such beauty."

He took his hand away, and Raham turned to stare straight ahead down the road. Why would he say these things? The same he had spoken when he first saw Hannah.

She looked back at him, "Why do you say those things about me? The same you spoke about Hannah. You said you were searching for her, that she was the most beautiful girl you had ever seen. What do you know of her? Why do you search for her? To marry? And then you say those words to me. I may be young, Malak, but I know when a man is full of himself."

Raham pulled her horse away, but Malak grabbed the reins and stopped her.

"Whoa, now. You misunderstand me. Yes, I was searching for her, but not for me to marry. She is the wife of a king. She is to be the wife of my king. I have been searching for her for several weeks after the king ordered me to do so. She is to be my king's wife. Hannah is truly a remarkable woman because she is a new creation of a new world. My king has been waiting for her to realize who she is. The world around her sees the scars, but my king sees her remarkable beauty."

Raham stared at Malak in confusion. What he said made no sense.

"But you are a different matter. I see you for who you are. I walked naked from the water and finally found my clothes. I sat for most of the day and night before my horse returned, thinking of you, Raham. Not Hannah. She is not for me. She was born to be the wife of my king. But you. Well, my thoughts were about you."

Raham turned away, her heart beating fast, her breathing labored. She had never felt this way before. And then she thought of Hannah. Hannah had fallen for the man. She had given him a lock of her hair.

"Malak, Hannah is taken by you. Did you see the lock of her hair that she tied around the sword she returned?"

"Yes, I have it here," he answered.

"Then, you need to keep your thoughts about me to yourself. She thinks you love her and that you are a gentleman, which she has dreamed about her whole life. You need to figure this out because if you hurt my friend, I will kill you." Raham warned and spurred her horse to the front. But her thoughts were filled with the fact that this man, a Bene Elohim warrior, was in love with her and not Hannah.

107

Malak watched her ride away, thinking that she would most definitely do such a thing. What a strange feeling he had for this girl. Why he was so infatuated by her puzzled him. Yes, she was truly beautiful, and in the short time he talked with her, he immediately loved her tenacity, honesty, and bravery. But he knew nothing about the girl except that she was Faireadoiri, which he had to admit meant a lot to him and that she was just who she was, and that seemed to be enough. He shook his head and noticed his horse had turned his head to the side to look back at him as if to say, "Yep, you in love, boy."

"Mind your own business," he scolded and spurred his horse onward.

After a few moments, Malak saw that the wagon tracks had turned from the trail.

"Hold on, Raham. The wagon has left the trail," Malak called to her.

Raham stopped and backed her horse as Malak caught up to her. There was a bit of awkwardness between them for a moment because of their last conversation, but they had more important things to worry about.

Malak pointed off to a distant grove of trees that set back against a low ridge, the evening sky glowing red from a setting sun. A tiny whisp of white smoke marked the presence of a campfire.

"Looks like they are setting up camp for tonight. Let's walk the horses from here and get as close as we can. There looks like a rise where we can hide the horses and see into their camp," he said.

They both dismounted and walked their horses as they followed the wagon tracks until they were just below a low ridge dotted with pine and cedar trees. A small stream meandered around the base of the hillside. They tied their horses and crept quietly up the hill to a rock outcrop where they could see down into the valley on the other side.

A single wagon was parked next to the trees, and a campfire burned nearby, lighting up the evening with dancing orange-white light. The sun slowly disappeared behind the tree line as they spied on the camp. They could see several men walking around the camp. Two sat by the fire, but they did not see Hannah.

And then Raham pointed to the wagon. Someone moved in the brush, and Hannah suddenly appeared just outside the fire's glow. She stood by the wagon, looking away from the camp into the gathering shadows. Raham's heart leaped with joy. She had been right!

Malak whispered in her ear, "We will wait until fully dark and then we will get her."

How? Raham thought.

She looked over to her partner. He lay beside her, his arm touching hers as he extended his telescope to look over the camp more closely while there was still enough light to do so. She noticed his muscled arms covered with tattoos.

She turned away. What in the world was going on, she thought. She had never had feelings such as the ones that welled up inside her in the presence of this man so close to her. She had to think of something to break this trance over her.

"Malak, do you know anything about the carpenter?" she finally asked.

Malak looked over to her and placed the telescope down in front of him, "How do you know of the carpenter?"

"Hannah said her mother told her before she died to go to the village and look for the carpenter, and he would tell her what to do next."

"Yes, I know the carpenter. He travels between the realms. He is very close to the king." Malak answered.

Malak sat up and placed the telescope back in its protective cover, "Did Hannah have an amulet?"

"Yes, she does. I have seen it, but she keeps it around her neck all the time and hides it, even from me."

Malak started to say something but suddenly looked away toward the setting sun.

"Horses coming. Look, the men are reaching for their weapons. Somebody is coming!"

CHAPTER NINETEEN

I stand by the wagon closer to the campfire and within sight of hopefully a friend who will help me. I see Clint hiding in the shadows. I know now that when he thinks he can, he will come to me again. I do not know what he wishes to do to me, but I fear him. The sun is finally setting, and soon it will be dark. I look around me for a weapon. Anything will do. My only hope is to scream if Clint comes or have some type of weapon to defend myself. But I find nothing of any use to me.

The other men are across the wagon from me. I back against the wagon and think of the chain around my ankle. I pick it up and gather the links in my hand. I can use the chain as a weapon if need be, but it is awkward.

The evening wind shifts, and the smoke from the fire blows over the wagon and swirls around me. I look over to where Clint had been standing and, in alarm, see that he is no longer there. I take a step away from the wagon just as a hand closes over my mouth, and Clint flips me hard on my back to the ground and sits over me. He gags me as I fight to escape, but he is too strong.

"Shh, now, girl. I just want to play with you. If you stay quiet, I won't hurt you," he whispers.

He holds both my arms down with his knees and pulls down my night dress, revealing my breasts to him. He stares and smiles at me. I twist away but cannot escape. He reaches down, and my hand comes free, and I strike him as hard as I can with the chain at his face. He jumps back in pain and raises his arm to hit me, but he suddenly falls away from me.

"You sorry, rascal. I told you if you hurt the girl again, I would give you a whippen," Travis warns.

Clint pulls a knife and swings but misses, and Travis pushes him back against the wagon, stabs the boy, and then slashes with the knife. Clint groans and cries in pain and slides down the wagon, falling to the ground at my side, his throat cut and blood gushing forward.

"You stupid boy," Travis says and leans over me, holding the key in his hand.

I hear horses out in the darkness, and Travis turns away in alarm and then back to me.

"Hear, let me unlock the chain. I'm done with this mess. I should have never helped," he whispers,

He unlocks the collar around my ankle and stands. There is a great commotion by the campfire as horses ride in the darkness. I hear screams and galloping horses.

"Slavers!" someone yells, and Travis pulls me up. The fear in his eyes is very evident to me.

"Run girl! You must get out of here!" he shouts and turns just as a man dismounts across from him. Travis rushes the man, and I turn and run into the darkness.

I hit the brush at full speed and trip over the vines and brambles, falling hard into the small stream. I hear fighting behind me and the cries of pain and death. Horses gallop past me. I had heard of Slavers and knew that I needed to find a place to hide. They killed men but would capture children and women to take to the seaport to sell. And I run knowing that most likely Travis had died to save me.

I am barefoot, and I feel the pain as thorns and rocks tear at my feet, but I must get free of this place to somehow find a place to hide and then try to get back to the village safely.

I cross the stream again and find myself out in the grasslands. I run through waist high grass as horsemen gallop around me. Did they somehow see me run from the wagon? Suddenly out of the grass, a shape emerges, long hair swirls and someone pulls me down into the grass. I pull away from the person in terror.

"Hannah, it's me. It's Raham."

I stop and see my friend and savior sitting in the grass next to me. All I can do is grab her and hug her as tight as I can.

"Come on, we got to go. Your gentleman is near, and we have horses."

My gentleman?

She helps me up, and we run toward a rocky outcrop that swells upward into the night sky above us. I see the shape of a man silhouetted against the sky holding a sword, and suddenly, two other shapes emerge, and I hear the metal clash. Sparks fly outward.

And then horses gallop past us, and something grabs at my legs, and both Raham and I fall under the weight of a heavy net. Raham stands up under the weight of the netting,

111

sword in hand, but a horse pulls, and the net slings her back down to the ground, her sword falling away into the grass.

Large, bearded men pull at the ropes, and the netting tightens around us both. We are pulled in the net back toward the wagon. I see the men fighting on the high ridge above us. One falls under the blow of a heavy broadsword, but several more rush upward. The last I see is the taller man falling back away over the rocky ledge.

We are dragged back to the wagon past several bodies. It seems the Slavers had killed everyone. I see Travis lying by the wagon, blood pouring from an open wound through his stomach. He had died trying to save me.

"Who travels with empty wine barrels?" one-man shouts in disgust and kicks over the barrels. They roll out from the wagon.

"That makes no since. A wagon full of wine barrels is worth a fortune, but they are all empty." another one says.

Our captor drags Raham and I up to the wagon. He dismounts and begins to unravel the netting, releasing the pressure on us.

"It's not all bad, boys. Look what I got," he says as he pulls the net from us, causing us both to roll out like two fish from a sea net.

Raham immediately jumps up and kicks the man in the groin, grabs his sword, and swirls beneath his upraised arms in the Faireadoiri way, slashing for his stomach with the blade.

"Whoa now, girl!" a second man behind shouts and pulls at the rope that is still under her feet, causing her to miss. She steps back and turns to face the second man, but another swings a club, hitting the back of her head, and she falls next to me, unconscious.

The one man laughs loudly as the first bends over in pain from being kicked, "She bout gutted you, boy."

Another man stands over us, "Tie them up. They will bring more than wine at the market. But if any of you ingrates messes with them, I'll cut it off. You hear me? They only pay for unsoiled girls at the market. I'll not lose a sale because one of you can't control your urges."

They tie our arms and legs and throw us both in the now empty wagon. In a few minutes, we are traveling in the dark across the prairie. I see two horses tied behind the wagon and recognize them as Raham's and the gentleman's. So, he must be dead, I think. I lay back next to Raham with no hope left in me, but then I look over at my friend. She is so much stronger than I can ever be.

112

Suddenly, I hear a shrill whistle out in the darkness, and the gentleman's horse jumps back at the sound. He fidgets and fights and bites at the reins until he suddenly frees himself and before anyone can do anything, he runs off into the darkness. And I have hope again.

CHAPTER TWENTY

Malak fell back into the crevice of the rocky crag below him and down into a dark hole, his sword falling next to him. The fall hurt, but it saved his life because none of his attackers dared climb down into the rocks after him. He set up and checked himself and found that he only had a few extra scars to add to the many he had over his body. He found his sword in the dark and stood, looked upward, and whistled as loud as he could several times. Hopefully, his horse would hear the whistle and return. If not, he had a long walk ahead of him.

They had been attacked by Slavers, which meant that they would most likely head to the port. The girls would bring a high price, and he had to get to the port before they were sold and shipped overseas. There were a lot of evils in the realm that he did not understand, and the sex trade for young girls was the evilest of all.

He sheathed his broadsword against his back and looked up. He would have to climb his way up the cliff, which would take a while, but he had to do so, one step at a time. Hopefully, by the time he made it to the top, his horse would have returned. After an hour of hard, slow climbing and falling back to the bottom on two occasions, Malak finally made it to the top of the ledge. He only had one more pull, and he would be free. He pulled himself over the lip of the ledge and saw his horse standing below him, looking up at him.

"Some help you are," Malak remarked.

The horse neighed back and shook his head.

Malak fell outward on the ground next to the rock and lay for a moment, staring at the sky, breathing hard.

"You try doing that. You couldn't climb out of the stall, much less a rock cliff."

The horse shook his head again and snorted.

Malak set up and laughed at the horse and then a dark countenance fell over him. He had to find the girls and free them before they made it to the market. If not then, he would tract them down to the ends of the earth, but he wanted to get them while they were together.

Raham, he knew, because of her beauty and the fact that she was Faireadoiri, would go for a small fortune to a rich man for his personal pleasure. Hannah, on the other hand, because of her scars, would be sold to a brothel. If he could only save one, with great sadness, he knew that he would have to save Hannah. She was worth more to the king than all other women because she was the new creation of a new realm. Malak did not understand what that truly meant, but it was not his place to understand. It was his place to make sure that the bride for the bridegroom was ready.

He stood up, brushed the dirt from him, and climbed down the rocky outcrop to where his horse stood. He mounted the animal and rode toward the campsite where the wagon had stood. On the way, he saw a familiar sword. He jumped down from the horse and picked it up. It was Raham's Faireadoiri blade. He secured it in his pack and mounted again, riding to the glowing campfire.

The empty barrels lay scattered around the dead bodies around the fire. He spotted the wagon tracts and began following them. There was no road, just two-wheel tracts on bent grass that were easy to follow even in the dark.

Malak followed the tracts for the rest of the night, never stopping until suddenly he saw a shape in the dark before him. He reined in the horse and sat for a moment, studying the scene before him. The shape was an empty wagon. He cursed because he knew that he had been tricked. He turned back down the trail, trying to find where the horses had left the wagon.

He had to backtrack for over an hour before he saw where the horses had left the trail and ridden off toward the south. He settled into a full night of trailing them, knowing that he had lost valuable time.

After another hour or so, the night became even darker as clouds formed up against the horizon and covered the stars. Distant thunder rumbled, and lightning flashed in the distance. Malak stopped and dismounted, pulled a leather cape from his pack, threw it over his shoulders against the strengthening rain, and mounted again.

The wind blew hard over the prairie as thunder rumbled and brilliant flashes of lightning bounced across the heavens. Waves of heavy rain fell, and all hopes of following the trail were lost as the ground became soaked by the flooding rainfall. Both horse and rider lowered their heads against the terrible storm and continued toward the port city where the Slavers were sure to be going, or so Malak hoped.

Finally, after a long night of riding through the storm, the clouds blew away, and the morning sun cast a slanting light through the mists. Malak did not stop, however. He had to get to the port city as soon as he could.

Unknown to Malak, another band of horsemen had ridden through the night. The captain had been told that the girl had been found and was waiting for them at the camp by the cliffs by one of his men. He had led his men through the night and had arrived at the camp in the early morning hours, only to find the dead men and the girl gone.

"What could have happened?" one of his men asked.

The captain shook his head in disgust. So close, he thought.

"Most likely, Slavers. They must have the girl. That means they are heading to the port," the captain answered.

That meant at least a week's travel back across these forsaken plains.

CHAPTER TWENTY-ONE

After riding in the back of the wagon through the night, we suddenly stop. The leader shouts commands to the men in a language that I do not understand. I look at Raham and see that she has regained consciousness. I see blood-matted hair across the side of her face. She watches every move of the men as they approach like a cat ready to strike, but her hands and feet are tied, as are mine.

"Come on, you pretty. You first," a man speaks, standing before us only as a dark shadow in the night.

Raham struggles at first, but there is no way she can free herself. He picks her up with ease and sets her on her own horse that had been tied to the wagon. He ties her to the saddle. He then returns and picks me up. I almost gag at the smell of him as he places me on the horse behind Raham and ties us both together so that if one of us falls from the horse, both of us will.

The man then replaces the bridle with a long rope that he ties to the pommel of his own saddle after he mounts his horse. The men are all mounted now, and we leave the wagon on the trail and turn away in a different direction. I have no idea where we are or in what direction we travel. All I know is that this nightmare is still ongoing, and my hopelessness grows with each passing minute.

Raham and the gentleman tried to save me, but now she is captive as well. And all of this is because of me. Even though I am glad she is with me, I now wish that she is not. She would be free, but now she is a captive, just as I am. She is here because of me and will suffer the same as I will suffer. Raham is the only friend I have. She is the only true friend that I have ever had, I think. And I wish with all my heart that she is not with me now, even though the only strength that I have is because she is in my presence.

We ride on through the night, everyone in a single file line, following some trail that the men know. The wind begins to blow, and thunder rumbles off in the distance. Flashes of brilliant lightning crash in the heavens above, highlighting massive storm clouds with white light.

The night grows cold, the air wet with the approaching storm, and I begin to shiver. I hold tighter to Raham, who is slumped forward on the horse. I worry about her. She had been hit very hard and had been out for several hours. She seems to waver between consciousness.

And then the rain comes hard. Thankfully, the men dismount and begin to pull shelters from their packs. At first, I think that they will leave us on the horse to weather the storm, but a man unties us and places us on the ground, one at time. He then throws a heavy blanket and tarp over us. I grab the blanket and pull Raham next to me as the rain strengthens. Lightning crashes above us and with every strike, the horrible thunder rumbles like cannon fire.

I pull the waterproof tarp over the blanket, pull Raham even close and pull the tarp over both of us. At least now we are dry, and our combined body heat begins to calm my constant shivering. Raham moans and turns. Even though it is dark, there is enough light with each lightning strike, that I see her open her eyes. Another strike and I see the confusion for a moment and then it is dark again.

"Hannah?" she questions.

"I'm here," I answer, and she reaches a hand to my face.

Another flash of light and I see that she is fully awake now and holding one hand against the side of her head.

"Ifreann fuilteacha! That hurts," she exclaims.

I cannot help but laugh because I know her words and respond, "Bloody hell indeed."

"Where are we?" she asks.

"I don't know. We have been riding all night."

The heavy rain continues to pelt the tarp, which leaks in places. I reposition the tarp, and the leak stops. The storm intensifies as it passes directly overhead, and the lightning crashes constantly now, with thunder instantly roaring after each strike. The wind increases, and we both hold tight to the tarp to keep it from blowing off. After a few more moments, as the storm travels past us, the wind subsides, the lightning and thunder fade, and the rain continues as a steady downpour. The worst of the storm seems to have passed us by.

"Did they get Malak?" Raham asks.

"Who?"

"The gentleman, the Bene Elohim warrior. His name is Malak. Did they capture him as well?" she answers.

118

So, his name is Malak, I think. What a strange name.

"No. I think I saw him fighting on the rocks when they got us, but I'm not sure. But no, they only captured the two of us."

"Then he is dead then," she says, and I hear the sadness in her response.

I sit up, "No. Raham. I thought so as well, but soon after they put us in the wagons, I heard a whistle. And then his horse. They tied his horse to the wagon as they did yours. His horse untied the knots and broke free after I heard the whistle. So, I don't think he is dead. I think he called for his horse."

Raham lays her head back and pats my leg. "Then he will save us. He must," she says and positions herself closer to me, "I'm sleepy, Hannah. There is nothing we can do now but wait and sleep through the rain."

I pull the tarp closer against the rain and soon fall asleep as well.

The tarp is pulled from us suddenly, awakening me from a fitful, cold sleep and causing me to roll out from under the blanket, now damp and useless in keeping me warm. The sun is barely above the horizon, casting a pale light across a wet grassland, streaks of pink and violet streaking across a partially cloudy sky. The morning is cold. I am wet and shivering and see that my nightgown is muddy and torn. I pull what is left of the dress around me and set up.

Raham sits up and shakes the hair from her face. She pulls the muddy red locks back away from her head and gathers them together into one long rope that seems to be held together by mud and caked blood. I see a dark gash across the side of her head above the ear from where she had been struck by the club. She looks over at me and cringes as she touches the wound, which is caked with mud mixed with blood and hair.

A man stands over me, blocking the rising sun. He throws a roll of clothing at me, "Change into this girl. At least it will keep you a bit warmer."

I grab the clothes and see that they include a pair of cotton pants and shirt. Another man kneels before me. His face is dirty and covered by a partial beard as if only a portion of his face can grow a beard. He hands me a piece of bread and a canteen of water. He then does the same to Raham and they both walk away.

119

"We leave in a few minutes, so do whatever it is you girls do and be ready," one orders.

I shake the dirt from my pants. They smell of horses, but they are better than the muddy nightdress that threatens to fall from me if I stand up. I look around to see if any of the men are watching and quickly cloth myself. They are too big for me, and I must hold the pants at my waist when walking, but they are warmer than the dress. A few minutes later, we are tied on the horse, and our guard reaches over and takes the rope and ties it to his saddle, and once more, we head off down the trail in a single line.

For the next two days, we ride from sunup to sundown, with few stops during the day and for only a few minutes each. The men feed us bread and water in the morning and again at night. Otherwise, they leave us totally to ourselves except to place us on the horse in the morning and take us off at night and throw us the blanket and tarp. For this I am grateful, but each night I wish for the warmth of their fire.

Raham says very little during the day as we ride. Like me, she perseveres through the days and cold nights with the hope that Malak will find us and free us. I think of him as we ride. He is of the tribe of Bene Elohim, who are great warriors of a race that is not of this realm but of a higher realm. Raham speaks highly of his tribe and more so of him at night while we wait for sleep to finally take over our tired bodies, but sleep is difficult because of the cold and constant discomfort.

She told me how they had met by the place where he found us in the water and I realized suddenly last night that she is very fond of him, infatuated by him as I am. I asked her why he was searching for me, but she would not tell me even though I think that she knows.

I lay under our sparse shelter and see the warm glow of the fire that the men sit around and wish that I could feel that warmth myself. Raham is asleep beside me, and I look down at her peaceful face and wish that I too could find peace.

Something about her is different than before, but I cannot quite figure out why. Before she had fallen asleep, she had apologized for failing me. She seems to have lost confidence in her abilities, and I watch her sleep and pray that she will gain her confidence again, because it is the only thing that has so far saved me, even though in her mind she thinks that she has failed me.

I lay back against her. I need to sleep. My body aches from the constant riding; I am filthy beyond belief and smell like horses, sweat, mud, and blood. My body aches for peace of sleep, but I lay wide awake. I do not know who to hope for, who to pray to, who to call to for help and then I think of the amulet. It still hangs around my neck by some miracle. I flip it end over end in my hand. It is small and shiny and seems to absorb light, but it has no light of its own. It is just silver metal on a simple chain that has the shape of the wooden structures that I keep dreaming about. Mother had said not to show it to anyone until I knew who to show it to. But how can I know who?

I hold the amulet in my hand and cry softly for my dead mother, who gave her life to save mine. I think of Raham and her family, who have sacrificed so much for me, thinking that I am something that I do not believe I am. I think of everyone who is chasing after me. Why? And finally, I fall asleep.

I wake up suddenly from a deep sleep to the sight of a man standing over me, holding the tarp and blanket that had covered me. Raham stirs beside me. The man throws us bread and water.

"You have ten minutes, girls. Today, we will reach the port," he says and turns to gather the horses.

Raham refuses the bread and stands up and stretches. She does not say a word to me, and she looks around the camp as if she is counting the men. I worry that she is still in the depressed state that she was yesterday, but she looks down at me after a moment and smiles.

What?

I see light in her green eyes again and she holds up her bound hands to stretch and while doing so points toward the ridgeline above me. I look at her questioning and she stretches again, and I follow where her hands point toward.

I scan the ridgeline and at first, see nothing but the mountain cliffs, broken tumbles of rock, and scattered cedar trees and brush, then back up against the cleft in the rock, I see the faint shape of a horse in the brush and higher up on the slope I see a man's shape for just a second before the shape disappears behind the rocks. Looking back to where the horse had been, I only see the brush.

121

Raham sits back down beside me and takes the bread and eats it in two quick bites. She then takes her water, drinks a bit, and pours the rest over her hair and face. As she does so, she mouths one word to me.

"Malak!"

I look back up to the ridge but see nothing. But how does she know?

A few minutes later, we are bound to our horse again, but at least today we know that our journey across the grasslands is almost over and that Malak is somewhere close. We ride single file, and I see that the men also seem to be tired of the trip.

Both Raham and I scan the ridgeline as we ride, but through the morning, we see nothing. And then just after we stop at mid-day to take a break by a spring of water by the trail, I see a horseman standing next to a tree on the ridge.

He is closer than before, and I know that it has to be Malak because this man rides a black horse, and a black cape flutters in the wind. Malak sits on the horse and watches us but no longer hides as the first time we saw him in the morning. He sits his horse sky-lined against the ridges in plain sight, and in a few moments, one of the men sees him reins in his horse, stops next to the trail, and watches as we ride by on the trail.

Malak turns the horse then and disappears behind the ridge and a few minutes later, he appears again, but this time he is further down the slope. This time a second man stops and waits by the trail as we ride by. What game is he playing?

I can tell that the presence of the warrior on the hill unnerves the group until finally the leader turns his horse around in the trail, "It's just one man. We are almost at the port. You men get back in line."

We ride on for several miles, and then suddenly, I see Malak again on his horse, standing directly in front of us on the trail. What does he think he is doing? He is one man against at least twenty.

The group stops on the trail at the sight of a warrior and horse that from this distance is just a black figure silhouetted before an afternoon sun. He sits on his horse and leans forward, then stands in his stirrups as if he is stretching. The horse side steps across the slope.

"What is he doing?" I ask.

122

Raham turns her head to me, "I think he is counting them. I think he wants to attack, and by the oath of the Bene Elohim, he can never yield to less than nine, but there are twenty-one men in this group, so he will need to think of something else."

Raham points to the men nearest us, "Look, Hannah, look how the men are afraid of him."

I look over and see the fear on the faces of the closest men and then back at Malak. I would be afraid of him as well, I think. He sits again on his magnificent black horse, his cape blowing in the wind. The metal of his shield on the horse's flank sparkles in the sun. I think of the time I saw him by the pond, his muscled arms, the tattoos, his brilliant eyes.

"He is definitely a sight to behold, your gentleman," Raham comments.

I think now that she is taken by him, and I feel a bit of jealousy. Raham is so much prettier than I would ever be, I think.

"Oh, hell with this!" I hear the leader say, and I turn to see.

He points to the three closest men in the line to him, "He is only one man. Go see what he wants. And if he doesn't leave, kill him, and you can split what you find on him," he orders.

The men look at their leader incredulously.

"Go! Or by the gods, I'll kill you here and now!" the leader shouts.

The three men draw their swords and spur their horses up the trail toward Malak.

"Bad mistake," Raham states and looks over at the guard next to us, "Yea, you all better run. When he finishes with them, you will be next," she taunts.

"Shut up," the guard orders.

"Just saying. That's a Bene Elohim up there. I give these three about two minutes. Then he will take all of you next," Raham continues.

"I said shut up!" the guard orders and, this time, slaps Raham hard across the face.

The slap knocks her back against me, but she recovers. She is the Raham I have known before now. She wipes blood from her face and stares defiantly at the man.

"Your time is coming," she states and this time the man completely ignores her as he turns his horse to the side and pulls them off the trail and behind the other men.

As the three slavers ride toward him, Malak sits back in the saddle and draws his broadsword, holding the weapon down and to one side of the horse. He leans over the horse and seems to pet the animal on the neck. The horse turns his head, and it seems to me that Malak is saying something to the animal.

Malak sits back up and holds the sword up just as the horse rears upward and paws at the air with his mighty hooves. I am awed by the sudden transformation as horse and man become one monstrous creature. The horse slams his hooves down and paws at the ground, kicking up a swirl of dust and turns briefly to the side before turning directly forward toward the three men rushing up the hill.

Malak leans forward and the horseman gallops forward casting a racing, dark shadow on the grasslands. The three slavers spread out and rush forward. Malak guides his horse toward the center man, who realizes that he is the target and tries to turn to the side, but Malak's warhorse crashes into the man's horse, biting at the horse, who rears up in fright.

The man swings his sword and misses. Malak slices across the top of the horse's head and cuts the man's throat. The horse falls over, and the man flings out wildly in the air, his sword arching high in the sky end over end, red blood spraying and casting a pink mist in the sun's light. The man falls dead in the grass. The horse stumbles up and runs away as Malak turns his mount, who has galloped past the other two.

"That's one," Raham taunts the guard, who pulls them back and away from the others.

The leader points at three other men, "You three! Kill that man!" he shouts.

The men pull their frightened horses back and refuse, staring upward as Malak charges forward toward the second slaver before him. Malak's warhorse attacks first as Malak swings his broadsword. The slaver ducks the first blow, but his horse rears up in terror as the warhorse bites at her neck. The rider falls backward, landing hard in the brush on his back. The warhorse rears upward, and the man screams as the horse stomps the man.

"That's two," Raham taunts.

124

"Shut up!" the guard shouts as his horse fidgets backward from the fight on the hill after seeing the great warhorse wound a horse and kill the rider.

"Just saying. Your best bet is to leave us here and ride away. Otherwise, he'll get you as well." Raham says louder so everyone can hear her.

Raham continues, "That's a Bene Elohim warrior. Even the Faireadoiri fear the Bene Elohim. You better run. I've heard that when they are tired of killing their enemy, they stop to eat and send their warhorses to finish the job."

I roll my eyes at my friend's statement, but then again, it could be true. What do I know about such things?

"I told you to kill him!" the leader shouts, but no one moves.

Meanwhile, the third slaver, seeing the demise of the other two, tries desperately to turn his horse away, but it is too late. Malak pulls his horse to one side of the dead man under the horse's feet and squares up on the approaching slaver, whose horse turns suddenly in fear. Malak strikes, there is another spray of blood that glistens in the afternoon sun, and the man falls face down in the dirt as his horse runs away.

"Cowards!' the leader shouts and draws his sword.

"He is only one man!" he screams and charges.

One man who just killed three of yours, you fool, I think.

No one follows, but the rest of the slavers suddenly turn their mounts away as one unit and flee across the grasslands, pulling us along with them,

I look over my shoulder as we run and see Malak charging toward the oncoming slaver, who seems to be a better warrior than any of the other three. Their swords clash, and sparks fly as metal scrapes against metal. The horses turn and fight each other as the two men parry each other's blows. Dust rises, and the two warriors are suddenly hidden by the brilliant sun. We gallop behind the hill, and I can no longer see.

We ride as fast as we can now, our guard pulling us behind him. The men are frightened and ride toward a city by the sea that suddenly reveals itself as we gain the top of the ridge and descend to the other side. Luckily for them the port city is near or else, I am sure Malak would have eventually killed them all one by one.

CHAPTER TWENTY-TWO

The men only slow their horses when they finally approach the gates to the city by the sea. I am immediately affronted by the terrible smell of the place as we enter the wooden gates on the road filled with mud and standing blackened water.

Beggars line the entrance to the town and fade back into the shadows at the approach of the slavers. Like the village of Glenmorrow, the main street through the center of the town is filled with street vendors, but there is nothing redeeming about the appearance of this town. Everything seems worn, dirty, and broken down, like a recent storm had blown through the place and ripped many of the structures apart, and no one bothered to rebuild them. They only covered the holes in the roofs with tarps and supported the leaning walls with blackened beams.

We turn down a side road, which reveals a lane that follows a row of low buildings to the port and several ships docked by the wharfs. Several taverns line one side of the street, and scantily clad women lounge along the boardwalk. At the sight of the slavers, the women saunter forward to the line of men on horseback. Several of the men lean down from their horses and grab at the woman. Some even pull them up on their horses as they laugh and then drop them back down with a promise to return as soon as they are paid.

As Raham and I ride by, the women look up at us and stare, and I turn my face away from their gaze. I had never seen such women as these. Raham stares straight ahead and says not a word as they mock and taunt us with lewd comments, which surprises me.

I am tired and sore and seem to smell even worse than the city itself, which says a lot about how filthy I am. As bad as this place seems, at least soon, I will be free of this horse. Maybe even they will put me somewhere where I can sleep under a roof again and not on wet, cold ground under a leaky tarp.

I see a large stone building that extends all the way to the wharf, and across from the stone building, there is a large open-sided wooden shelter. I see a group of people across from me by the wharf looking away and into the open-sided structure.

Several of them hold their hands up one by one as one man shouts, "Two hundred gold pieces. Do I have two hundred and ten?" a man shouts.

"Okay, two hundred and ten, do I have two hundred twenty? Two hundred twenty," he continues.

"You won't find a better work crew. Fresh off the boat, they are hard workers," the man says as I look through the crowd to see who he is talking about.

"What is this place?" I ask Raham.

"Slave market," she says like she is declaring a disease.

I see past the crowd now and see five men standing in a line and chained together at their ankles.

We thankfully turn past the road and down a side street to where the men pull their horses up to a barn across from the wharf and dismount. A large woman walks from the barn and looks over the group of men and then sees Raham and me sitting bound on the horse.

"Is this all you have?" she asks, "Where's Hunter?"

Our guard answers, "We were first attacked by the queen's men and then just today again. Hunter is dead, and yes, this is all we have,"

He hands the reins to the woman, who looks curiously up at us.

"Are they unsoiled, or did you ruffians spoil them?" she asks.

"We have not touched them. Hunter said they would bring a high price at the market," the guard states.

"Okay, okay. It is something. Go inside, and each of you will be paid, but only half your rate. Two girls are not enough for the full rate. And If I find that you have spoiled them, I will not pay you at all," she warns.

"Lord girls, you look a sight," she says after she looks us over, not seeing my scars as my hair covers most of my face.

"Get them down and take them to the first room. We need to get them cleaned up and dressed properly. The girl's sale is soon," she orders and walks back inside the building.

127

The guard cuts the ropes that tie us together and pulls us from the horse. I almost fall, but Raham catches me as the man stands close over Raham, his foul breath sickening. He takes a lock of Raham's hair and twirls it in his hand as he inspects her like she is some type of animal. He then steps to me and does the same. He pulls the hair back from my face and sees the red scar down on my cheek, across my ear, and down the side of my neck to my shoulder.

He strokes the scar and inspects it even closer as if puzzled by its existence, "You would be a pretty thing, except for that."

He steps back to Raham and pulls her dress away from her neck, "You know, after you clean up, I may buy you. I may even buy the both of you. Oh, what fun we should have."

He grabs her hair and pulls her toward him to kiss her, but Raham spits in his face and jerks her head back. He slaps her, but she remains steadfast before him. He curses her and pulls violently at her hair, and she falls in the mud on her knees. He hits her again across the side of the head, and she cries out in pain as her wound from before is opened. Raham covers her face with her bound hands, and he raises a fist to hit her again.

"No!" I scream, and with all the strength I have in me, I hit him in the groin, and he leans forward in pain. I kick him as I cry in rage. He groans in pain and falls to his knees before me next to Raham. Men laugh all around me as I take his greasy hair in my hands to hold his head and knee him squarely in the face. He cries out, and blood gushes forward, and I hit him again and again as I scream, and the men laugh as he falls over into the mud. I stomp on his stomach, and he rolls over, trying to get up, his eyes wide. I kick him in the side again and again until one of the men finally pulls me away.

Raham stares up at me in astonishment at the rage I had just released and nods her head approvingly, and another man pulls her up, and they take us into the building, leaving the guard lying in the mud groaning in pain. I could not believe what I had done, but I felt no remorse for hurting the man.

Raham spits in his face as we walk by and kicks him again.

"Okay, that's enough," one of them orders and then laughs at the guard on the ground, "She just about killed you, man."

I see his eyes as we are led away and the rage and hate, and I fear that if he ever got the chance, he would kill both of us for the humiliation that we had just caused him. But then again, I did not care.

128

"I didn't know you had it in you, Hannah," Raham remarks.

"I didn't either, but I was tired of his foul stench," I respond, and we both laugh despite the impossible position we are still in.

Our guard takes us into a room and closes the door behind us. We hear the distinctive click of the lock. The room is totally bare with a small, caged window that looks out over the harbor that allows fresh sea air in, which is a welcome relief to the awful stench of the place. The walls are cold, gray granite, the floor is cobblestone.

We are in the room for only a few minutes and then hear someone outside the door and jingling keys. I instinctively grab Raham's arm, and she steps close. I feel that I cannot take much more, but what choice do I have? Hopefully Malak has reached the city by now. He must know that the slavers have taken us here.

We stand before the door, and I take a deep breath to steady myself for whoever or whatever is coming through the door. The person finally finds the right key, unlocks the door, and pushes it wide open before us revealing a girl, not much bigger than myself. She wears a simple gray dress and white apron and holds in her hand towels and two sets of clothing that are neatly folded, as well as two sets of shoes.

"Follow me," she says softly and turns away.

For a moment we both stand at the door, and I cannot speak for what Raham is thinking, but I am thinking that instead of following the girl, we should turn the other way and run from this place. The girl turns and steps back in front of the door.

"Look, don't make it hard. There is no escape from this place. The doors are locked from the outside and guarded. I am to make sure that you are properly bathed, clothed, and fed. If you don't come with me, the guards will strip you naked here in this room and bathe you, and I assure you that you will regret not following me," she states and stares at us, "It's your choice."

We heed her warning and step out from the room and immediately notice a guard standing down the hallway in front of the door leading to the outside. Through the window across from the door, I see the ships in the port outside.

"Good, now come with me. I have warm baths for you," the girl remarks and walks down the darkened hallway leading deeper into the building.

129

We follow the girl as she turns one way and then another down the hallway, lined with granite rock and windowless, the only light coming from small candles at intervals on small ledges on each side of the hallway. We reach a wooden door at the end of the hall, and the girl hands each of us our own towel, a simple dress, and a pair of shoes. Seeing the shoes, I look down at my feet, remembering that I have been barefoot since being taken. My feet are red, scarred, and filthy.

The girl unlocks the room and as the door opens, bright light floods the darkened hallway. We follow her through the door, and she turns and closes the door behind us.

We are in a very large room with a row of beds down one side of the wall. There are several vanities, a few tables, and several chairs as well. I count at least twelve beds, but there is no one in the room but the three of us. On the far side of the room, there are two large tubs with steam rising upward from the hot water inside.

"You need to thoroughly clean yourself and throw your old clothes down the laundry bin. Miss Harriet will be in shortly to inspect you. Don't clothe yourself until after she sees you," the girl orders and then leaves the room, locking the door behind her.

"What is this place?" I ask.

Raham looks around the room. She places the clothing on a vanity and walks over to one of several windows. They are set high on the wall, and she must stretch herself to just barely see. Metal bars cover the windows. Because they are so high, all she can see is the blue sky. She then checks the doors to see if she can somehow pick up the lock, but there are no locks. The doors are bolted from the other side.

"Looks like a prison," she comments.

"What can we do? Raham, they intend to sell us at the slave market."

"I don't know, but we'll think of something. We must. Plus, Malak is sure to find us," she answers.

She takes the clothing and walks over to the bath. She tests the water, "Right now, I think we'll feel much better if we just do what the girl told us to. At least we can get rid of these awful clothes and be clean."

130

As usual, Raham sees the good in all bad situations. A few moments later, we are both in the bath, which immediately begins to soothe my tired muscles. There is soap that smells of the ocean, and I take some. The water is hot in contrast to the room itself. Steam rises slowly, swirling around us, and the water turns brown quickly because of my filth. I scrub myself the best I can and then take my hair and do my best to clean it. Raham does the same, and I notice how tenderly she cleans the wound over her ear of the caked blood and dirt.

After a few moments, the door opens with an overly loud screech and the same woman that first greeted us outside steps in. I jump at the sound of the opening door and drop the soap. The woman walks in to stand in front of us. In contrast to our surroundings, the woman has a kind face, but knowing what she does here overcasts her kind appearance with an ugly evil.

"Did the men violate you?" she asks.

Raham shakes her head, no, but I do not understand her question. They treated us horridly the entire trip. Is that what she means?

She looks directly at me, "Child, did the men have sex with you? Did they rape you?"

Raham speaks, "She knows nothing of men. They did nothing to her in my presence, but I do not know beforehand."

The woman sighs and motions with her hands. "Stand up and let me see you."

I hesitate and look over at Raham. "It's okay, Hannah. Do as she says."

I stand up, as does Raham. The room is suddenly cold against my wet skin. She stands directly in front of me, and I see that she is taken aback by the scars. She follows them down my face and across the side of my body to my waist with her stare. She reaches out to touch them and turns my face to see the side of my neck.

Then she suddenly reaches down, and I jump as she touches me between my legs. "Did the men touch you here? Did they do anything to you here?"

I shake my head no, thinking to myself that she has violated me more than any of those men did, even as bad as they all were to me.

131

The woman steps back. "Okay then, dry off and clothe yourself. You will eat and sleep in this room until we find a buyer for you. A Faireadoiri such as yourself will bring me a handsome price to the nobility," she states as she looks over Raham. "But you girl is worthless to me. I think it will be the brothel for you," she states when she looks back at me.

I think of the women on the streets as we came in. Was I to be one of those? I would kill myself first, I think and stare at Raham in complete hopelessness as the woman leaves us.

I begin to cry then, falling back into the water. If only I could go home to my little cabin in the mountains, to see my mother again, to stay hidden away from all the horrors of this world. I sink below the water and think that I will end it now. All I must do is breathe deeply in the water and I would leave this horrible place. I would end my life that has no hope. My scars had doomed me to be like one of those horrible women by the road that were used by men for things that I knew nothing about but seemed to be worse than anything that I could imagine. I had been told that I was the wife of a king, but how could that be with my terrible scars? No king could ever wish to marry me.

In desperation, I take a deep breath under the water and immediately feel the incredible pain that comes with water being sucked into my lungs. I gasp and struggle to rise, and then strong hands grab me by my shoulder and pull me up. I violently cough up the water and gasp for air as Raham hugs me tight. I cling to her, the only friend I have in this horrible world I have found myself in, and cry deeply, uncontrollably, as she holds me tightly above the water.

"It's okay, Hannah. I promise you that we will be free again. It's okay. We will find a way. Help will come. You will see." She soothes.

I continue to cry, but less so until finally there is nothing to cry about left within me. How can one so young as Raham says she is so wise beyond her years? The Faireadoiri are truly an amazing race to breed such strong people so young. After a few moments I suddenly stop crying. There seem to be no tears left within me.

"You, okay?" she asks.

I shake my head, yes.

"Good, because I am freezing and so are you," she states and drops me with a splash back in the tub.

132

I pull myself out of the water and grab the towel to dry, embarrassed at myself for what I had just done.

"Sorry. I just lost it," is all I can say.

Raham looks up at me as she ties the leather shoes. "It's okay. We are in this together, and we will get out of this together."

After a few moments we are dressed in similar cotton dresses that button in the front and flair out some at the hips and hang down to just above our ankle high, leather shoes. I think that my dress is the most comfortable dress that I have worn in a very long time.

The girl from before brings us food, and we both sit at the table. I think that tomorrow may bring horrible things, but on this day, there is food, we are dry, and we have a bed in which to sleep on. And I feel that right now, that is enough for me.

CHAPTER TWENTY-THREE

Malak lay on his back and stared at the setting sun. He looked to his side and took hold of the hilt of his blood-stained sword, the point still embedded in the slaver's chest. The man lay open eyed and dead beside him. Malak turned his head in the other direction and was rewarded by a wet kiss from his horse. He pushed the horse away and sat up. The animal snorted at him and prodded his back with his nose.

"Well, that didn't work as I planned," he commented to the horse. The horse hit the back of his head lightly with his nose as if to say, "No kidding."

"Stop that," Malak ordered, "I could have used a bit more help, my friend."

The horse shook his head and prodded Malak again.

"So, you think I have lost my touch, do you?" Malak remarked as he surveyed a bloody wound across his thigh. He stretched his shoulders and felt the pain on one from the impact the slaver's sword had made, luckily with the flat side. Malak had to admit that the slaver had been a worthy adversary, well-trained as a warrior. He admired the man's fighting ability even as he loathed what he did as a slaver.

Malak may have knocked himself unconscious as he fell backward from his horse with the last attack. How long had he been lying on the ground, he thought. The sun was quickly retreating behind the low range of distant hills. His horse pushed at him again.

"I know. I know. I got to get moving. You know, you could have been more help there. Maybe it is you who are losing his touch," Malak remarked as he stood.

The horse snorted, shook his head, and stepped back from Malak.

"Oh, come on, old man. Can't you take a joke?" Malak said as he mounted the horse.

The slavers had to be heading toward the port city, which is just a few miles away. It would be dark soon, but that was okay with Malak. He knew where the slave market was and where they would most likely take the girls. He would find his way through the town by way of the water and try and find a way to get them out, hopefully before the next market.

The slavers had ridden across the grassland, creating an easily followed trail. Malak followed the slaver's trail until he climbed over a low rise and saw the port city stretching below him in the dark. The wooden gate was already closed for the night leaving scattered nomads, beggars, and travelers to set up their camps outside the palisade. Their individual campfires lit up the road leading into the town, but Malak stayed clear of the light. He led his horse across the slope of the hill toward the bay.

After a few moments of following the outline of the wall, Malak heard crashing waves out in the darkness. The salt air blew upward from waves that crashed against a rocky cliff. Malak dismounted his horse and cautiously walked up through thick salt grass growing on sand dunes to the cliff edge. He heard the ocean below him but could not see down into the dark void. Off to one side, he saw the lights from several ships anchored in the harbor and closer in, the wharf lights. The wooden palisade extended to the edge of the cliffs and then turned inward toward the wharf for a short distance, rows of houses constructed against the walls on the inside. Several balcony lights glowed from above the walls.

"Well. boy, it looks like I'm going to have to climb down to the bay from here," Malak commented to his horse as he pulled the broadsword from the scabbard and swung it over his back and tied it tightly in place.

"You stay out of sight now and listen for my call. And be quick about it if you hear my whistle," Malak said.

The horse shook his head and pushed Malak forward as if to say, "Go on with it then."

Malak had a 100-foot section of rope. He hoped it would be enough. He fastened a loop and tied the rope to one of the few trees that tenaciously grew on the exposed escarpment. He pulled on the rope, tested his weight on the tree and then lowered himself down into the darkness as his horse looked over the edge of the cliff toward him from above.

135

Malak did not need the rope for the first section as the cliff was somewhat at an angle and covered with rock outcrops, but about twenty feet down, the cliff suddenly broke off directly down into the blackness. In the dark, Malak felt around for a foothold below him, but there was nothing. Only a black void and the crashing waves far below. He grabbed the
rope tightly and released himself from the rocks. He swung out and then back and found a foothold, but the face of the cliff was straight down at this point and seemed to be so to the ocean, but he could not be for sure.

Malak slowly very carefully lowered himself down toward the waves, which seemed to be further down than he had anticipated. If his rope was not long enough, then what could he do in the dark? The rope had to be long enough, he thought. He continued to lower himself and the sound of the crashing waves grew closer, but he could still not see anything below him. And then he realized that the end of the rope was only a few feet below his feet. He swung himself around so his back was against the rock and tried to see anything below him. The ship lights were almost even with him now, so he had to be close to the ocean. But was there a sandy beach below him or rocky crags that could break his legs if he jumped down?

The waves were close enough that he felt the salt spray as they crashed against the cliff wall below him. Malak felt with one foot until he found a narrow ledge. He placed his weight on the ledge and pulled himself over to one side. He found another ledge and lowered himself to the very end of the rope just as a wave hit him squarely on the back, the force knocking the rope away from him, and he grabbed with his hands at the rock face. Another wave hit him, and he fell back into the ocean below in a seething pool of crashing water that pulled him down and then knocked him back up against the cliff wall. He struggled until he found his footing on a sandy bottom against the cliff wall. A few moments later, he finally found a place where the cliff broke away, and the shoreline extended away from the cliff, forming a barrier island that jutted out toward the ocean and protected the inner bay where the ships were docked by the wharf.

Malak crawled out of the waves as they crashed over him until he finally emerged out of the water and onto dry land. He pulled himself up at the edge of the docks and looked back from where he had come. The high cliffs rose above him, black and ominous against the night sky. He thought he saw movement at the rim which must have been his horse.

He leaned against the pier for a moment, collecting himself from the ordeal and breathing deeply. Above him, the pier extended back into the shadows, partially illuminated by several small fires burning in metal barrels. Several men walked by the nearest barrel, the shapes casting shadows over the fire, and Malak leaned further back against the post, partially under the pier itself. They talked quietly to themselves, and one laughed.

The men walked back toward the street away from him, and Malak climbed out from the pier and emerged on the cobblestone street that ran alongside the wharves that were full of trade goods that had recently been unloaded from one of the ships. He noticed a guard by one of the fires and several men lounging on the street. A woman shouted to one of them, and the men laughed at her words. Another woman appeared, and the men followed them up the street.

The street was lit by lanterns, and several taverns were situated between larger, stone buildings. He heard laughter and music from the closest tavern. Malak needed to find a place to dry himself and mingle with the people to see if he could find information on where the slavers took their captives. He knew this town was known on both sides of the ocean as a place to buy and sell slaves. The girls had to be somewhere near, but he did not know where to begin to look. He also knew that the slavers would be near as well. That did not concern him too much. He could take care of them, but that was not his mission. He needed to find the girls, free them, and get out of the town as quickly as possible.

Malak gathered his shoulder length hair to wring the water out as much as he could. He noticed a clothesline in an alley and helped himself to a towel to dry himself somewhat, but he was soaked from head to toe. He placed the towel back on the line. It would have to do; he thought and left the alley and walked to the nearest tavern. He was hungry, thirsty, and cold.

He stepped up on the boardwalk and stood a moment at the entrance, looking over the batwing doors. The room was full of people, sailors, workmen, women, and a group of possible slavers sitting together at a table back against the bar. He did not know if they were the same slavers he had encountered, but they were dressed very similarly. Smoke filled the room; a man played the piano next to the entrance, and men gambled and drank and harassed the women who laughed and drank and harassed them back.

Malak pushed the batwing doors apart and walked in and no one seemed to notice him. He stopped briefly at the door until he spied an empty table in the corner opposite the piano and away from the bar. He walked to the table and took a seat, his back to the wall. From there, he could see the entire room.

A woman walked over, "Well, hello. You lookin for a good time, dear?" she asked.

"No, just a bit of food and drink and a place to get out of the cold for a bit."

The woman shrugged, "Your loss. We have beef and bread, whiskey, beer, and mead."

Malak answered, "I'll take some beef, bread, and water."

The woman eyed him strangely, shrugged her head, and walked back to the bar. She returned a few moments later with a plate of sliced beef and bread on a wooden plate and a flask of water. She lay it down in front of him, and he gave her two coins.

"You sure you don't want something else. The water here tastes like the ocean," she remarked.

"No thanks, this will be fine."

The woman left him to himself. He began eating the beef, which tasted pretty good, but the bread was stale, and the water tasted like fish. As he ate, he listened to the people all around him, hoping someone would say something that would help him. If the townspeople saw Raham, they would know that the slavers had captured a Faireadoiri, which was a rare thing.

Malak motioned for the waitress to come back, and he ordered mead to drink. She was right. The water was undrinkable. When she returned, he finished the last of the beef and drank. The mead was warm, sweet, and very strong. He focused all his attention on the five slavers at the table across from his.

138

"That girl bout killed you, man," one man said and laughed. His voice was slurred by too much drink.

A second one turned, and Malak saw his face. He recognized the man as the one who had been leading the girls because of his half-beard and thinning hair. One eye was red and swollen. "You just wait until I get my hands on that little bitch. She won't sell at the market. Who would want a girl scarred the way she is? I bet I could buy her."

"Oh, leave it be," another remarked.

"No way. She's got it comin," Half Beard said and drank from his flask, the beer running down his beard. He was drunk as well.

"You won't get a chance to buy her. I heard that a nobleman already heard that we brought in the Faireadoiri girl, and he will buy her tonight. The other girl is her maid, so he may take them both."

Half Beard slammed his flask down and stood up, "Well then, I better get my satisfaction now," he said and staggered toward the door.

The others just shrugged and let him leave. Malak waited a minute and walked out the door behind him.

CHAPTER TWENTY-FOUR

I lay in the bed next to Raham and neither one of us can sleep even though we are exhausted from our journey of the past few days. After eating the meal prepared for us, the servant girl had come in, taken the dishes, and left without saying a word. Thankfully no one else had bothered us. Even though I desperately needed sleep, sleep eludes me. Raham lay on her back beside me totally still. I look over and see her eyes glimmer in the candlelight. She lay awake, staring up at the ceiling.

Music plays somewhere off in the distance. A wagon travels by the window, but otherwise there is no sound except for the piano music that floats on a night sea breeze blowing in through the open windows and refreshes the air in the room. I pull the blanket up in defense of the night air.

I fear sleep because with it comes wild dreams that haunt my night and sometimes even my days. I also fear waking up in the morning to face whatever new horrors waited. Now, I am warm and lying in a bed with a full stomach and a roof over my head. But the fear of tomorrow keeps me from sleeping. If I stay awake, I stay in this moment of peace. But if I sleep, I will wake up in the morning to face an unknown fate that frightens me.

I want to talk with Raham, but what can I say? What can she say that will make our situation any better? Earlier, I had wished to kill myself. The fear of what lay ahead had been too much for me to bear. Raham had saved me. She had brought me back with the promise of hope. The only thing I have left is hope, hope that somehow Malak is out there, somewhere close, and he will save us.

I look back over to Raham. She still stares at the ceiling. "What?" she asks without looking at me. "We need to sleep, Hannah."

"I know, but I cannot. I fear what will happen when I wake up."

She reaches over with her arm and pulls me close to her. "I do as well. But we cannot let fear overcome us. We do not have a spirit of fear, Hannah. We must subdue fear, master it, bend it to our will, and use it to overcome what will happen tomorrow. Malak is out there. He will not stop until he rescues you. Hannah, we both will do whatever it takes to get you to where you need to be."

"I don't understand why you say such things. Why does Malak seek me? Who am I that you both say such things? That your family said the same even though they never knew me?" I ask. I really did not know. I lay my head on her shoulder like I used to do with Mother.

"Hannah, I don't know the answers. All I know is that you are the Bean an Ri and it is my job to help you in your journey, wherever that journey takes you. On the night when we left my parents, I knew that I most likely would never see them again. But that is okay because I always knew since my creation that I am one of the Faireadoiri whose only job is to guide the Bean an Ri. I was trained from birth to do so. When you showed up in our camp, I knew that it was my time. That is all I know; all I have ever known. Your mother told you to seek the carpenter, and that is all we need to know."

I cannot fathom what she just told me. I could not understand what she said. But I know that I must accept it. Something deep inside me says that what she says is true, and that is the hope that I have. But what of Malak?

"But what of Malak? Why does he search for me? Why does everyone seem to be after me?" I ask.

"Hannah, Malak told me that he is searching for the wife of his king. When he saw you by the ferry, he immediately knew that you were the one." Raham looks down at me, her eyes glistening in the light. "Hannah, I know the Bene Elohim. They are a higher race. They travel between the realms in ways that even the Faireadoiri cannot do. I know for a fact that once they are given a mission, they will accomplish that mission. He has been tasked with finding you. He has found you, and he would travel through the very gates of Hell if he had to. Don't worry, Hannah. Whatever happens, you will be saved."

"But what about you, Raham? Will he save you as well?" I ask.

Raham smiles and looks away to the ceiling and then back to me. "I hope so, Hannah. I really do, but you are the only one truly worth saving." She looks away again. "But I hope he will save me as well."

141

I think a moment of her words and remember the many things she has said of him since we had been taken by the slavers. I know that she even dreamed of Malak in her sleep. I know that I am naive about men and love, but I do understand more than people think that I do. I know that Raham has feelings for the man. Part of me is jealous, especially now that I know Malak is searching for me, not for himself but for his king. But I remember the way he looked at her that day by the pond and the way that she looked at him.

"You love him, don't you?" I state.

She looks down at me, her eyes wide, "That's crazy, Hannah. How can I love him? I don't even know him." She shakes her head and turns away, and I sit up in bed.

"Oh, you do. You are smitten by the man. I see it in your face, I hear it in your words," I say, and she looks back at me, her eyes wide. "I even hear it in your sleep. You are in love with him. Is he with you?"

She blinks and looks away, "I'm sorry, Hannah. Are you mad?"

"Why would I be mad? I admit I was jealous at first a few days ago when I realized that you were in love with him. I still am, I guess. He searches for me, not for himself. But I see that you are truly smitten by him."

I lay back down. Part of me, a part that I wish to push deep inside myself and forget, is terribly jealous. Raham is beautiful. I am not. That is the truth. I still do not believe that any king would want me. Why would he? But why would a king that I never knew and who has never seen me send the Bene Elohim to search for me? I have so many questions. But Mother said to find the carpenter, and he would explain, and that is what I must do.

"I don't think you have anything to worry about, Raham. Your gentleman will save you just the same as he will save me."

With that statement I close my eyes and soon fall asleep.

I stand at the threshold of an overlarge, double door made of elaborately carved, dark wood. I look down and see that I am wearing a beautiful white gown embroidered with lace and pearls. My hair is free around my shoulders except for a few trusses that are braided with the same lace and pearls. I feel the presence of people all around me and turn my head to see thousands of men and women standing in the courtyard below the stairs that stretch as far as I can see among golden towers, walls, fluttering flags, and banners.

142

I feel totally at home in this place, as if I have always lived here, even if the place seems like a dream from another time, place, and realm. Something about the place is very familiar, but I cannot fathom why I think so. I know that I belong here. That this is my home. That this has always been my home. To my right, the mountains stand tall against a brilliant sky, the flanks covered in trees of all colors, brilliant in the sunlight. Flocks of multicolored birds playfully fly among the trees. Butterflies flutter aimlessly among the meadows covered with brilliant flowers. A cool breeze blows over me, filled with the scent of the flowers.

I hear no sound except for the breeze flowing through the courtyard. The people behind me all stand totally still, no movement, no sound, all staring up at me. I walk up the steps to the door as if I know what I am to do, but I do not. I am just mesmerized by the door and what lies beyond it.

There are two massive warriors standing before me, one on each side of the door. They are fully covered in brilliant golden armor, only their faces visible to me. One is a man, and one is a woman, both somehow familiar to me, but I cannot remember why. They stare straight ahead at full attention, and just as I step to the door, one turns and opens the left door, and the second turns and opens the right door. They hold the doors open to me, and I step through the threshold. The man stares beyond me, but the woman looks directly at me, and when I look at her, she smiles and winks at me. I know her, I think. But how? She looks beyond me, and I step through the door, and it closes behind me.

I now stand in a very large room, twice as long as it is wide, with vaulted ceilings. Massive wooden columns line both sides of the room. The columns are beautifully carved with a variety of animals in vivid detail. They seem to be living, breathing creatures that move around the columns. The floor is blue marble that appears as the ocean on a calm day. I look closer at the floor and see fish swimming in the marble. Brilliant shafts of multicolored rainbows swirl across the ceiling, and I notice birds flying within the ceiling panels and trees, grass, and flowers growing within the walls. The room is alive with all of creation.

143

I am the only person in the room. For a moment, I stand in wonder at the beautiful creation of the room itself, but then I see movement at the far end of the room. I take a step forward, and immediately, I stand at the other end of the room, facing a throne before me that sits in front of a forest of trees that grows in the wall itself, fully alive, the leaves fluttering in the wind, the scene full of animals and birds that play. The entire room is one large, living organism. The throne sits empty before me. There are two wooden chairs before me, very simply made in contrast to the rest of the room.

I suddenly see myself sitting on one of the chairs, a king sitting beside me, holding my hand in his. How can this be? I am standing here before the throne while sitting on the throne next to the king. How is that possible?

The figures disappear and I am standing alone again in the room that now appears to stretch in all directions for as far as I can see.

And then two men stands before me, one dressed as a king, and one dressed as a normal workman. The king is handsome beyond belief and wears a purple rope and crown. He smiles at me and holds out his hand, but I look at the second man. He is also handsome, but ruggedly so with a short beard and hair, dark eyes that shine brightly and a loving smile that I have known from before. But what is before?

I know that I must make a choice, and I choose the king who takes my hand and leads me to one side. The other man lowers his hand and I see sadness in his eyes as he steps up to the throne.

I am now standing in the forest in a simple dress holding a basket full of mushrooms, holding a tree as the earth shakes around me.

I wake up suddenly. Someone is opening the door to our room in the dark. The candles had burned out as we slept.

"Raham!"

"I hear; get up, Hannah. Someone is coming in. Maybe this is our chance," she orders.

The door opens allowing light to enter the room. The first in is the large woman from before holding a lantern. Behind her are two guards, one who lights several lanterns in the room.

"Get up, girls, and stand in the light," the woman orders, and Raham and I stand and walk over to the light. I grab Raham's hand in mine. Fear wells up within me, but I remember Raham's words. I take control of my fear and use it to my advantage. I try to, at least, but it does not seem to work.

"You are in luck. We have a noble gentleman from across the ocean who is looking for a Faireadoiri, and maybe he will take the both of you," she states.

Another man walks in. He is very tall and dressed like a dandy with long, flowing robes and jeweled hands. His hair is longer than my own, falling over his shoulders to the base of his back. In the light, I think he wears makeup. I have never seen a man dressed in such a way. He walks up to me in a characteristically female way, one hand on his hip and another touching his cheek. He stands before Raham, who, although taller than me, is only as tall as the man's shoulders. She stands before him, staring at him with a defiant glare.

"Oh, my dear one. You are quite the specimen. Beautiful red hair of the likes I have never seen before." He looks over to the woman, "Is she pure? Good. She is very beautiful. She will be most welcome in my court."

He walks around Raham, and she turns with him.

"Watch her, my lord. She is a Fairedoiri warrior," a guard cautions. "Watch the dark haired one as well. She almost beat one of the slavers to death yesterday."

The man circles Raham and steps away, "Of yes, you are a warrior. I have never owned a Fairedoiri. And a redhead. So rare. So intriguing." He looks over at me. "Now for you. A warrior as well. You have the body of a Fairedoiri, but your face. You are marked." He pulls my hair away from my face.

Before I would have lowered my head in shame, but I stand straight and stare at him with contempt, even hatred as he inspects me. He shakes his head no and looks at the woman, "I will only take the red head."

"You will pay the price? I will give you the other for free," the woman answers.

"No, only the red-haired one. Give the other to the guards," he states and turns and walks out the door. "Take her to my ship. We set sail as soon as everything is loaded."

145

"No!" Raham screams. "She is my maid. She has always been with me!"

"I already have maids," the man says from beyond the door.

Raham rushes the door and a guard steps in her way. She hits him square in the face with her fist and he steps back and faulters. She grabs his sword, but the second guard pushes her away.

"Chain her!" someone shouts as I rush forward as well in desperation. I grab at the man's face and claw him, drawing blood. He screams and backhands me with his fist. My head explodes in pain, and I fall back against the bed.

"Get the other one! Good god, she'll kill you given the chance!"

I stand up. Raham struggles desperately, but the woman chains her arms together and jerks the chain hard, causing her to fall on her face on the floor. The second guard hits me again, and I fall back on the floor, dazed. Raham screams at them in her own language as they drag her out the door, shutting me in the room.

"What do we do with the dark-haired one?" I hear a man ask.

"I'll rent her to anyone who will have her until she is used up, then I'll take her down to the brothel. She will never be worth more than that," the woman answers.

I lay on the floor in a heap. I want to cry, but this time, I swear I will not. I must do as Raham said. I must take control of my fear and use it to my advantage. Malak must come. He had to, but I fear for Raham. Will he be able to save her as well?"

CHAPTER TWENTY-FIVE

I lay on the floor until my head clears of the pain and stand up. I taste the salt and iron flavor of blood as it runs over my mouth and feel the cut across my forehead. Another scar, I think. I crawl up on the bed and peer out the window. There is currently one ship in the port, so that must be where they are taking Raham.

I must get free of this place, but how? I check the back door to the room, but it is locked. The front door is locked as well. I check each of the windows, but the bars across the windows are secure, all except one. I can twist it, so there is a possibility that I can twist it free of the cement that holds it to the rock wall.

I pull the bar, and it moves as cement chips fall away. I continue to work with the bar with all my strength, desperate to break it free. With each pull and twist, the hole in one side of the cement widens until the rod seems clear. But now I need to release the other side. That side is tighter, but as I pull on it, the cement begins to fall away ever so slowly. I don't know how long I work, but eventually, the rod pulls free. My hands are bloody from the work, but the rod is free, and there may be enough room now for me to crawl through the window.

I pull myself up enough to look out the window and realize that I seem not to be on the ground floor of the building. The cobblestone road is at least twenty feet below me. That means I will need to go out the window feet first and jump to the road, which could injure me, but anything is better than my current situation.

I climb back out of the window and realize for the first time, that I am barefoot. By candlelight I find my shoes and put them on and as I am tying them, I hear someone outside the door. I desperately try to climb out the window feet first but cannot, so I give up and pull myself up headfirst into the opening.

"Oh no, you don't," a man's voice calls from the shadows, and someone pulls me from the window by my feet and throws me hard to the floor on my face. I turn and grab for the bar, but I see a boot kick the rod away from me.

I crawl quickly backward away from the man to the wall and pull myself up by the bed. The man lights a lantern and then a second one. "Oh, no, we will have none of that. You owe me, girl. You made a fool out of me. Now you will pay. Oh, you will pay, you will. All night long, you will pay. Yes, you will."

I suddenly realize with terror who the man is. He is the one that I beat yesterday, the man with the half beard. I desperately break free from his out-reached arms and jump over the bed, kicking it back to him. He staggers and falls. He smells of beer, and I realize that he is drunk.

I run toward the door, but he reaches out and trips me, and I fall hard to the floor. He recovers himself grabs my legs and pulls me toward the bed as I claw at the floor and scream.

"Screaming won't do any good in here, girl. People hear screams all the time in here and no better than to see. You are mine for the night you are. And you owe me, yes, you do. All night long, you owe me."

He staggers as he drags me, but even though drunk, he is twice my size and too strong for me to break free. He flips me on my back, and one leg frees, and I kick him as hard as I can. He curses me, but before I can escape, he grabs me again and throws me up on the bed on my back, knocking the breath from me. I am desperate now, but I will not give up. I will never give up again. I will always fight to the very end. Whatever happens to me, I owe it to Mother, to Raham and her family, and to Malak to fight for my life. They are willing to die for me to protect me. I will fight to the very end.

Half Beard jumps on the bed, and I kick at him again. He falls on top of me, his heavyweight crushing me, but my hands are still free. I claw at his face, pull at his beard, and gouge his eyes, but he grabs at my hands and then hits me hard in the face with his fist, dazing me, and my head swirls. I cannot pass out. If I do, all will be lost. I must keep awake. I lay still for a few seconds to allow the dizzy spell to stop, but by doing so, he has my hands pinned down as well. I have trouble breathing because of his weight.

"Oh, you are a fighter, that's for sure. Come on, girl, this could be fun for you. It truly can. It doesn't have to be so rough on you," he says, and I spit in his face and struggle again to free my hands, but I cannot.

148

Well, if you going to be that way, I'm goin to tie you." He takes a rope and ties my hands together and then ties the rope to the bed rail. He pushes against me spreads my legs and pulls up my dress.

The terror and fear come forward, and my old self would be crying and begging for him to stop. But my new self will never do that again. I work at the rope as he drunkenly tries to disrobe himself while sitting on me. After a moment, I can loosen the rope, and with all the strength I have in me, I hit him in the nose that I know I most likely had broken earlier with my fists.

Blood sprays over me, and he grunts and falls away. I quickly roll off the bed and struggle to get up, but he swings out and knocks me down. I see the rod pick it up and stand just as he rushes toward me. "I'll kill you, girl," he screams.

I swing the rod and hit him across the face, and he falls back hard on the floor. I turn and run for the door. The door is very heavy, but it is unlocked, and after a couple of pulls, I can open it. I see a man standing at the door and swing the rod at him, but he parries the blow with a sword.

"Hannah?" the man asks.

"Malak?" I say in amazement, holding the rod before me like a sword against his broadsword. I hear Half Beard swearing and running toward me. I drop the rod draw Malak's short sword from his scabbard and turn to face the evil that threatens me.

Half Beard stops when he sees the sword in my hand, and in his drunkenness and rage, he apparently does not notice Malak standing behind me. Half Beard pulls his own sword and raises it high over his head to strike downward. He swings down, but I duck and swirl under him in the way Raham had done and I now remember in the way that Mother had taught me as a child. His sword swings through empty space, but mine strikes true and tears a gaping wound through his mid-section, almost cutting him in half. He staggers backward and drops his blade, his eyes wide with pain, and I hope the fear of dying to a girl that he wished to violate and kill. I step back from him as Malak steps forward beside me. I hold the sword, trembling, crying now softly as my rage subsides. Half Beard falls at my feet. I turn and look up at Malak who gazes down at me. I give him the sword, and he wipes the blood off Half Beard's cloak and sheaths the weapon.

I grab Malak then, holding him tightly, "You came."

"Yes, I did. But it looks like you didn't need me," he says.

I step away and look at the man on the floor. I had never killed a man before. I think a moment about that and realize that I have no remorse, no quilt. He deserved to die. I look up at Malak and smile. "Maybe not, but I did need the sword. I never should have given it back to you."

Malak turns his head to the side and looks at me in a strange way and then looks around the room. "Where's Raham?" he asks.

"They took her, Malak. Earlier tonight, some nobleman came and bought her. They took her to a ship. We must free her," I answer him and walk to the door. I look in the hall and see a guard lying on the floor.

"We have to get you to the carpenter first, Hannah," he says as he gently takes my arm.

"What do you know of the carpenter?" I ask. "That does not matter, we need to get to that ship before it sails first."

"Hannah, the carpenter can prove to you who you really are. There are many people searching for you. There are several that are already in the city. We must get you out of here."

I pull away from him and turn to face him defiantly. Raham has told me why Malak searched for me, but that does not matter. Only Raham matters to me now. "Malak, I will not go with you anywhere until we free Raham first."

He shakes his head. "Fine then. If you will not help, then at least give me your sword, and I will free her myself." I glare at him until he turns away. I continue, "I have spent the last few weeks running from people I do not know. I have seen my mother die trying to protect me. I have seen everyone place their own lives at risk trying to save me from something that I do not even know, including you and Raham, and I am tired of it all. These people wished to sell me as a slave. That man tried to rape me. He would have killed me. And I am tired of running away. I know that I must find the carpenter and maybe he can make me understand why my life has turned upside down. Maybe he can explain the horrible nightmares. Maybe he can answer my questions. But first, whether you help me or not, I will free Raham."

150

I stand before him, staring up to the man, my fist balled tightly, my heart racing, my breathing labored, my head aching and he stares back at me, shakes his head and smiles. "Okay, my lady. I must obey you because you are the wife of my king. So, I give you my sword and I swear my allegiance to you forever more."

My eyes grow wide as he kneels before me and takes my hand in his. I try to gather my composure and try to slow my heart rate. What is he doing? He bows his head and kisses my hand lightly as he places his broadsword, point to the floor before me with his other hand. He looks up at me, and I hold my breath for a moment. "I pledge my sword to your protection, life for your life. I will forever be your servant as the bride of my king. I am Bene Elohim, and know that my word is forever true." He smiles at me again and rises.

I am totally speechless, not fully comprehending what he really said. "Does that mean we go and get Raham?"

"Yes, but first, we need to get ourselves free of this place."

CHAPTER TWENTY-SIX

The men dragged Raham from the stone building and out on the street as she struggled the entire way, trying to free herself. Once on the street, they threw her on a wagon as people walked by while paying no attention to what was happening to her. One man stopped to look, but a guard pushed him away, threatening him with an upraised sword, and he fled down the street.

Raham's main concern was for Hannah, but she could do nothing now to help the girl. Hopefully, Malak would reach her in time if he was even close. He had to be close. He knew that Malak would risk everything as she would to save Hannah. But would he make it in time? She had heard the awful plans that evil woman had for Hannah. Hopefully, Malak would reach her in time. If not, hopefully, Hannah would be able to withstand the awful things that were in store for her. Raham did not know for sure that even she could do so.

The wagon turned down the street that ran alongside the wharf, and Raham saw a drunken slaver walk by, and then, to her astonishment, she thought she saw Malak standing in the shadows watching. The man in the shadows had to be him, she thought. All she saw was a darkened form in the half-light, but the man had to be Malak. She leaned over the rail and looked carefully as the man stepped briefly past the light, and Raham saw his face. It was him! She thought of calling for him but knew that she could not. He had to get to Hannah first. She knew that. Hannah was the only one worth saving, so she lay back into the wagon to await her fate and think of how she could escape.

The wagon stopped, and a man pulled her from the wagon roughly.

"Easy now, idiot," the nobleman scolded. "She is chained. Surely you can handle her now without hurting her." He looked at Raham. "You will be such a wonderful addition to my collection, my dear," he said and touched her face.

152

Raham glared at him and turned away. His time would come, she thought. He laughed at her like a girl does and walked away as Raham stared after him. He dressed like a woman and acted like a woman, but he was a man. She had never seen someone like this person before.

And then she remembered something her father had told her a long time ago. There had been an ancient evil race of men who enslaved women from all over the world, treating them like trophies. They collected women and especially wished to collect Faireadoiri women, but they rarely could. To his knowledge, they had all been killed years before, but they were a race of mankind that could emerge at any time. Could this man be one of those?

One of her guards laughed and whispered to the other one, "I doubt he would know what to do with a woman." He looked over at Raham. "What a waste. Girl, we should take you with us. At least you would be with real men."

Raham looked them both up and down with disdain and laughed, "I don't see men. I see lapdogs who kiss the asal of a dandy for scraps. Take these chains off if you think you are real men and see how long before I an bheirt agaibh a choilleadh." She spits the last words in her native tongue.

"What did you say, girl?" one asked.

"Unchain me and find out. All I know is when I am done with you, you will never be able to be with a woman ever again," she said and turned to follow the dandy up the gang plank to the ship.

She thought of jumping, but with her hands and feet chained, she would drown. She would bide her time, knowing that Malak was surely on his way to find and save Hannah. The guards followed her up the plank, one of them holding the chain that bound her. When they reached the deck of the ship, she saw several sailors eying her as if they had never seen a woman before, much less a Faireadoiri woman. She stared back at each of them. She feared what might happen to her, but she would not let anyone see her fear. She did not have a spirit of fear. She would harness the fear, control the fear, and use the fear for her benefit. She would not let the fear control her, but she would control the fear.

"Take her to the room below mine and lock her in. And for goodness' sake, take off these chains. She is but a girl. She may be Faireadoiri, but she is only a girl and where will she go? We will be in the middle of the ocean. And besides, the chains will ruin her perfect skin," the dandy ordered and looked at Raham. "You see, child. I mean you no harm. I only wish to add you to my collection. You will be well taken care of. I promise."

The guards took her to the forward side of the ship to a door that led down to the lower deck. They walked behind her as she slowly made her well down the steps to a darkened hallway and then to the end of the hall to an open door. They led her in and as one watched her with a drawn blade, the other took the chains off. They then went back to the door.

Raham rubbed her sore arms and smiled at them. They were afraid of her, she thought. She could use that fear to her advantage, and as they watched her, she swirled her hands before her and blew across
her hands and turned their palms outward toward the two men who backed away, their eyes wide with fear.

"Botun mor, botun mor, botun mor," she chanted, and they slammed the door, locking it.

"Witch! That what you are," one shouted.

Raham laughed and wondered how long it would take them to figure out that all she said was, big mistake, three times. She was not chained, which was a big mistake for them to make. The door was locked, and the windows were too small for her to get through, but she could get out. She inspected the lock to the door. It was a simple lock and all the Faireadoiri knew how to pick almost any lock that mankind knew how to make. It was a secret talent that they held close for times such as this. Sometimes locks took a while, but this lock was old and well used. Also, the metal was encrusted with salt from years of being exposed to the ocean air.

She knelt and looked at the lock more carefully. All she needed was something to serve as a pick. She looked around the room and finally saw a small iron pin that held a door to a cabinet in place. She worked the pin loose and then found another and did the same. She returned to the door, and after a few moments, she made the right connection, and the lock opened. That was too easy, she thought. She placed the two pins in her dress pocket, carefully opened the door just a bit, and peeked outside.

One man stood guard at the bottom of the steps, his back facing her. Easy prey, she thought. Raham took a chair in her room and worked one of the wooden legs loose, trying not to make any noise that would alert the guard. She then quietly opened the door very slowly until it was half open and stepped out into the hallway. She crept up to the guard, and before he knew she was there, Raham hit him hard over the back of his head, and he crumbled to the floor. She left the chair leg on the floor and took the man's sword. She tested the weapon. It was not as good as her own, but it was sharp and well balanced.

Raham pulled the unconscious man back into the room, locked the door, and then walked back to the steps that led up to the deck. She noticed that it was now early morning. Soon, the whole ship would be awake, so she needed to get off the ship and go back to the wharf. But first, she needed to see if her suspicions about the dandy were correct.

Upon reaching the deck opening, she poked just her head above the floor and looked around. There were two sailors on the far side of the ship. They were working with the ropes and had their backs to her. She gathered her dress up climbed fully out onto the deck and ran quickly over to the nobleman's room. She checked the door, and it was unlocked. With a final look over her shoulder she entered the room and closed the door behind her and then locked it.

The room was dim and full of shadows that gathered in the corners away from the window's early morning light. A vanity covered in clothes was situated below the window next to a large, canopy bed and two chairs and a desk. A second, closed door was across from her on the side wall away from the window.

155

Raham held the sword before her and looked toward the bed, where she saw movement from behind the veil. She stepped cautiously forward until she saw a woman turning under the covers. Her arm was tied to the bed. When the woman saw her, she pulled herself up, her eyes wide with fear. Raham motioned for her to be still and walked up to her. She was a young girl with long black hair and dark eyes. Her face was bruised, one eye swollen, her hair matted and tangled. Her dress lay in a heap on the floor beside the bed.

Raham kept her eye on the closed door and thought she heard movement in the other room. She picked up the dress and threw it at the girl and motioned for her to hold her arm up. Raham took the girl's arm and cut the rope with her sword. The girl quickly dressed, and Raham went back to the outer door.

Something seemed off to her, but she could not figure out what it was. She needed to just leave things be and get off the ship, but if there was one girl tied up in the room, there might be others in the back room. She would never forgive herself if there were others back there, and she could have saved them but did not.

She motioned for the girl to stay quiet and edged her way to the second door, her sword raised before her. She heard someone cough, and something fell with a loud bang.

The whole room seemed full of evil, the very air smothered in something dark, ancient, and of another realm. What was it? Why did she feel this way? What was this place that she had found herself in? Never before the past few weeks had she ever felt such darkness all around her, but now, with each passing day, she felt it grow ever stronger like the air itself was some malignant organism that drew strength within the realm and would soon suffocate all who breathed it.

It had all seemed to start when Hannah had suddenly appeared on the prairie, Raham realized with full clarity. Hannah was the key. She had to be. Something about her had opened the realm up to something dark and sinister. Raham shook her head. Why had she just now come to that conclusion? Was the room playing tricks on her reasoning? Or was the danger real?

Suddenly the door opened, and the nobleman stepped out. Raham backed away from him in shock. He stood before her dressed only in loose fitting cotton pants, his tattooed chest bare and his face covered with blood. He leered at her, his eyes bloodshot, his eyes yellow as he casually took a towel and wiped the blood from around his mouth and face. Behind him, in the other room, Raham saw two women lying on the floor with their necks cut, yet there was very little blood.

At first, Raham panicked at the grisly sight, but she could not let the evil of this place infect her with fear. Overcome fear, bend it to your needs, use fear for your own purpose.

"Well, well, my dear. Most unfortunate. You were never to see this. Oh well," the man said and motioned with his hand.

There was movement beside her and she turned just in time to see the flashing knife in front of her face. Raham jumped back as the girl rushed her, her eyes bloodshot and yellow as well. She screamed, an unearthly scream of a banshee. Raham distinctively swirled back, her sword raised in front, and the girl impelled herself on the sword as she clawed at Raham's face with one hand and thrust the knife forward with the other. She missed and embedded the knife in the wall directly behind Raham's head, the blade cutting a small section of her red hair. Raham scrambled back in a panic and turned just as the man lunged forward. He had no weapon and misjudged Raham's ability. Raham pushed the girl off the blade, and she crumbled dead on the floor. Raham side stepped and slashed sideways with the sword. The man screamed as the sword slashed away his arm and blood sprayed over the floor. He staggered back and Raham slashed a second time and the man fell dead.

Raham stood totally horrified at what had just happened. It had been so quick, she thought. If she hadn't turned around in time, the girl would have killed her. What evil was this? The man had drunk the blood of the girls. Was that what he had planned for her?

Raham staggered back against the wall and dropped the sword. Her breathing quickened, the shock of the evil she had encountered causing her to become dizzy. Something dark swirled around the room over her. The shadows gathered strength in the corner of the room and settled over the bed and formed a black shape that was almost human, but not quite. Raham stared in horror. She fought the fear that welled up within her. Control fear, subdue it, use it.

157

Whatever evil lay within the dark mass that hovered over the bed had no control over her, she thought. She was Faireadoiri. She could overcome all fear, her thoughts screamed to her, and she regained her composure as the mass swirled in midair and then quickly shot away and disappeared.

Raham looked down at the bodies below her and quickly noticed that the two sets of eyes that stared back up to her in death were no longer bloodshot and yellow. The man had blue eyes and the girl had brown.

Men shouted from behind the door, and someone banged on the door. "Get the keys!" someone shouted.

Raham jumped back! She had to get out of this place! She ran to an open window and peered out and saw the ocean below. The door opened behind her, and men rushed forward. She climbed out the window just before they grabbed for her, and she jumped.

CHAPTER TWENTY-SEVEN

I follow Malak as he cautiously leads me down the hall toward the outer door of the building. I see another guard lying on the floor who moans and rubs his head. He sits up, looks up, and is rewarded with a kick to the head. He falls back unconscious again.

We run down the last hallway and exit the building on a deserted street across from the wharfs. The sun is forming on the horizon, casting the water in a morning glow.

"There, Malak. The ship. That must be where they have taken her." I pull at Malak's arm and point.

"There's a boat," he responds. "Hurry! It looks like they are making their way to leave. We'll have to be quick."

He runs across the street to the dock that extends out into water where a small boat is tied to the dock. I gather my dress up to my knees and run as fast as I can to catch up to him. Malak quickly unties the boat throws the rope in, and jumps in behind it. He turns back just as I catch up to him, breathing heavily, and holds out his hand. The boat backs away from me, and I jump across the void. He catches me and places me into the seat and sits back, grabbing the oars.

His strong arms pull the boat swiftly out toward the ship. I watch as he strains against the oars and with each pull, the boat shoots forward. I suddenly realize that I totally trust this man. I place my life in his hands even though this is only the second time that I have been with him. When I first saw him by the ferry, my heart had quickened at his gaze. When we had encountered him at the pool, I had fallen in love with him in a child's dream, but with the knowledge of why he had searched for me, I no longer felt that way about him. Oh, to be sure, I am infatuated by him, but I know that he is in love with Raham, even though she denies that. And that is okay.

Men shout from the deck of the ship, and I see them running. Malak hears the sound as well and turns briefly to see. He pulls even harder as he sees the mask swirl outward as the ship prepares to set sail. I wish I could help him, but all I can do is watch.

"How will we get on board?" I ask.

"There is a rope ladder to the back. See it? We will pull the boat up to that point. Something is happening and they seem to be running forward. Can you climb?" he asks.

My face darkens in a frown at that remark, and he laughs. "Sorry, of course you can. We climb up, and you take the short sword. After what I saw before, I know that you have been trained in its use."

He pulls hard again, and the men shout, and there is some commotion, and suddenly, we hear a splash in the water forward of the ship. Malak turns the boat to get a better view, but we see nothing at first. And then men lean over the deck as the ship begins to sail away, searching the waters below them. One points toward us.

I see a flash of red in the water and point excitedly, "Malak! It's Raham! She jumped from the ship!"

Malak turns the boat sharply toward where I point, straining to see, and I see his face light up when he sees the red hair of the girl as she desperately swims away from the ship, "I don't think she sees us!" He turns the boat and pulls hard on the oars to intercept her.

"Raham!" I scream.

She turns suddenly and floats, looking frantically around until she sees us. She dives back under the water and swims toward us, and Malak continues pulling the boat forward. A few moments later, Malak pulls on the oars and stops the boat. He leans over the edge, searching for her, but we are both looking in the wrong direction. The boat shakes a bit, and I turn to see her hands grabbing the rail. Malak grabs her and effortlessly pulls her into the boat like a fish.

She falls to the bottom of the boat, her red hair covering her face as she coughs, breathing hard and trembling. I jump down to the bottom and pull her up in my arms, wiping the hair away from her face. She looks up at me and then to Malak, her eyes wide.

"Oh, Raham. I thought all was lost. I thought I had lost you." I say as she pulls herself up to the seat, still breathing hard from her swim.

She catches her breath finally and looks over at Malak who is smiling widely at her. "What are you doing here? You idiot. You should have gotten her away from here. I can take care of myself." She scolds him and then sighs. "I'm sorry Malak. That was unkind. But still, why are you here? You should have left me. Hannah is more important than both of us. I know that more now than ever."

160

"She wouldn't let me, If I didn't agree to save you, she would have come herself." Malak answers, still smiling.

Raham sighs again and looks at me and then back at Malak as I smile as well. "What? Malak? Hannah? What are you doing?"

"I'm happy to see you again, Raham. I thought I had lost you as well," he answers, and Raham suddenly blushes and looks away.

For a few moments, I hold my friend tightly to me as she recovers from her ordeal, whatever it was. I see that the arm of her dress is covered in blood, and her hand is cut. Malak continues oaring, but not toward the wharf. He is taking us across toward the cliffs up the beach from the city itself.

Raham sits up. "I'm okay. That swim took it out of me," she comments and looks at Malak with eyes that must have showed something to him that I did not see for he looks back at her in alarm.

"What happened up there?" he asks.

"I'm not sure, but it ain't good. There is an evil on that ship that I have never seen before. Malak, something terrible is in the land. We must get Hannah to the carpenter and quickly."

"Yeah, I have felt it as well, ever since the earthquake. There is a darkness over the land from ancient times," he remarks.

I remember the dream I had the night before. I had awoken suddenly in the forest of my youth on the very day of the earthquake. The day before all of this had started. I think of what they say but choose not to say anything. I feel for the amulet. I want to show it to them, the only friends I have in the world, but I know that I should not. Mother had said not to show it to anyone until I knew to do so. It is not the time. So, I say nothing. But I know in my heart that whatever Raham had experienced on that ship and whatever Malak had seen started with me. And I know now for a fact that I must see the carpenter, whoever or whatever the carpenter is.

Raham suddenly looks around, confused. "Wait. Malak, where are we going?

"We can't go back to the city. Last night, I saw the queen's men. The one's searching for Hannah. I know a place up the shore in the forest of the Bene Elohim where we can find shelter and supplies. They may also know where to find the carpenter."

For at least an hour, Malak continues rowing around the sandy headland that shields the port from the open ocean and, thankfully, shields us from being seen. I am amazed at how he continues rowing without it seeming to affect him. I am amazed at this strength. I look at Raham and see how she looks at him. I smile to myself. Something happened between them after I was kidnapped. Even if Raham refused to admit it to me, she is in love with him, and he to her as well.

"Hold on, girls. The waves are angry today," he warns.

We are approaching the shoreline below cliffs that rise at least a hundred feet up above the crashing surf. Malak stops rowing and keeps us behind the breaking waves, but the boat rises and drops dramatically with each approaching wave. I grab hold of the rails in alarm as does Raham.

"Raham, take an oar. Hannah do the same. Pull back on the water and keep us behind where the waves break," he orders.

We both do as he says and strain against the current to keep the boat steady. To my surprise, Malak stands up in the boat. What is he doing? I look over at Raham, who looks as surprised as I am.

"Malak, what are you doing?" Raham asks, but he ignores her. Instead, he holds back his head and whistles a high-pitched whistle that is much louder than the waves that crash before us. He looks upward to the cliff, and I do as well. I had heard that whistle before on the night when Malak and Raham had tried to save me from my kidnappers. He is calling for his horse.

He whistles a second time, and I see movement on the high ridgeline. A horse suddenly emerges to the very edge of the cliff. Malak points up the coastline, and the horse nods his head but stands still on the cliff. Malak lowers his arms and shakes his head. More dramatically, he points again, and the horse nods his head but stands still on the ridge, looking down at us. I can't help but giggle at both. Malak hears my giggle turns his head and glares at me and then points again to the horse and then up the coast.

"You wait till I get my hands on you. Dumb as a rock sometimes," he mumbles and points a fourth time at his horse and then up the coast. This time, the horse nods his head and turns and runs along the ridge up the coastline.

Malak sits back down and takes the oars from us. Both Raham and I smile at him but do not say a word. I watch the ridgeline and see that the horse follows us as we row up the shoreline until the cliff recedes when it is no longer present, and then the horse suddenly stands at the very edge of the waves, waiting for us. Malak turns the boat toward the shore, and we hold tightly as we ride the waves onto the beach. Malak jumps out, grabs the rope, and pulls toward the shore. Raham and I jumped out and helped push the boat through the surf until we grounded the vessel on the shore.

Malak walks up to his horse and takes hold of the reins. "You know you made me look bad in front of the girls back there." I hear him say. The horse nods his head yes.

Malak pets the horse and leans his forehead to the horse's head in greeting and I see the love and attachment that each has for the other. The horse steps back, looks at both Raham and I and then lowers his head and pushes against Malak's chest.

"Yea, we finally got them both together again," Malak says, pats the horse and walks to the saddle bag where he retrieves a canteen of water. I honestly believe that the two can talk with each other.

Malak gives the canteen to Raham who thanks him and drinks and then passes the canteen to me. I am parched with thirst and the water is cool, sweet, and refreshing. I take several gulps and give the canteen back to Malak who takes a drink and places the canteen back in the bag.

Raham walks up to the horse and reaches a hand up to him. To my amazement, the horse bows slightly to her, and she rubs the side of his head. "What a beautiful animal you are. I wonder whatever happened to my own horse," she says sadly. She looks over to Malak, who is searching for something in one of the packs tied behind the saddle. "Where are we Malak?"

He points up the coast, "About a day's journey, maybe less, maybe more, is the Bene Elohim Forest. There is a cabin not far from the ocean where we can find supplies and horses and with any luck information on where the carpenter is." Malak finds whatever it is he is looking for. "You must be starving. I'm afraid all I have is dried beef," he says and gives Raham the beef.

She tears a piece for herself and gives the rest to me. I eat the beef like it is prime rib and then forget that I did not save any for Malak, but he seems not to notice. He is looking up at the shoreline.

163

"If you guys can make it, we will go a bit further up the coast away from the city and find a place to camp for the night. Hopefully, I can find something for us to eat on the way," he says and looks back at us. "You can ride the horse. I will take the bow and scout ahead. There are birds in the marsh grass. Maybe I can get one for us."

"The horse is yours, Malak. I can walk," Raham says.

"I know you can walk, Raham. You and your Faireadoiri pride. Look down at yourself, girl. You are barefoot. You are exhausted. The both of you are. Now, you both can ride the horse, and I will find us something to eat."

They stare at each other as I look on. I may not know much, but I can tell when two people love each other and can't quite admit it to each other. Go ahead and kiss her, Malak. You know you want to. Raham gives in and steps back. She takes hold of the pommel and mounts the horse and reaches down to me and I mount behind her. At least this time, we are not tied together on the same horse.

Malak retrieves his bow and quiver of arrows and hands the reins to Raham. "Stay along the ocean until you see a river. Then turn upstream at the forest. That is the borderlands of the Bene Elohim. There is a good camp among a grove of oaks at the river that grows almost down to the ocean. If something happens, tell the horse to find me and give him free rein. He will find me. I should not be too far ahead of you and hopefully will have found us food."

I cannot help myself. "So, he will listen to us, right? He won't do what he did with you at the cliffs," I say, rather proud of myself for the joke. Raham cannot control her laughter.

Malak shakes his head and pulls at the halter, "See what I told you. You made me look bad in front of the girls." He looks up at me as the horse nods his head. "He dislikes it when I order him around sometimes. But he loves the ladies. He will listen to you. Won't you boy."

The horse shakes his head, yes. I swear the horse can understand us, I think. Malak gives one last look over the horse and then jogs off into the dunes.

164

Raham prods the horse, and he sets a slow, easy trot up the coast. I hold tightly to Raham, and after a moment, I finally ask her what happened on the boat. She tells me, and I am horrified by the story. What evil has spread over the land, and how am I involved? I then share with her my experience, and I realize that we had grown even closer than before because we had gone through a terrible ordeal together, and we had survived. Afterward, my exhaustion overcomes me, and I fall asleep to the gentle rhythm of the horse's gait.

I awaken with a start. Raham sits on the horse in front of me and the horse is standing still. "Is everything okay?" I ask.

"Yea, we are at the oak trees. Do you smell smoke?" she asks.

I breathe deeply and catch the scent of smoke in the air. The horse trots a bit further to the very edge of the trees and Raham points ahead to a small fire burning beneath ancient oaks on the banks of the river that flows into the ocean to our right. I see Malak standing by the fire watching us. I also smell the meat cooking and realize again how hungry I am.

Malak had killed a rabbit and we had eaten well. I lay on a bed of pine needles that Malak had made for us. Raham lay beside me. Malak stands on the other side of the small fire, his back to us, looking out over the ocean. I love the sound of the waves crashing out in the darkness, a constant rhythm that is leading me to sleep. We said very little as we ate. We were all so tired. Much had happened to each of us, yet somehow, we had all been able to come together. But the constant strain of the past week had exhausted me, and I quickly fall asleep.

I wake up suddenly and set up an alarm by myself in the pine bed. The fire glows merrily nearby. I feel its inviting warmth. The night air smells of wood smoke and the ocean. Out in the darkness beyond the fire, I hear the ever-present crashing waves.

I set up, looking for the others, and saw Malak sitting on a log on the other side of the fire facing the ocean. He had to be exhausted as well, I reason. Raham walks up and sits down beside him, gathering her long dress around her knees. Her hair is free, and she touches the log she is sitting on. She gathers her hair together and then lets it down again.

The two sit silent and still for a few moments, her head level with his shoulder. She turns to say something to him, but I cannot hear what she is saying. He looks down at her for a long time as she talks and then leans down to her as I watch, spellbound. They are both of a higher race, I realize, human but not quite human. I know that they are in love with each other. At first, I had been jealous of that. Why could he not be in love with me? But now I am happy for them. But I am still so confused about myself. If I am the Bean an Ri and the king wishes for me to be his wife, then why does he not search for me himself?

Malak leans down further, and I think he wishes to kiss her, but Raham pushes him back and he stops. And then suddenly she pulls herself even with him and kisses him. He places his arm around her, laughing and she leans her head on his shoulder and I soon lay back down and fall asleep.

166

CHAPTER TWENTY-EIGHT

I feel warmth on my face and wake up to bright morning sunshine. Raham lies sleeping next to me on her side. I had slept better than I had since all of this had started, and for once, I did not have any dreams. Malak is on his knees before the fire, smoke blowing up and around his head. He seems to be cooking something over a flat rock that he had placed over the coals, but I cannot see what he is cooking.

He looks back at me with a wide smile. "You like eggs, Hannah?" he asks.

I sit up and pull myself out of my bed, slowly. My entire body aches as one hurt muscle. "I love eggs. Where in the world did you get eggs?"

Malak points over toward the river, where I see several hens scratching at the dirt along the riverbank. "The forest around here is full of them," he comments as he takes a wooden fork and flips the eggs.

Raham wakes up and stretches, "I smell food."

She crawls the short distance to the fire and scoots herself up beside Malak. Before she would have made sure the fire was between him and her, I think. I walk over and sit on the other side of him.

"Are they done?" I ask.

"Sure, but careful they are hot," he answers and impales one on the fork and hands it over to me. I take the egg from the fork and wave the fried egg a bit to cool it and then eat it in two bites. I see that Malak has cooked several of them and we each eat the eggs until we are full, washing them down with the last of the water from the canteen.

"What do we do now, Malak?" Raham asks.

"We are not far from a Bene Elohim cabin where we can find supplies. Hopefully, the guardian there will know where the carpenter is and will have news of the king." Malak answers and stands. He whistles once, and his horse trots up a few minutes later.

Malak greets his horse in the same manner as I had seen him do before. He places his forehead just above the horse's nose, "Good morning, brother. Today, you see an old friend."

The horse raises his head and turns to Raham and then back, "Now none of that. Let's get you saddled."

I am always astonished at the conversations Malak has with the horse and must ask. "Malak. You talk with him like he can understand you, like he talks back."

Malak pats his horse, "I think maybe he does. We have been together for my entire life. Each Bene Elohim has a horse for life, and we are tied to them in a way that we can't understand." He throws the saddle over the animal. "I don't understand how, but I feel him answering me."

The horse waits patiently as the pack and shield as well as the bow and quiver are attached to the saddle. This time Raham mounts the horse without complaint and Malak helps me up. He then leads off down a thin trail that runs along the riverbank.

"No complaint this time, Raham. You are rather compliant this morning, aren't you?" I tease.

Raham straightens her back and I cannot help but continue.

"Soooo, you going to tell me what happened last night between You and Malak by the fire."

"Nothin, nothin at all," she answers,

"Well then, maybe I should ask Malak."

She turns back to me, "You wouldn't dare."

I squeeze my friend tightly, "No I wouldn't. But you got to tell me. Is that the first time you ever kissed a man?"

Malak looks back over his shoulder and I duck my head back. Did he hear me?

"Hannah!" Raham exclaims, and Malak shakes his head.

We travel along the river for several hours until Malak stops. "Stay here a bit. I think the ford is just over there," he orders and steps off the trail and into the thicket.

He emerges a few minutes later from the undergrowth. "There is a ford just below. The cabin is not far on the other side from here," he says and leads his horse through the brush to the riverbank.

At this point the river is only thirty to forty feet wide and shallow. The water runs swiftly over rocks that glisten in the sun. Trout dart away from us back into the deeper water as we enter. The water is only waist deep to Malak at the mid-point and we make it across the river easily to the other side.

"The guardian should be nearby. She probably already knows we are here." Malak comments.

We follow him down a woodland trail under a cathedral of giant trees, some of them over five feet in diameter. I look up into the trees toward the blue sky above and see mostly a mantle of green leaves and gray branches. Birds flutter among the treetops.

And then, to my surprise, I see a face briefly between the branches, a flash of brown and green, and then swirling leaves. "Malak! Somebody is in the trees!"

Raham jerks her head up, and the horse stops and turns, pawing the ground with his hooves.

"Easy now, boy. It's okay, Hannah, it's only Nasar." Malak says.

"Who's Nasar?" Raham asks.

"The guardian of this place," Malak answers and draws his sword.

"Should we be alarmed?" Raham asks, but Malak ignores her. "Nasar. It's Malak."

I hear a swoosh above me, and the horse turns toward the noise. I see another flash of brown and then swirling leaves. And then I swear I hear a soft giggle, like a child. A horse neighs further out in the forest, and Malak's horse straightens his ears at the sound and neighs in return.

"Come in, Nasar. You got me. I surrender." Malak steps away from us looking around him, holding the sword in front of him. "Don't worry. It's a game she loves to play." Malak turns away from us, searching the deep forest toward where the other horse is hiding.

A young woman suddenly materializes from the brush beside us. She wears brown pants a green shirt and mantle that is fastened at her chest with a brooch with the same crest that I had seen on Malak's sword. Her hair is blond and braided. Her eyes are icy blue, her face small and round, her lips full and red, her face flushed. She smiles widely and holds a finger over her lips for us to be quiet. The horse turns to her and bows slightly, and she pets him and steps to the other side, holding her sword before her. She takes another step away from the horse as Raham and I watch in astonishment.

Malak suddenly swirls, and their blades cross. "Almost, but not quite," he says, and the girl swears softly and shoves her sword point first into the dirt in submission. Malak does the same, and the two hug each other. What in the world is going on?

After a moment, she pulls herself away and looks back at the two of us. She whistles, and the other horse emerges and runs up to her. Malak's horse steps forward, and the two greet each other like old friends.

Malak steps up and helps me to dismount. He then turns to Raham, but she ignores him and dismounts herself and steps forward, facing Nasar, eying her with suspicion. I smile. Raham is jealous, I think.

"This is Nasar, my sister," Malak says. "And this is Raham and Hannah."

"A Faireadoiri, brother. My, you have been busy," the girl says and smiles at Raham and then looks at me and her eyes grow wide.

Oh, here we go again, I think. She steps up to me and looks over at her brother, "You found her. Malak. Oh my God! You found her."

She takes my hand and bows to me and steps back. "Hannah. I am honored to meet you. We have all been searching for you. The king himself has searched the north country for you." She looks over to Malak. "Where did you find her?"

"It's a long story, Nasar. We need supplies, the girls need clothes, and we need to find the carpenter."

"Sure, come on. The cabin is just up the trail." She says and we follow her up the trail, the horses following along behind us.

We walk through a forest of thinning trees, the understory open, the ground covered in a thick bed of leaves. Shafts of warm sunlight slant between the trees. Clouds of small insects swirl through the lights. The forests here remind me of the one above my home, a place of peace and solitude. I look through the trees and see a jumble of broken rock in one place, like a wall that had once stood high but, in some ancient time, had fallen in on itself. The path led toward the rocks, and between a gap, I see the walls of a wooden structure.

The Bene Elohim cabin is constructed of dark red logs with three levels and is surrounded by a large porch. Several chimneys rise above the roof. A sliver of white smoke floats upward from the nearest chimney. Potted plants with multicolored flowers hang at intervals around the porch. A vegetable garden lies to the side of the cabin in a small meadow.

"Any of the family here besides you?" Malak asks as we pass through the gap in the broken rock ledge.

"No, only me big brother," Nasar answers and looks over her shoulder at Raham and myself. "I believe I have clothes for the both of you. And a hot bath and hot meal." She looks back at Malak and takes his hand in hers. "Brother, it's so good to see you again. And to have found her, Malak! The king was here just a week before. He said the dragon has awakened, Malak."

Malak looked at her in alarm, then back at Raham. A dragon? Don't tell me a dragon is also searching for me. I am only Hannah, a girl whose mother is dead, a girl who only remembers living in the forest of my youth. And then I remember the horrible dream of the dragon searching for me in the forest, a witch woman standing in the darkness.

I stop suddenly just as we reach the porch. The others keep walking until Raham realizes that I have stopped. "Hannah, you, okay?"

My face must have shown my sudden horror when I remembered the dream as all three of them stare at me.

"I have seen the dragon, Malak," I state.

"Where, Hannah? Where have you seen a dragon?" Malak asks in shock.

"In my dreams. Ever since the night my mother was killed. Just after I first saw you at the ferry, I had horrible nightmares. Many times, a dragon hunts for me, and a witch calls to me. There are times when I am standing in a forest like this one or a beautiful meadow, and I see a wooden structure like this." I take my hands and make the shape that I see. "And then there is fire, there is an earthquake, there is a horrible dragon that tries to kill me, there is a witch woman that I can't see but a shape of, but I hear her call to me."

I begin to tremble as the memories of all the dreams flood forward. I want to cry, to hide myself and run away, but where would I go? These are the only friends I have. They have all sworn their allegiance to me. Control the fear, bind the fear, use the fear.

Raham takes my hand, "It's okay, Hannah. We are with you. You are safe with us, even in your dreams. We will find the carpenter, and you will see. You will know."

Nasar walks up to me. She is taller than I but not as tall as Malak. I see a great resemblance to him. Malak is a beautiful man. And Nasar is a beautiful woman. Both seem to be of another worldly race of people as does Raham, for that matter. I smile at her.

"Come into the house, Hannah. You are safe here. Let's get you a bath and a hot meal. You need to sleep, and I promise that even bad dreams cannot enter through these walls. Tomorrow, you will see the carpenter." She looks at Malak. "He is close. He has set up his shop not far from here, almost as if he knew that you were coming."

We walk into the front room of the house, and my fear and anxiety immediately vanish. I stare in wonder all around me, as does Raham. The inside of the front room is huge, far larger than the entire house seemed to be from the outside. A vaulted ceiling rises far into the heavens as if it would continue forever, and I see no roof over me, only a clear blue sky that vanishes into a brightly colored rainbow.

A marbled fireplace is to one side, with a cheery fire burning within. The room is full of beautifully carved chairs, couches, and tables. One table is covered with a chess set of silver knights standing at least a foot high. The opposite wall from the fireplace is covered with hard-bound books that fill the entire wall upward into the rainbow lights. What wonder is this place? Who are the Bene Elohim to live in such a magical place?

Raham walks over to the books and slides her hand over the leather, looking at Malak in wonder. Her gaze questions him. "What is this place, Malak? Who are you, really?"

Malak takes her hands in his, "My home, Raham. The place of my birth. The birthplace of the Bene Elohim. From before ancient times, the Bene Elohim have lived here. We come here from our travels to rest, to find comfort. To share our love."

Nasar suddenly stands between them, looking first at Malak, then at Raham, then down at their hands, and then at me.

"They're in love," I say matter of fact and shake my head.

Raham drops her hands and steps back. Her face flushes. Nasar inspects her closely, looking all around her.

"What are you doing?" Malak asks.

"Checking to see if she is tied up. Did you come willingly, or did he force you to with a terrible curse if you didn't?" she asks.

"Oh, good grief, sis."

"I came because I am Faireadoiri and Hannah is the Bean an Ri. I can't explain why I am in love with your brother, but I am."

"Oh, lord. Okay brother. At least you have picked well. Let's get you guys some food. And Raham, I can tell you about my brother," she says and turns, pointing to the hallway that leads further back into the house.

We follow her to the hall, and I look back to the front room, but it is now only a small parlor with a chair, couch, fireplace, and a single table. I step back into the room, and it immediately opens as before. What magic is this?

"I'll tend to the horses," I hear Malak say behind me as I follow the girls down the hall.

173

CHAPTER TWENTY-NINE

The captain stood before a wooden door at the market house. His men still mounted on their horses and up along the cobblestone street behind him. They had followed the slaver's trail until they found four bodies lying in the grass at a point where the trail had turned away from the road to the port city. Someone had attacked them and had gotten away. His scouts had found the tracts of one horse leading away from the fight and the slaver's horses traveling straight to the front gate.

Who could the attacker have been? Some bandits, perhaps, but that would be foolish for one bandit to attack a slaver party. There was only one race in the realm that would attack an entire slaver party. He pounded on the door again and swore his bad luck. A lantern lit in a back room.

If the attacker had been a Bene Elohim warrior, then he must have been searching for the girl as well. By this time, word had to have gotten out and all the Bene Elohim would be searching for her. Even the king himself would be searching for her. But how had word gotten out? No one knew about the girl.

He pounded on the door again. It was early morning, and the entire port city was just coming to life. The early sun covered the port city in a glow of light as fog swirled over the water and through the streets. He had forced his way through the city gate at the protest of the guards until they saw who he was and had led his men to the market. The market would be the only place the girl would be, and with any luck, she was still there.

The door opened and a frightened servant girl in her night dress peeked around the door, holding the lantern before her. He stepped away from the door. Even the captain did not see the need to frighten a poor servant girl any more than she already was.

"Is your master home, girl?" he asked.

"Yes, my lord. She is. She is asleep." The girl answered, her voice trembling.

The captain eased his tone, "Then wake her up and tell her the captain is here to see her right away. It is most urgent."

She shook her head yes and quickly ran back into the house. A few minutes later, another lantern was lit, and the captain heard a voice call out to the girl, swearing at her.

"But, madam, it is a captain and his men. They say it is urgent for you to come."

A few minutes later, a very large woman came to the door.

"You the master of the market?" the captain asked.

"Yes, what is this about?"

"Do you have a girl just brought in by the slavers with it in the past couple of days?"

"Yes, two were brought in, but we sold one to a nobleman who immediately took her to his ship."

The captain pushed the door in, and the woman backed up in fear, "You sold her! You sold her before the market!" He backed out the door and looked toward the docks. He saw two ship's lights in the port. "Which ship?"

"I'm not sure, captain. What have I done wrong? She was a Faireadoiri, very rare to capture a Faireadoiri and the nobleman paid more for her than ten girls."

The captain looked down at her, "No the one I am searching for is not Faireadoiri. She has black hair and a scar." He shows on his cheek and neck where the scar is. "Down the side of her face and shoulders. Down her side."

"Yes, that is the second one. We still have her."

"Take us to her," he orders.

"You will pay? I have rented her out for the night."

"No. I will not pay. You will give her to me. And for your sake, she better still be alive."

The woman grabbed her keys and hurried from the house and down the cobblestone road toward the stone building by the wharfs. The captain motioned for two of his men to follow him. Upon reaching the building, the woman stopped quickly in front of the door and stood for a moment. The door was ajar.

The captain drew his sword and pushed his way past the woman. The other two men did the same. A guard lay on the floor before him. Across the other side of the hallway a second guard stirred, groaning. An inside door stood open, and the captain rushed forward and into the room, the woman immediately behind him.

175

Before them on the floor lay a dead man, his mid-section cut through, and congealed blood spread outward across the floor, almost black in color. The captain turned to the woman, his face red with rage, and the woman backed away in fear.

"You rented her out! You fool! You allowed her to escape!" he screamed and backhanded her across the face, breaking her nose and knocking her back against the wall. She cried out in pain and grabbed her face, blood pouring over her hands. The captain raised his sword but stopped and regained his composure.

"Why is she so important? She is worthless. Her scars make her worthless." The woman stated between her gasps.

"You fool. She is worth a hundred times the Faireadoiri, a thousand times. She can destroy us all!" he said, sheathed his sword, and stormed out into the street. He looked wildly around him. They had to be close, but where?

He motioned for his men, and they galloped quickly down the road, the sound of so many horsemen on cobblestone causing the townspeople to emerge from their homes to see what was going on.

"Search house to house," he ordered. "Shut the gates and make sure no one leaves the town. She must be here somewhere!"

The men spread out across the town, breaking into the homes and stores to search, indiscriminately ransacking houses and shops at sword point. A few drunken slavers at the tavern still hung over from their night, resisted, but they were quickly cut down, and the townspeople cowered in fear as the soldiers continued their search.

The captain stood on the wharf and waited as his men searched the town. The girl had to be somewhere nearby. Or someone must have seen what had happened at the slave market. For most of the day and into the afternoon, they searched. Finally, one of the soldiers brought someone who said he had known what had happened. He was a drunk and a beggar in ragged clothes that smelled of horse manure. He described who had to have been a Bene Elohim warrior who had broken into the building. A short time later he emerged with the girl, and they had not left town, but had run to the wharf and gotten on a boat. They had rowed out to the ship.

"Are you sure?' the captain asked.

"Yes captain, yes. The two of them rowed toward the ship, but they never made it, they did. They turned and rowed up the shoreline around the headland. I thought how strange it was for the two of them to do such a thing, I did. Now can you pay me? The soldiers said you would pay," the man said and held out his hand.

The captain ignored him and motioned for the nearest soldier, "Gather the men. I know where they are going."

"Hey, captain. The soldier said you would pay me," the man shouted.

"Pay the one what he is worth," the captain ordered the nearest soldier, who turned, drew his sword, and stabbed the man who gasped, his eyes wide in pain. The soldier withdrew the bloody sword, cleaned it on the man's cloak, and pushed him back into the water, where he floated on his back, blood drifting away from his body.

The captain mounted his horse and led the men along the wharf to the edge of town, but on this side of the headland, there was no way to continue up the shore because of the cliff walls. He sat for a moment, watching the waves crash against the cliff walls, and then noticed something moving unnaturally along the side of the cliff. He retrieved his telescope from his saddle bag and looked carefully along the cliff until he saw a rope dangling on the cliff wall. So that was how he had gotten into town in the night, he thought. He swore to himself and turned. They would have to go out the front gate and ride along the top of the cliff until they could reach the shoreline.

They found the boat on the beach late in the afternoon and footprints in the sand heading north up the coast. They followed the footprints until they finally disappeared with the rising tide and the darkness of night. His men needed rest, and so did he. The trail was gone because of the high tide, and he did not won't to lose them in the dark. Plus, he had a good idea where they were heading. He just didn't know how far the forests were. They made camp for the night in the low dunes along the shoreline.

The next day, they continued their search, slowly working their way north along the coast. Every now and then, they would find a horse track or a place where someone had stopped to rest the horse. They followed the trail until, finally, the captain saw a tree line off on the horizon.

He spread the men out, and they slowly and methodically worked their way up the coast until they reached a grove of oaks that grew alongside a river that emptied into the ocean. They found a camp just before dark and stopped again. The captain first thought of crossing the river and continuing the search, but the forests were unknown to him and foreboding. Plus, they were within the territory of the Bene Elohim, best traveled throughout the day.

CHAPTER THIRTY

It is night again, the first night in the home of the Bene Elohim. I lay in a warm bed in an upstairs room, warm and safe. A low fire burns in the fireplace in the room, the orange light from the fire dancing on the walls. It is very late, and we have been telling Nasar of our terrible and yet wonderful adventures. I cannot believe that it has been almost two months since I left my home. So much has happened, most of it horrible. However, I feel that I have grown so much and have persevered through so many trials. I have made new friends and have found that I am able to overcome fear. I still do not know why everyone thinks that I am the wife of a king, that I am beautiful and desired. I don't understand why I have these dreams that haunt me, But I am excited now because in the morning, I will finally see the carpenter.

To me, that is one of the most ridiculous mysteries of this journey. What could a carpenter tell me about who I am? A carpenter, for heaven's sake, a man who builds things from wood. What could he know? Why is it so important that I seek a carpenter to tell me what I must do, who I truly am? But at least tomorrow, I will fulfill what my mother told me before she had died saving me.

I try to sleep, but I am too excited about possibilities, about all that has happened, about the wonderful time Raham and I had talking with Nasar. She is truly a wonderful girl, older than the both of us in a way that, like Malak, seems to make her ancient. Like she has always existed. I realize that the Bene Elohim seem to have always been alive in this realm. I know that sounds strange, but that is the best way that I can describe their age. It is much the same with the Faireadoiri. They are so young but seem to have always been. Raham says she is but fourteen years old, but to me she is eternal.

We took a bath, ate dinner and talked of things like I always dreamed girls would do. Nasar had let us pick out new clothes. We had fixed each other's hair and talked of Malak and even the king, which is strange to me. They say I am to be the wife of the king. Sometimes they say I am already the wife of the king. But I do not know the man. How can I be his wife when I do not even know him?

Finally, Malak came in and he and Raham walked through the gardens hand in hand and then she returned, flushed and I see the love that she has for the Bene Elohim warrior. Would I feel the same way about the king when I finally meet him?

I asked her about love once before and she said then that she had never been in love. Tonight, she shared with me that Faireadoiri will find a mate once in their lives, and it will be instant. They would simply find their mate, and they would know for sure, and it would be settled. She said that the Bene Elohim were the same, but she had never known a Faireadoiri and Bene Elohim who had mated. I hope that love will be that easy for me, I think. But what choice do I have? Everyone seems to think that I am the wife of a king. There are those around me that have sworn their life for me. And there are those out there who wish to destroy me for who they say I am. I still see my scars and say that I am not worthy to be chosen as a wife for the king of this world.

I look over at Raham, who sleeps in a peaceful sleep. We have been through so much together, and I think strangely that maybe I have known her for some time before my dreams, but how can that be? So many questions and no answers. Tomorrow, the carpenter, whoever he is, would have to answer them, or I will go crazy with the continued asking of them in my mind.

Oh, my lord! I cannot sleep! I sit up in bed and quietly walk over to the window and lean out, breathing in the fresh forest air. The night is a little chilly, but not overly so and I stand and look out over the trees. The night sky is brilliant with a multitude of stars and a full moon that casts the forest below me in a half light. I look down and see Malak and Nasar standing below me. Don't the Bene Elohim ever sleep?

"You truly love her, brother? A Faireadoiri. I can't believe it."

"Yes, I do, Nasar. From the first time I saw her, I knew that she was to be my mate. And like us, sister, love falls on the Faireadoiri the same way." Malak answers.

"She is a fine young lady, Malak, a Faireadoiri warrior no less. But you do know what lies ahead of us all. There will be times that she will be in realms separate then the one that we are in. She is destined to be in mankind's world while we travel in other realms."

"Yes, I know, but time in nothing. You know that. We will always be able to be together in this realm, this place, even when we are apart, we will be together. And when the age is done, we will be here, in this place, in this realm. I have talked with her about this, and she knows, and it does not matter."

"When Hannah realizes the truth, it will all change," Nasar comments.

"We need to get some sleep. Nasar. I will watch for a while," Malak says.

"No, brother. I will take the watch. You have not slept in weeks," Nasar says and steps away from the tree she is leaning against. "I sent one of your birds with a message for the king. Hopefully, he will be here soon. It's truly good to see you, Malak. I have been at Sateria for too long."

They both walk back inside, and I stand at the window, totally confused by their conversation. More mysteries. More questions. I walk back to the bed and lie down, pulling the covers over me, and try to sleep.

I am sitting in a grand ballroom at a table that stretches out of sight toward a distant fireplace. I sit at the head of the table beside a chair that is empty. All the other seats are filled with people, both men, and women, all elegantly dressed in their finest clothing. The table is full of foods of all types. The people are all eating and drinking, laughing, and talking to each other as if I do not even exist, but I know that I belong at the head of the table. I know that the table and everything on it is meant for me, is in honor of me. I look down and see that I wear a beautiful wedding dress. I touch the side of my face and feel the wrinkled skin of my scars, but when I look at my reflection in the silver vase before me, I see no scars. I realize that I am beautiful. My hair is elaborately decorated with pearls that glow a bright white in contrast to my raven-black hair. I look down again and see the amulet shining brightly on its simple chain on my breast.

I jump when I realize that a man's hand is over my hand, which is gloved with white lace like a lady's. I look over at the chair beside me and see the king, I know he is the king, even though he does not dress like what I always thought a king would be dressed like.

181

He smiles at me, takes my hand in his, lifts it to his face, and kisses it lightly, and the crowd shouts with joy and applauds. My chest flutters, my heart skips a beat, and my breathing quickens at his touch. He places my hand back on the table and then softly caresses my face. He pulls an errant strand of hair away, leans in, and kisses me.

I wake up suddenly, the dream so real that I look around me to see where the king had gone. But he is nowhere. I am lying in my bed. But the dream had been so real. I still feel his kiss, I smell the food, I feel his touch. My heart beats fast and my breath quickens, and I sit up. Raham stirs beside me. I lay back down and close my eyes. I long for sleep again so that I can dream such a wonderful dream again.

I walk in a forest among low-growing flowers under ancient trees that grow far above me into the very clouds. Birds fly between the branches. The air is sweet, the sunshine warm, and the forest floor soft with a thick bed of leaves and ferns. The ground is cool to my bare feet. All around me, the forest is full of life, and I twirl in the sunshine, run among the trees, chase the elusive butterflies, and splash my feet in the pools of water by the stream.

I know this place, I think. This is my home. This has always been my home. I lean down at one pool and see myself and see the scars that have burned my flesh. I turn away from the scene. How can anyone ever want me? I am a burned one. I am disfigured. I am ugly. I turn away, saddened by the sight of who I am, and see a man walking toward me through the trees. He is dressed like a woodsman with rugged pants, a shirt, and boots. He smiles widely, and I see that he is the king. I run to him, and he holds out his hands and takes me in his arms and kisses me, and I no longer worry about what I look like because I know that to my husband, I am the most beautiful of women.

I wake up again, my heart racing. I still feel his strong arms holding me. What is going on? The dreams are so real. What is this place that would cause me to have such wonderful dreams? I fall back asleep.

I wake up to bright sunshine that streams into the room and over my face through the window. My dreams are still fresh in my memory like they were real. I sit up and look around.

Raham is gone and I see that she has dressed and has taken her new weapons given to her by Nasar the night before. I jump quickly out of bed and dress myself. I see Malak's short sword and sheath lying on the dresser. The hair ribbon I had given him at the hot springs was tied tightly to the hilt. I latch the belt around my waist. Malak must have worked on the sheath and belt because it fit perfectly around me. I lace my new leather shoes and look in the mirror. Nasar had given me riding pants and a shirt plus a half skirt that fit over my pants. She had commented that a true lady should always wear some form of a skirt. I like the outfit. It was made for outdoor use and for riding.

I run down the steps and to the kitchen, where a plate of food sits. Where is everyone? I think. I am too excited to eat and hurry out the front room that opens to the heavens above me when I enter and resumes its smaller form when I walk out of the room and onto the front porch.

I see Raham standing with her back to me and looking up at Malak and Nasar, who are both mounted on their warhorses, fully armed for combat. What has happened? Malak leans down and kisses Raham and she steps back as he turns his horse and rides off into the forest. Nasar rides across the yard in another direction as Raham turns and walks back to the house.

"What's wrong, Raham? Why are they leaving?"

She steps up on the porch. I see that she is armed with her sword and a new crossbow, tied to her back like I had seen her do before. "It's okay, Hannah. Nasar scouted the trail back toward the river last night and saw a group of soldiers camped where we had camped by the river. Malak believes they are the same ones that are after you." She must see the look of terror that crosses my face. "It's okay, Hannah. They will watch them. You and I are to go to where the carpenter is. All will be fine. The soldiers are entering Bene Elohim land. That is a big mistake on their part. Nasar has alerted the king and he is on his way, Hannah. I'm not sure how long it will take him, but he is on his way here."

My eyes grow wide at what she says. The king is on his way here. My heart races. I think of the dreams. Is the king the man of my dreams or is the man of my dreams just a figment of my imagination?

Hannah smiles at me. "Don't worry. Today is your day, Hannah. Everything you have gone through leads you to this day." She takes my hand. "Now come with me. I've got a surprise for you."

183

She leads me around to the back of the house and I see for the first time, a barn, and stables. There are several horses in a corral beside the barn and two are tied to a post in front of the barn. Both are saddled. They are beautiful animals.

"What is this?" I ask.

"A gift from the Bene Elohim. From now on, we don't have to ride on the same horse." She walks up and pats the first horse, which is a brown and white mare with three stocking feet and a long main.

The second is a shiny black mare with only one small white spot on her nose just below her eyes.

"Mine?" I ask in wonderment.

"Yes, yours. Malak said he picked that one for you because she matches your hair," Raham answers as she mounts her horse.

I walk to the front of my horse and greet her like I have seen Malak do. The horse lowers her head, and we touch forehead to nose. I mount the horse, and she sidesteps a bit as I adjust the reins.

Raham looks over my horse and makes sure the gear is tight against the back of the saddle. "She is well trained, Hannah, so let her lead. She knows what to do. Nasar said the carpenter's camp is but an hour's ride from here."

She gives her horse a slight kick, and the mare leads off up the trail. I hold on tight as my own horse follows. The most experience I have had with horses is riding on the back of one with Raham, so this is quite a new experience for me. After a few moments, I realize that the mare seems to know that I am inexperienced, and her gait is smooth, and she runs along the trail easily. I settle in, holding the reins and keeping my legs tucked against her flanks, and she does the rest.

After a few minutes Raham looks up toward the sky and suddenly reins in her horse. Mine slows down as well and stops just behind the other horse. Raham holds her gloved hand up in the air, and I hear a flutter of wings above me. I duck down in alarm as the bird flies over my head. A hawk lands on Raham's hand and she turns and places the great bird on a perch behind her saddle.

She smiles at me. "Malak is full of surprises. This is one of his birds. She will be our eyes and ears. If we need anything, we can place a note in this little compartment, and she will take it to him. Nasar sent one to the king as well last night and it returned this morning with a note from the king that he was on his way." She urges her horse on and mine follows.

184

We ride through the forest as the sun rises behind us, the shadows under the thicker canopy retreating away from us like a living organism. After a while, the forest gives way to an open forested savanna with majestic pine trees growing over rich grass meadows. Buffalo grazes off in the distance. As we ride closer, they look at us but continue grazing, not interested in our presence.

We ride toward a dark tree line that grows at the base of mountains that climb high into the clouds, the upper flanks bare of trees, snow and ice on the extreme summits glistening against the rising sun. I have never seen such a beautiful country before. The trail leads across the savanna and enters the forest among a jumble of granite rock and tangled vines that grow across the rocks and into the trees.

Raham stops before entering the forest, looking across the tree line. "There should be signs of the carpenter's camp. Nasar said he camped just inside the trees across the savanna."

She turns her horse and rides back from the trees and away from the trail, searching for any sign of an encampment. At first, we see nothing, but then I see movement just above the low rise where the trees grow sparser than near the trail.

"Look Raham. I see something. There is something moving up by the trees," I say and point as the tree line seems to move and swirl like the wind is blowing, but there is no wind.

We look further up the slope and suddenly see a large, multicolored tent among the trees. Had that been there before? Next to the tent are several wagons and horses.

"That's strange. I swear there was nothing there before," Raham comments.

I rein my horse on the crest of the hill and can see the carpenter's encampment fully now. There are no people anywhere around, only the horses standing to the side of the tent, which is the size of a major building back in town. The tent is round with a dome room supported by massive timbers. A small sliver of white smoke drifts upward.

Is this where I am to finally meet the mysterious carpenter who is to answer the many questions I have? Is this the man who I am to finally reveal the hidden amulet that I have not shown anyone as my mother ordered to do? My heart races with anticipation and excitement.

185

Raham dismounts as do I. She takes a small piece of paper, writes a note, and places the paper in a small pouch tied to the hawk's talons. She unties the bird and touches her gently. "Go to Malak," she orders and raises the bird up.

The hawk takes flight swiftly and flies off across the savanna from where we had just traveled. I look over to the tent and wonder what I am supposed to do. There seems to be no one anywhere around. All is quiet, all is still. Even the horses by the tent seem to be statues with no life in them like they had been placed there as decorations.

"Hannah, you have to go on the rest of the way yourself," Raham comments softly, and I look over at her with fear.

Control the fear, use the fear, subdue it,

I calm my heart and breathe deeply. Why am I afraid? This is the one thing that my mother told me to do before she died.

Raham takes the reins of my horse, "I will stay here and watch out. You go on ahead. Don't worry, Hannah. This is what you must do to see for the first time who you really are." She smiles at me. "Don't worry. I will be right outside, waiting for you. I will be right here when you come out."

I nod remove my leather riding gloves, and place them securely in my belt. I straighten my dress, reposition my sword, and step forward to the tent, and immediately, I am in a swirl of lights of the rainbow. My body swirls around as the lights swirl around me. They fly over and under and all around me, brilliant individual colors flying separately like they are alive and then merging into one myriad of colors. I look around me and see for just a second a bright white light off in the distance and then the rainbow returns, and the lights disappear as fast as they had come.

I stand before a wooden gate in a beautiful garden, full of flowers, shrubs, and trees. Birds flutter among the shrubs. The door is made of oak and has massive iron hinges that secure the door to an ancient oak tree with branches that spread out in all directions and cast the door in deep shadows.

Where had the tent gone?

I look around and see Raham and the two horses standing where I had left them. Raham looks off into the distant savanna, her back to me. She is only a few feet from me, but when I reach out to get her attention, she disappears and re appears far off in the distance. I turn back to the door and tentatively reach out to touch it, to see if it is real. The wood is rough and cold to the touch, but it is real.

The door opens on its own revealing the inside of a large room filled with beautifully made furniture. I step inside and the door closes behind me. The room is warm and comforting and I feel no fear of being inside. The room smells of freshly sawn wood.

A man stands with his back to me in the center of the room at a workbench filled with tools and pieces of wood of all shapes and sizes. The floor is covered in sawdust. The man is working on something, but I cannot see what it is he is working on. He is a large man with dark skin and muscled shoulders that bulge under a brown shirt as he works.

"Hold on. There, finished," the man says and turns toward me with a smiling face and holding a small horse in one hand and a carving knife in the other. He holds the horse up and inspects it closely. "Ah, perfect." He holds it out to me. "What do you think?"

The horse is carved from some type of reddish wood, and I am amazed when the horse moves in his hand as if alive. And then I realize in amazement that the carved figure is alive! The man carefully sits the horse on a shelf against the wall and places the knife back on the bench.

"I am so glad you have come to see me, Hannah," the man says.

The man reminds me somewhat of Raham's father, James, and then again, he has some of the characteristics of Mr. Spivey. That's strange, I think. I know this man. I am totally at ease in the room with this man who I have never seen before, yet for some reason, I feel as if I have known him my entire life.

"How do you know my name?" I ask, not knowing anything else to say.

He ignores my question and turns, waving his hand over the room. "Sorry for the mess. I have been so very busy as of late," he says. "There are so many things that I wish to create."

187

"You are the carpenter?" I ask and he answers me this time. "Yes, yes child. That is what I am called in this realm. I love to build things from wood. It's a hobby of mine. I see the beauty in all things and then work to bring it alive. Like the horse I just made."

I look over at the horse and see that there are several more. They run and play along the shelf on the wall that he placed the horse on. What magic is this?

"Let me show you something," he says and walks over to a pile of broken pieces of wood. Some of them are full boards with beautiful, swirling grains, others just bits of timber, the bark still on them. Some are burned and I cringe at the sight of the blackened wood. He pushes a few of the boards over and digs deeper into the pile.

"You see, all of them have a life within. They all are precious to me, because I don't see them how they appear in the pile. I see them the way I have created them to be. Oh, here is the one," he says.

He pulls a disfigured, blackened piece of twisted wood from beneath the smooth boards and holds it up to me. "See how beautiful this piece of wood is?"

I do not see any beauty at all. I see the twisted wood, the blackened bark, the dirty soot from a past fire. The carpenter takes the wood in his hand and gently brushes the dirt away. He then takes the wood and places it in a bucket of water and washes the wood until the blackened soot is all gone.

"You must see through my eyes, Hannah. Not imperfections, but the true reality. You must see through the mirror that is the eyes of your creator." He takes the wood from the water and takes a towel and gently dries the wood and I see that the fire scars are no longer visible.

He holds the piece of wood up to me. "Now what do you see?"

"Nothing but a piece of wood that you have cleaned."

He smiles with a low laugh. "It's okay. Let me work on it a bit and then you will see the life that is hidden within," he says and picks up a small carving knife. "Come with me and let's talk in the garden."

I follow him through the room and out onto a veranda that lies under the shade of several large oaks and surrounded by beautiful flowers. He sits on one bench, and I sit on the other across from him. He immediately leans over the wood and begins to shave off portions

188

of the bark with the knife. I sit uncomfortably with my hands in my lap, not knowing what to do or say.

For a few minutes he carves on the wood as if I am not even present and then without looking up, he says, "You have a story to tell child. So, tell me. Tell me everything."

"Where do I start?" I ask.

"It's usually good to start at the very beginning."

CHAPTER THIRTY-ONE

Nasar lay in the tall grass, only her head above the hill's crest. She could see the river below, but only partially through the thick grass that covered her. Her horse stood behind her hidden from the men by the river by the ridge line. Malak crawled quietly up beside her; his own horse hidden as well.

"Quite the assembly, don't you think?" she whispered.

Malak peered over her shoulder and was surprised by the number of warriors who camped just across the river from them. There had to be over a hundred men, he reasoned. He scooted back down the hill and sat up. "More than I thought there would be. How do they know for sure that she is here?"

Hannah pointed. "Look at the tent, the coat of arms. Malak, the dragon is here. That must be how they know for sure she is here. The dragon has second sight. She would know the Bean an Ri is close. They know the legend, Malak. They must have known that the Faireadoiri had helped her, that Raham is with her. So, they know that she is to meet the carpenter and the dragon knows that the carpenter is in the land of the Bene Elohim."

Malak crawled back up to the hill for a second look. He saw a white tent back against the large oaks at the very edge of the sea. It had only been a few days before when he had camped there with the girls. How had they assembled such an army so quickly? They must have trailed him from the city. They must have been right behind him when he had come to free Hannah.

The red dragon was painted on the doors of the tent, but the doors were open, which meant that the dragon was not present in the camp. If she was present, the door to the tent would always be closed even if she was not inside.

"No, Nasar, the dragon is not present now, but they have set up the camp for her, which means she is expected. So, we have time. Hopefully, the king will make it before she does." Malak stated and sat back up behind the hill again, looking out over the sky behind him.

Wings fluttered and the hawk landed just below him in the grass. The bird stood there quietly, staring at first Malak and then Nasar, his head turning from side to side.

Malak reached over and took a paper from a pouch below the bird's neck. He read the note as Nasar waited.

"They have found the carpenter's camp. It is on the trail at the edge of the savanna, maybe an hour's ride," he said and gave the note to Nasar.

Malak took the note and turned it over. He looked around for anything to write with but found nothing. So, he cut his finger and reached over and plucked a feather from the hawk, who pecked at him for the theft. He dipped the feather in the blood at the wound and wrote. He waited a while for the blood to dry and then rolled it up and placed it in the pouch.

"Sorry, my friend," he said, petting the bird. "Take it to Raham. Quickly now!"

With a great heave upward amidst a flush of mighty wings, the great hawk rose quickly upward and away through the trees as Nasar and Malak watched him go.

Nasar sat up and looked over at her older brother. "Well, brother. I guess we need to do what we do best," she stated.

Malak grabbed her hand in his and they both stood up.

"You know sis, if Hannah does not see who she really is, this sacrifice, our sacrifice in all the realms will be for nothing."

"Yes, but I think she will. If she does see who she really is, then all our sacrifices will be just a blur, a second of time, a flash of light. Don't worry, Malak. The king is on his way. Hannah will see and the Shadow Realms, Sateria, the realms of humankind, will all be just a dream and the true kingdom will always be."

The two warriors walked back to their horses and mounted. They rode up to the top of the ridge among a scattering of large pines and sat side by side on the ridgeline above the encampment by the river and waited. The camp was only a few hundred feet below them on the far side of the river, so it only took a minute before one of the warriors spotted them. He called back to the camp in a language that neither Malak nor Nasar could understand.

A large man stood by the fire and walked over to the edge of the river by the man who had called and looked up toward the two warriors on the hill. Malak had seen the man before. He was the captain. Several other warriors mounted their horses and rode to the edge of the river behind the captain.

Malak challenged, "I see that you have mistakenly entered the realm of the Bene Elohim. If you will pack your belongings and leave the way you have come, you will find adequate shelter, food and hunting just on the other side of the forest. I will excuse your mistake and we will wait here until you leave."

Malak's horse turned his head to look back at Malak and snorted at the challenge. Malak stood silent. Nasar could not help but laugh silently.

The captain shook his head and called back, "We seek the queen's servant girl who has crossed into the forest. We have no fight with the Bene Elohim. We will take the girl and leave."

"Oh, I see. So that is how it is to be. Then we do not excuse your mistake, captain. You have illegally entered the lands of the Bene Elohim and you will immediately leave or suffer the consequences of your stupidity," Malak responded as his horse snorted and stomped his hooves in agreement.

"Well, that should do it, brother. You just called the captain stupid," Nasar commented.

The captain shouted back, "Let's see who is stupid, Bene Elohim. You are only two!"

"That should be plenty," Malak shouted back. "Well, what are you waiting on? You wish to invade the lands of the Bene Elohim. Then come on!"

The captain motioned to the horseman and nine of them lined up by the river. They crossed the river and stopped. Other warriors mounted their own horses across the river as the captain stood motionless. Malak leaned down and patted his horse, whispering something in the horse's ear. Nasar had seen her brother do this time and time again just before he would charge his enemy. He drew his sword, but Nasar reached over and grabbed his arm.

"Malak, wait. Look, he has sent just nine warriors to challenge you, He knows our code that we must never yield to less than nine. He wishes to draw us into him. Look behind. He has ranks of nine warriors in line." She pulled her quiver of arrows and swung it over her shoulder and her bow. "Draw them into our forest, brother. Let's take them on a chase through our realm," she said and turned her horse suddenly and retreated into the shadows of the deeper forest.

The captain laughed. "It appears the girl has no wish for this fight," the captain shouted as his men laughed behind him.

The nine warriors walked their horses forward. Malak looked behind him until he saw his sister disappear into the treetops as her horse trotted off into the forest behind her. And then he suddenly charged toward the first troop of nine.

'Kill them both!" the captain screamed.

Malak was among the nine in seconds, swinging his mighty sword. The first died instantly before they had a chance to react to his sudden charge.

Malak's warhorse charged directly into the second warrior's horse as Malak slashed his bloodied sword at the third, who veered away, the warrior colliding with the second and both fell as their horses panicked and reared upward away from the mighty warhorse. Malak pulled his horse to the side and rode past the others as one fell back with an arrow through his throat.

Other horsemen splashed across the river and Malak turned and raced back into the shadows of the forest on the ridge as another warrior fell from Nasar's arrows. He turned his horse on the ridge to see. Four lay dead and another wounded by the river. The second troop of nine charged toward him as all the rest spread out and crossed the river. His horse reared up and he charged the second troop as they struggled to get to the top of the slope. The first fell under the horses' hooves as a second flipped back over the third, an arrow through his chest. The others spread outward. A sword flashed near, and he parried the blow, his broadsword breaking the lesser blade in two on impact. Malak retreated deeper into the forest on one of the winding trails that only the Bene Elohim knew by heart as several arrows flew past him from the trees above.

The forest was very thick now and difficult for horses unless a trail was used. In places he knew that his pursuers would only be able to ride in single file. For a moment he did not see any of the warriors but could hear men off in the distance. He turned his mount and stood on the trail facing back the way he had come.

A warrior suddenly appeared on horseback before him on the trail, startled at the sight of him. An arrow flashed, but the man raised his shield just in time and the arrow embedded itself in the shield. The man charged forward, and Malak rushed to meet him. The horses collided at full gallop, the impact knocking both men back. Malak held tightly as did the warrior and both swung forward with their swords. Malak's warhorse lowered his head and brought it up suddenly, biting the other horse and drawing blood. The horses both screamed, Malak slashed forward, but the shield met his blow. The warhorse turned sideways as another arrow flashed across the horse's flanks and embedded itself into the warrior's thigh. Blood gushed outward, spraying over both horses and Malak's sword swung true. The man fell back from his horse as Malak backed away and another warrior pushed forward over the dying man on the ground only to be pinned against the tree by one of Nasar's arrows.

Malak retreated down the trial again. He saw a glimpse of Nasar running above him on the giant limbs of the ancient oaks. He was always amazed at her ability to do so.

Her horse stood just down the trail and upon seeing Malak, the mare turned and galloped away. Malak stopped on the trail again and listened. Men shouted in the distance, but he could not understand their language. It seemed that they had dismounted and were spread out in the forest. There was only one trail where a horse could be used, and he stood guard on it. As warriors attacked, Malak killed and retreated.

For a long while, Malak stood on the trail as Nasar kept watch high above him in the trees. All was silent. What were they doing? What were they planning? They had lost many warriors so far, so they must be changing their tactics, he thought. But what would that be?

Suddenly a warrior appeared on the trail. An arrow flashed overhead, but the man was prepared and diverted the arrow. Several arrows shot upward from behind the warrior as he retreated down the trail.

194

"Bowmen!" Malak shouted and quickly dismounted, holding his shield before him. "Back, boy! Get back!" he ordered his horse. "Nasar? Nasar, you okay?"

"I've been better brother."

"Are you hurt?" Malak asked the trees above him, watching the forest in front of him.

"I'll be okay. They only winged me," she said, and a bloody arrow dropped on the ground. "Malak, they have outflanked us. I see horsemen riding across the savanna. They are heading toward the girls."

Malak looked toward the savanna in alarm but could only see the dense forest and the narrow trail that led toward the distant light of the open fields. Another arrow shot upward toward his sister and Nasar swore and returned the fire. The arrow caught the warrior who first shot in the chest, and he fell out onto the trail.

"Malak. You need to get out of the forest. You need to help the girls. I will be okay. It's only a small wound. I will hold them off as long as I can and then I'll join you." Nasar said and Malak could hear the pain in her voice.

Malak did not want to leave her by herself but knew that what she said was true. They had to keep Hannah safe until the king arrived, until she had time to talk with the carpenter, until she believed who she truly was, and until she would unite with the king once again. Then, all of this would only be a flash of light.

Malak suddenly smelled smoke and heard the distinctive crackling of a fire. Where was the smoke coming from?

"Malak! They have set fire to our forest! They are killing the forest, Malak!" Nasar screamed.

Smoke shot upward suddenly, and orange flames flashed in the undergrowth, gaining strength as the wind pushed the flames upward into the treetops. Someone was setting fire all around them.

"Nasar, you got to get down!" Malak shouted as several arrows landed all around him, one embedding itself in a tree, another hitting the saddle on his horse who jumped away. Malak pushed the horse back, holding the shield to cover himself, and watched the trail where the shots had come from. The fire gained strength, a heavy smoke spreading toward him, dark and full of embers, that landed all around him. The leaves were dry and several small spot fires erupted close by.

Nasar struggled as she tried to climb down. Malak saw that she had been hurt worse than she had said. Several more arrows shot upward into the tree, almost hitting her as she jumped the last few feet, coughing from the smoke that was worse in the tree's crown.

Malak backed away from the hidden bowmen and the approaching fire, keeping himself between them and his sister as she struggled to get on her feet. Her shirt was blood-soaked. Her bow lay broken on the ground, her quiver empty and she held the wound at her side with one hand.

"Only winged?" Malak stated in alarm.

"I'll be fine, brother. The arrow didn't go too deep," she stated as she reached for her horse who had trotted up at the sight of her falling on the ground. Malak helped her mount and then he mounted his own horse as the fire raged all around them. The trail led toward the field, and he followed Nasar as they raced ahead of the fast-spreading fire toward the safety of the open meadow. Dark smoke enveloped them as embers fell over them like snow. Nasar faltered on her horse and at one point almost fell, but she held on tightly, leaning down against the mare's neck. They both emerged from the forest with the fire only a few feet behind them. Malak turned back to make sure they were safe but saw nothing but dark smoke and raging wildfire.

He looked over to his sister. She held her horse's neck tightly, her face ashen, staring in horror as her beloved forest died before her in a catastrophic blaze, the trees cracking, the living greenery turning instantly into a blackened death as the flames rushed forward. Malak dismounted and caught her as she fell. He lay her down gently on the ground, all the while watching around them to make sure no warriors approached.

He checked her wound. She had been shot in the side and she was bleeding, but he had seen worse wounds, but not on her. He found moss growing on a rock nearby and packed the wound to stop the bleeding after washing it with water from his canteen. The whole time, she stared at the fire, and he saw that she was crying. But not from the pain, he knew. She cried because of the death of the forest that she loved.

After a few moments, she collected herself and pushed herself up. "Malak. You need to go. I can't go any further, but you must help the girls."

"Can you ride, sis?"

196

"Some. I'll go to the springs," she answered and saw the worry in her brother's face. "Don't worry. I'll be fine. The springs should help to heal me, and they will never be able to find it. You hurry on. I'll see you when you get back."

Malak helped her back on her horse and she trotted off toward the mountain crags as the fire continued burning through the forest. Malak mounted his own horse. Nasar had seen horsemen riding the trail toward the savanna. He knew he could ride cross country and gain on them, because the trail made a wide arch following the natural contours of the land. He could ride straight across the slope and hopefully catch up with them before they reached the girls. Or so he hoped.

CHAPTER THIRTY-TWO

Raham walked her horse over to a rock under the shade of a tree and sat down, watching the great savanna out in front of her. Hannah had been with the carpenter for a very long time, which could be a good thing or then again, could be bad. She looked back at the tent which strangely seemed to be just a picture. Nothing moved. The horses stood perfectly still.

There were so many things that she did not understand. All she knew was that from the first time she had seen Hannah, she knew that she was the one called to be with her, to follow her wherever she went until she realized the purpose of her entire existence. She also knew that Hannah held the key to everything. All the realms that the Faireodoiri and Bene Elohim encountered ultimately were bound up with who Hannah truly was. Everything would continue to be disjointed, out of place, and uncertain, until Hannah realized that she truly was the Bean an Ri, the bride of the king.

Raham stood up and stretched, worried about Malak and Nasar. They had ridden out to delay the warriors, whoever they were, from entering the forest. Hopefully, they were okay. Hopefully, Malak was okay. It was strange, she thought. It was strange how she had known from the first time that she saw him by the hot springs that they were destined to be together. She had been shielded from men by her father, because as a Faireadoiri warrior, she was destined to serve the bride, but destiny had given her Malak as well.

She thought of her family as well. They had their own destinies, their own calling. Hopefully, if the realms could be joined, she would see them again as well. If only Hannah knew the power that she had within her. If only she could see who she truly is. Then all the sacrifices over a multitude of realms and eons of time would be worth it and all would be new in a flash of light. But now, she had a job to do. If warriors approached, she would fight to the end to protect Hannah and hope that the king will come in time to save them all.

The hawk suddenly landed on the saddle of her horse, startling her. The bird sat totally still, his eyes staring at her as she turned to greet him. She saw the paper rolled in the pouch and hesitated to take it out. The wording was in red, which was strange, but then with alarm, she realized the note seemed to have been written in blood. She pulled the note from the pouch and unrolled it, her hands trembling. The note had been written in blood.

She read the note.

At least a hundred warriors are heading your way. We will hold them off as long as we can. Hannah must have time with the carpenter. Otherwise, all will be lost. My heart will forever be yours. Malak.

She read the note again and looked at the bird. She did not have an answer. Her job was simple. If any of them made it through the forest, it was her job to protect Hannah until the king arrived. She placed the note in the small pocket of her dress and checked her crossbow. She had twenty arrows and her sword. Her father had taught her how to fight as a child. She was a Faireadoiri warrior, every bit as powerful as the Bene Elohim. And she had a few tricks that even the Bene Elohim did not have. She was also a Faireadoiri woman, and her mother had taught her as well.

Raham looked back at the tent. There were things to be done. If warriors approached, she would be ready. She cautiously walked up to the horses by the wagons, and they moved some when she got close. She led them up to the hill and put them by the tree. When she moved away from them, they stood still again like before. Her magic was not as strong as Anna's, but she knew how to make the horses appear to be warriors on horseback, but she would have to wait until the last minute before doing so, because her strength was limited. But at least for a while, she would have three mounted warriors fighting for her.

She looked among the wagons and to her surprise she found tar used for sealing barrels in several buckets. She took them and began spreading the tar across the grass along the slope leading up to her tree. She then placed wood by the tree and started a small fire and placed a small amount of the tar beside the fire. When she finished this she looked back at the tent. What was taking Hannah so long?

199

She looked up then and for the first time, saw billowing, gray and black smoke rising upward from the green tree line against the far horizon. The fire moved across the green and she realized that the forest of the Bene Elohim was on fire. She shielded her eyes from the sun's glare and watched the fire. Nasar and Malak were there fighting even now. How could only two of them stop a hundred? Raham had never felt more alone in her life.

CHAPTER THIRTY-THREE

I start at the beginning, or at least from the time of the earthquake when everything suddenly changed in my life. I tell the carpenter everything that had happened to me, everyone I had met, all the places I had been and all the dreams that I had. As I tell him about the dreams, they come alive even more and I feel that they are not dreams at all but are real. More real in fact than everything else.

At times, I cry as I tell of the horrible things I have seen, of the nightmares I have had. At other times I smile as I recount fond memories of the new friends that I have met along the way.

The room is warm and comforting, the air fresh with the scent of flowers and wood. The whole time I talk, the man sits to one side, working with his tools on the piece of burned wood that he had retrieved from the discard pile. He leans over the wood and sits to one side, so even though I try to see what he is doing, I cannot tell what he is carving from the wood. He seems not to be listening to me because he is so attentive on the work he is doing, but I know in my heart, somehow, that the carpenter hears every word. He has a way about him, a countenance of spirit that I trust and admire, even though this is the first time that I have ever seen him. Or is it? What a strange thought.

I finally come to the end of my tale to the point where I entered his workshop and for a while the room is silent. He stops carving on the wood and places the carving knife on the table but holds the piece of wood in such a way that I cannot see his handiwork.

"Hannah, do you remember anything before the earthquake?" the carpenter asks.

"Some, but for some reason my memory before is faded. I have always lived in the forest with my mother. We kept to ourselves. She hid me away from strangers because of my scars. Town people scorned me, they ridiculed me. But I am not sure anymore what is real and what is not."

He looks up at me with concern and I am drawn into his rugged face, his peaceful eyes. "It's okay Hannah. A lot of what you remember is not real at all. You cannot see that you were created as the bride of the king because you cannot remember who you are. You only see what you see. But I created you to be the wife of my son, the king. I see you the way I created you to be."

My eyes widen in disbelief, and he chuckles softly. "I know. That is a lot to take in," he says and stands up and walks to one side of the room where he picks up a mirror and walks back to me again. He holds the mirror up to me. "What do you see in the mirror, Hannah?"

I look at the mirror and see my reflection. I see a girl with dark eyes and long black hair, but most of all I see the red scars that cover the side of my face, neck, and shoulder and I know that under my dress, those same scars cover the side of my body down to my waist. How could I ever be beautiful? How could I ever be the bride of the king of this world? I turn away from the reflection, my eyes clouded by my tears because I know that I am the reason why I appear to be this way. My actions are why I am scarred. The truth of what I did to deserve my scars are in my dreams. So why would the king want me?

The carpenter sees my pain and what I have seen. I feel his compassion for me. "It's okay Hannah. But I see you the way I created you. You must see yourself in the same way," he states.

"But how? I am scarred. I am flawed. I have done this to myself." I cry. "My dreams are real?" He shakes his head, yes. I turned away from what could save me. I chose the wrong man. I turned away from the king. Then why? How would he still want me? How am I still the bride?

"Hannah, you just have to embrace what I have already done for you," he says.

I look at him in confusion. What is he talking about? What has he done for me?

He takes my hand in his and gently wipes away the tears. "Hannah your mother gave you something that holds the key to you seeing who you really are. It will show you what was done."

How does he know that? I never told him about the amulet.

Mother had told me not to show the amulet to anyone until I knew how to show it. Her words had not made any since to me then. But now I understand completely. I know for a fact that I am to give the carpenter the amulet. I reach down and pull the amulet from beneath my dress and pull the chain up over my head as he steps back.

I hold the amulet up to him by the chain, revealing a small silver cross in the same shape of the wooden structures that I had seen in my dreams. The carpenter takes hold of the cross and when he does, I feel a sudden jolt of energy surge through my body.

I stand on a rocky ledge under a night sky full of stars that twirl above me and then I realize that the rocky ledge is twirling, and the stars are still. I see far off toward a distant horizon as the ridge stops rotating. Orange and red lights flash on the horizon and then the sky opens around me, revealing flashing lights of the rainbow and high, shining gates that shimmer in golden light. And then the gates disappear, and I stand in a meadow with the wooden cross above me.

I am a little girl with golden hair and red boots looking up at the cross in a meadow, her abuse as a child only a faint memory because of the healing that resides in the cross. I am a young woman sitting at a kitchen table crying and holding the hand of the older version of the little girl, her life new and whole because of the redemption that resides in the cross. I am a wildland fire fighter pushing through the portals of failure and despair to ultimate victory because of the power that resides in the cross. I am countless men and women across all the realms of humanity. I look up and see the carpenter hanging on the cross, bleeding and dying. And then I am on the cross as well with him while at the same time I am standing below the cross.

And then the vision disappears, and I am standing in front of the carpenter. The cross is gone, but now the carpenter holds in his hand a small wooden doll that looks exactly like me, but with no scars.

He takes the doll and places her on the shelf as he had done with the horse earlier and the doll is alive and turns her head to look at me. Her long hair blows in the breeze, her eyes sparkle, and her smile radiant with pure joy and she has no scars. She is dressed in an elegant wedding gown that flows around her body and she twirls in delight and dances around the shelf as if she is dancing with a partner, but I only see her.

203

The carpenter points at the doll. "That is how I created you, Hannah and from before the creation of this world, I took your scars from you, so that you will be in the form that I created you to be. You are truly the bride of the king. That is who you truly are and by your willingness to give me the cross, you can finally see the truth that has been hidden from you since you appeared in the meadow after the earthquake." He holds up the mirror to me again. "Now what do you see?"

I look in the mirror and see the dream that I had. I see me walking to a giant door with two guards. I enter the door and walk up to the throne where a king stands at one side and a regular man stands at the other. I see now that the king is not what he appeared to be, and the regular man looks a lot like the carpenter himself, but younger somehow. I make the wrong decision and turn away from the true king.

I see myself scarred and then I see the king, the true king standing high on the ramparts of a great castle as a terrible storm approach and in the storm a great dragon rides the clouds, breathing fire and roaring like the thunder. The king has no fear and bravely draws his sword to face the approaching dragon. I see flashing swords and fire and portions of the walls collapse around the king, but he continues to bravely fight until he is fatally wounded and falls from the battlements among the collapsing rubble. The wooden cross appears in the storm as the dragon swirls above the cross and disappears. And the king climbs out from the cross itself and stares upward toward the retreating storm with the dragon and his bride.

The vision fades from the mirror, and I see myself now. I see the same long black hair and darks eyes, but to my astonishment, the scars are gone. I pull my hair away and look more closely. Where burned skin had been, is now smooth, beautiful clear skin. I gasp, my eyes wide and look over at the carpenter. He smiles at me.

"Now you see yourself, the way I see you. You are truly the bride of the king. He comes for you, but he has one more thing to do. Hannah, your friends are in trouble, but don't worry. You know who you are now. You are the key to everyone's salvation," he says and suddenly the room begins to swirl around me once more.

CHAPTER THIRTY-FOUR

Raham paced back and forth around the rock and tree, occasionally looking back to the tent, but could see no sign of where Hannah had gone. The hawk whistled high above her and dove down over the plain and then toward the distant fire that still burned across the horizon. She thought she saw dust and looked more carefully toward where the hawk was flying and saw horsemen galloping toward her. They were only dots on the grassland, but they were approaching fast. She counted at least thirty horsemen, but there could have been more even further away. The hawk circled back on the wind currents and circled above her.

Raham returned to her horse and greeted the mare by touching the mare's nose with her forehead. She closed her eyes and drew a deep breath for she knew that she may not possibly make it out of this fight alive. Malak and Nasar may already be dead, and she would have to continue alone. She thought of her family, of her destiny. She was Faireadoiri. Her job was to fight for mankind across the realms, but now she was in this one, she was fighting for time for Hanna. She would hold this ground to her last breath until the king arrived.

She mounted her mare and prepared her crossbow. She would fight first with this weapon from a distance. Then she would unleash her magic and she would charge her enemy with her sword in hand. Her horse pranced sideways across the face of the hill, her eyes shining bright. She was a warhorse of the Bene Elohim and knew what to do.

The horsemen approached to the base of her hill, charging faster now that they saw her before them. She looked back to the carpenter's tent one last time and lowered down to ignite her first arrow from the small fire by the rock. There were seven in the first rank and five immediately behind them. To one side there were at least a dozen more who seemed to be veering away from her and charging the tent.

Raham waited a few more seconds until the side rank was riding over the tar she had poured earlier and released her first arrow. She reloaded and shot a second one and then a third in quick succession. The arrows struck true and immediately a great wall of fall spread across the slopes between her and the horsemen. Several were engulfed in the flames and men and horses screamed. Several horses panicked and fled, partially on fire and at least three of the warriors were down on the ground in the fire.

The others veered away from the grassfire as it spread outward, following the tar, and igniting the dry brush. With her left flank secured. Raham turned and fired several more arrows into the other groups and ignited more fires across the slope until a great roaring grassfire engulfed large sections of the hillside between her position and most of the warriors. But a few managed to get through the fires and were climbing the hill toward her.

She sheathed the bow and drew her sword. She had only a few arrows left. Raham leaned forward to her horse the way she had seen Malak do before he charged and patted her horse on the neck. The horse shook her head and jumped forward and charged the closest warrior. Raham screamed the Faireadoiri war cry as loud as her lungs would allow so that the entire realm would know that a Faireadoiri was riding to victory.

Malak heard the war cry high up the hill and could see the fires burning ahead of him. His horse was winded from the wild ride across the savanna to catch up to the warriors. He reined in the horse and surveyed the scene before him. Several fires burned across the slope. Horsemen were trying to ride around the fire. Several horses ran past him, panicked, and riderless, their saddles burning.

He drew his sword and spurred his horse onward. A warrior saw him and turned and swung his sword. Malak paired the blow, his horse charged forward attacking the warrior's horse. The horse stumbled, throwing the warrior to the ground. Malak slashed downward, wounding the horse as he rode past toward the fire.

There was a gap in the fire and Malak rode toward it just as a second warrior saw him and charged toward him. Malak only had one thing on his mind and that was to make it to Raham's side. He rode past the warrior, ducking under the swinging sword and struck out with his own, cutting the man, but leaving him to his wounds.

206

The gap in the fire closed suddenly, but the warhorse was not afraid of fire. Malak held tight and the horse made one jump across the lowest part of the fire and landed in the blackened grass on the other side. The smoke swirled around him. He saw warriors riding across the slope away from him. Others rode closer. High on the hill, he caught a fleeting glimpse of wildly red hair and flashing swords. He turned his horse as a warrior appeared suddenly out of the smoke before him and ducked away from the flashing sword.

Malak drew back just as a giant hawk dived out of the sky and attacked the man's face with deadly talons. The man dropped his sword and screamed, grabbing at his face. The hawk twisted his body, giant
wings covering the man and then rose quickly back upward above the smoke. The man fell over, his neck broke, his face bleeding. Malak rode forward.

Raham's warhorse attacked the first warrior's horse causing a great panic and the horse turned away as Raham struck. Blood gushed forward and the warrior fell dead. One down, she thought. A second warrior rode past her, and she barely parried his blow. She turned toward a third warrior and the horses collided. Raham was not prepared for the collision and held tightly to the pommel to keep from falling away. She ducked low to one side and away from a flashing sword as smoke blew over her. She regained her balance and turned her horse to the side, parried a blow from one sword and felt the bite of a second one as it sliced across her shoulder and cut a portion of her braided hair, the red trusses falling over the horse's flanks.

The sight of her hair falling away enraged her even more. She screamed and charged forward and killed another before she was cut once again by a warrior behind her. She whirled her horse around in the smoke, blood sprayed across her face and her horse screamed in pain. In horror, she saw the gaping wound across the warhorse's neck as the horse fell forward throwing her over the fire and into the blackened grass.

Raham landed hard on the ground on her stomach, her sword flying high over the fire. She quickly flipped over and stood up and tried to run toward the falling horse, but she was hurt more than she thought. The warriors milled around the other side of the fire, not seeing through the smoke where she had fallen.

She jumped over the fire, slid across the grass to the dying horse and retrieved her cross bow. There were only three arrows left, the others broken or burning in the fire. Thankfully her horse was dead as the fire approached her. She killed the closest warrior before the heat became too unbearable and she climbed out of the fire, her hands burned, her clothes smoking.

Her rock was only a few feet away and with all the strength she had in her, she crawled the last few feet to the rock and set back against it, facing down the hill toward the chaos below. She saw several dead men and horses and several more still on the other side of the fire from her. Other horsemen rode past her toward the tent. So, she had failed. They would get to Hannah, but she was with the carpenter. Surely the carpenter could save them all.

Several warriors dismounted and walked toward her, their swords held low, almost dragging the ground. She was bleeding, her hands were burned, she was dying. But she had one arrow left and her knife. She tried loading the crossbow, but her hands did not work right. Her right arm lay limp at her side.

Finally, she placed the arrow and pulled back the bow. She raised the weapon and fired, but the string had been burned and the arrow flipped backwards and fell.

"Ifreann failteache!" she exclaimed.

She crawled up to her feet, leaning against the rock and noticed with great pride that the men stopped walking toward her as she stood. They feared her. And then she chanted the dara daoine draiocht song and smiled.

Suddenly three Faireadoiri warriors on horseback charged forward as her magic took control, taking the men by surprise. The warriors slashed with their swords, but Raham was weak, and she could only control them for a few minutes, but with satisfaction she saw all three of the men cut down before the three horsemen vanished in the smoke, leaving only the three horses that she had taken from the carpenter's camp standing before her. Her vision swirled and she thought she saw Malak in the smoke. She reached her hand outward but fell back over the rock.

Malak lost sight of Raham and then saw her again in desperate combat. He charged forward. Horses collided in the smoke and chaos of battle. Blood poured over his face as one man fell over his own horse, dead. He pushed the man off his sword as a great broadsword flashed forward, cutting him across the back. His horse swirled to meet the new attack. Malak killed another, but more pressed forward, but they were not trying to attack him. They were charging toward the tents that stood just over the crest of the hill.

And then he saw Raham fall back into the fire as he desperately tried to reach her, but riderless horses now pushed him back. How many warriors were there? How many had she killed?

Suddenly the captain emerged from the smoke and this warrior did not run past him. He spotted Malak and turned to attack him. The two warriors charged forward. The two great warhorses struck each other in their own combat and this time, both the captain and Malak fell backward from their horses.

Malak stood up, the captain recovering just above him. Beyond the smoke, Malak saw Raham crawling away toward the hill and three horses who stood motionless above her. She was still alive!

He swung his great sword and sparks flew outward as the captain parried the blow. The captain swung low, and Malak countered and the two traded blows. The two great warriors were an even match, but with each blow, Malak felt the strength leaving him. He knew he was bleeding from the wound to his back, but he knew he had to kill the captain here and now, or Raham could not survive and then Hannah would be taken as well. The captain thrust low, and Malak missed, but slashed forward as the captain's blade cut deep. Malak staggered back, holding the wound, and feeling the gush of warm blood over his hand.

The captain smiled, as he stepped back at the sight of Malak, but then he staggered and looked down in surprise. Malak had cut through his stomach. He dropped his sword and fell on his face in the blackened dirt, dead.

Malak stood for a second, feeling the strength leave him and looked around. Minutes before there had been raging fire, blowing smoke, screaming horses and the cries of war, death, and pain. Now all was silent except for the crackling of the fire. He staggered forward toward the hill. Raham lay over the rock, three dead warriors immediately in front of her. How had she done that?

A great flash of light exploded over the meadow on the wings of a strong wind that blew the fire back into the blackened earth. Malak staggered up the hill toward Raham and saw a warrior riding a great white stallion galloping across the hillside toward them. The warrior charged the remaining soldiers who turned their mounts to face him, but it was too late. The king cut them down in one final melee.

Malak was bleeding out from the wound across his back, blood dripping over the ground around him as he struggled to climb the hill toward his Faireadoiri love.

Raham reached out her hand to him and he fell before her in the grass, grabbing her hand in his. Malak pulled himself up beside Raham and pulled her small, broken body into his lap. He brushed her bloodied, red hair away to reveal her face. He smiled at her as his horse stood over them before bowing his head as another horse galloped up behind the tree.

Raham looked up to him. "I failed her, Malak. They got past me," she whispered. Malak wiped the dirt and blood from her face gently as his own strength weakened.

"No, my dear Faireadoiri warrior. You have not. The king is here." Malak answered her and hugged her tightly against the pain.

The king stood over them, the sun shining brightly behind him. He knelt before the two warriors as they lay in each other's arms. Malak looked up to his king who placed his sword on the ground next to him and took off his gloves. He placed one hand on Malak's shoulder and one on Raham's. Raham opened her eyes and saw her king for the first time. The realms flowed around them and through them. Would their sacrifice be worth it? Only Hannah herself held the key to that.

CHAPTER THIRTY-FIVE

I stare at the carpenter in fright, "They are in trouble. Please sir, please can you help them?" I plead.

"Oh, my child. Who do you see when you look in the mirror?" he asks and holds the mirror up in front of me.

I see myself with no scars, my hair long and braided, my eyes bright and free. I wear a beautiful white wedding dress. I begin to cry tears of joy and wonder. "I see the Bean an Ri, the bride of a king," I say.

"Then you have already saved them. Look, your bride groom comes," he says, smiles and disappears.

I stand at the ancient door by the oak tree once more. I turn and see the hill where Raham had been standing, but I don't see her. I take a few steps away from the door and when I do, the door disappears as well. I look out over a burned grassland, the smoke still lingering, small fires still burning in the tall grass. Dead men and horses lie all around the hill side and I hear movement and see my own horse and Malak's horse standing by a tree on the hill next to a large rock.

Where are Malak and Raham? The carpenter said I have already saved them, so where are they? I see two bodies by the rock below where the horses are standing and the shining red hair. No! They can't be dead! They must be alive! I know who I am! I remember everything! I understand now!

I run toward them, but suddenly the sky grows dark above me and I stop and look up in horror at a great red dragon flying in the sky, twin yellow eyes staring down at me. I stop and back away from the dragon, but then I realize that I am no longer afraid. I stop and draw the sword at my side as the dragon swirls over me and lands just a few feet in front of me. The dragon lowers the great head, but this time I stare at the beast. I do not have to run anymore.

211

To my surprise, the dragon swirls before me in a red cloud of smoke and a woman emerges from the smoke as the dragon disappears. She is tall and wears a dark shirt and pants, knee-high boots and a black cape that is fastened at her neck with a red brooch. A great sword is belted at her side, the pearled hilt exposed from behind the cape.

"Oh. I have finally found you girl. I almost had you, but the Watcher protected you. Then I reached for you in the forest, but you are a strong one. But no matter. I have you now," she says as she walks around me.

I turn as she walks, continuing to face her, holding my sword before me.

She laughs. "You think you can defend yourself with that thing. Look around you, girl. Look at all the death you have caused." She points toward the rock where my friends lay dead or dying. "Even the Bene Elohim and Faireadoiri could not protect you," she says.

"Look at them girl! You have caused their death. So many died because of you and to no end. I still have you. You are nothing. Look at you, scarred, flawed. Your decisions caused you to be so."

She stops and looks over at me differently than before, like she sees something for the first time and her eyes grow wide. I smile at her because I know that she can no longer see my scars. They are gone forever.

"No! That cannot be!" she screams.

She draws her sword and I step back. I will fight her. I am no longer afraid. The fear is gone. I have full control over it now.

"You think you can kill me, girl? Where is your king? Your bridegroom? You may be his bride, but he is not here when you need him the most."

I feel a presence behind me, a person that I have known for my entire existence, a man who died for me so I can live. A man that I have lived with in the Garden of God outside of this realm that is only a shadow created by my mistake. This Shadow Realm that is only true outside the cross. I know who I am. I am the Bean an Ri.

"No, I cannot kill you, witch, but my husband can." I say and step aside.

The king steps beside me and my heart flutters at the sight of him. He stands a foot taller than I. His hair is brown and falls to his shoulders, his eyes are dark like mine, his smile wide and beautiful. He wears a simple crown that keeps his long hair from his face. I sheath my sword and he takes my hand is his just briefly and I feel all eternity flow through me, an eternity of life with him.

"I killed you once, my lord. I will do so again," the witch spats and swirls in the cloud of smoke.

I step away as my king, my husband draws his broad sword and steps forward into the smoke with no fear. Lighting flashes above and the heavens break open with huge storm clouds that swirl in darkness and flashes of light.

I see only partly through the clouds. Fire shoots across the sky. The dragon roars. Blue and red lights flash as swords clash. The very ground shakes around me with each clash of the mighty swords and then suddenly there is a great flash, and the clouds roll away and reveal a blue sky.

The dragon is no longer visible, only the woman. She holds her sword before her, blood covering her body. The king stands before her, his sword bloodied as well. She swings, but she is weak. He parries her blow, and she screams and curses at him. She drives forward suddenly, but he is stronger, and she grows weaker with each blow. Finally, she swings high and the king ducks under her, swirls to my surprise in the Faireadoiri way and slashes her deep. She staggers back and drops her sword, and he cuts again and the great dragon, the witch called Rahab falls in pieces to the blackened ground.

The king steps back from Rahab's body, kneels and cleans the blood from his sword in the grass, stands and turns to me as he sheaths the weapon. My heart quickens, my breathing flutters at the sight of his beautiful eyes as he looks down at me. He is the man of my dreams, the king at the throne, the woodsman in the forest, the man standing by the cross in the meadow. I have known him for my entire existence. I remember it all now. I remember our life together in the Garden of God since my creation.

He steps toward me, and I step back nervously.

"I'm sorry," is all I know to say.

He smiles and takes my hands in his and looks at me with loving eyes. He takes a hand and pulls back the hair that covers my face and touches my cheek where the scars used to be.

213

"You are beautiful you know. My wife, my love," he says and leads me to his horse. "Let's go home."

THE TRUE REALM

A door opens before me, two armored guards standing at attention as I walk through, my gloved hand holding the hand of my husband, the king of all the realms. We enter a great banquet hall and to my great delight a ballroom. My husband leads me past thousands of warriors, farmers, woodsmen, women, and children who all bow as we walk up the center aisle toward a throne at the other end where two simple wooden seats stand next to each other on an elevated platform.

Down each side of the great hall, large windows show a world outside full of all the glories of the universe, mountains, valleys, forests, fields, great cities, multiple heavens, circling planets. All swirling around in pure life and love.

My husband leads me to the throne, and I sit first. He bows before me and kisses my hand and I blush and smile as the crowd applauds and then he takes his seat beside me. I look over to the side and see the carpenter, working at his greatest hobby, creation. He looks up at me and winks and then returns to his work.

The king, my husband motions and music begins playing from an orchestra that floats far above us on balconies of gold. The people begin dancing before me.

My husband leans over to me. "I have a surprise for you, my dear," he says, and I look at him strangely.

The great doors to the ballroom open and I suddenly shout with glee and stand up and immediately the music stops, and the people stop dancing and stare up at me as my husband chuckles. I have broken unspoken protocol, but I don't care.

Malak and Raham walk in the great hall, hand in hand. He wears an elegant suit and a flowing cape and for once, I see no sword at his side. Raham's beauty radiates, her small, round face glowing, her green eyes bright. Her hair is elaborately braided with strings of pearls, and she wears a beautiful, dark blue gown, the purity color of the Faireadoiri. And behind them, Nasar in her brown and green woodsmen attire.

215

I run to them and grab Raham in my arms and we hug each other. And then Malak, great huge Malak, picks me up in his arms and holds me tight, swirls me around, and then places me back down. He steps away and bows before me; takes my hand and kisses it.

"I thought you were all dead. I saw you on the field." I say.

"No Hannah. You saved us all," Raham says. Then she leans into me, a sparkle in her eye. "He is handsome, your husband," she says, and I blush again.

And then I see Raham's family and Mr. and Mrs. Spivey and all the Faireadoiri as they enter the hallway. And then standing in the crowd, I see my mother, who I now know was a Faireadoiri Watcher that had been with me during the time when I was lost to this realm. They all suddenly bow, and I turn to see my husband standing behind me.

"You wish to dance?" he asks.

He bows before me and takes my hand, and the music starts playing. I had always dreamed that one day a gentleman would bow before me and dance with me in a grand ballroom.

I am Hannah, which means Grace in my Lord's language and I am all of Humankind redeemed by the cross. I am the Bean an Ri, the Bride of the King.

Hannah saw a vision of herself while in the carpenter's tent. She saw herself as a young girl in red boots, an older girl at a table, and a wildland firefighter. If you wish to know more, then I suggest you read my other novels in the Realms Series. Shadow Realm, Gatekeepers Journey, Mackenzie's Journal, and The Garden House.

See how the realms swirl around us and see how the true realm of God is only found in the completed work of the cross of Christ.

Made in the USA
Columbia, SC
23 September 2024

42454139R00120